Angel dove at Ranyel, slamming into her. Despite the Garlock demon's size and strength, he knocked her to the floor against the wall.

Together, they fell in a tangle into the small breakfast table and two chairs. The furniture shattered.

Pain blazed through Angel as he tried to push himself up. Something tugged at his stomach. Glancing down, he saw that a long sliver of wood from one of the chairs pierced his side and jutted out four inches.

"Missed your heart," Ranyel growled, rolling to her knees in front of Angel.

The ovipositor from her abdomen probed him, bouncing across his chest, but at the touch of his dead flesh, the organ jerked back as though flame-broiled. Vampires couldn't be used as incubators for the demon young because their touch killed them.

Angel reached for the demon, seizing her bowling ball head in both hands. He groaned in pain as Ranyel yanked the splinter from his side and fisted it like a dagger.

"I won't miss again."

MEDIA TIE-INS

Angel™

Available from Simon Pulse

The Essential Angel Posterbook

Available from Pocket Books

ANGEL™

image

Mel Odom

**An original novel based on the hit television series
created by Joss Whedon**

SIMON
PULSE

New York   London   Toronto   Sydney   Singapore

Historian's note: This story takes place during the second half of the second season of *Angel*.

First Simon Pulse edition April 2002
™ and © 2002 Twentieth Century Fox Film Corporation.
All Rights Reserved.

SIMON PULSE
An imprint of Simon & Schuster
Children's Publishing Division
1230 Avenue of the Americas
New York, NY 10020

The text of this book was set in New Caledonia.

Printed in the United States of America
10 9 8 7 6 5 4 3 2 1

Library of Congress Control Number 2001099351

ISBN 0-7434-2750-5

To the *LATFB* gang, who can make the most
grueling road trip seem like fun

Acknowledgments

Eternal gratitude goes out to those people who wrote the best haunted house stories I've ever read: Shirley Jackson, Richard Matheson, Anne Rivers Siddons, and Stephen King.

Thanks also to Joss Whedon, David Greenwalt, Tim Minear, and the cast and crew of *Angel*; Lisa Clancy, Micol Ostow, and Liz Shiflett of Pocket Books; Caroline Kallas and Debbie Olshan, and my family.

prologue

"Aren't you going to answer that?"

Pulling up from the daze she'd been in, Faroe Burke looked at the sweating man standing before her. She blinked, gathering her thoughts, remembering that she was sitting in the stairwell that led to her studio/apartment above the boxing gym filled with the noise of leather gloves against bags and bodies. Until that moment, her whole mind had been occupied with the sketchbook she had resting across her knees.

"I'm sorry," she said, not understanding and feeling a little anxious.

Young and good looking, the guy would have caught her instant attention out on the street if she hadn't been so caught up in the sketch. He was fit, dressed in black boxing trunks and shoes, a towel thrown over his shoulders and well-worn boxing gloves dangling by their strings from one hand. His face and head were smooth-shaven, and his eyes were wide and intelligent, his dark skin unblemished.

1

She'd seen the guy a few times around the gym and she thought she had his name. It was Gunn, or something like that. She hadn't asked about him, not really, because the last thing she needed in her life was a boxer or someone off the streets of Los Angeles. If she showed up at the gallery show tomorrow with a new boyfriend that looked street tough, Lenny would just have cow. The thought was almost enough to make her laugh despite the rolling tension in her stomach.

"Your phone." The guy tapped his temple. "Your phone is ringing."

"Better catch your call before they give up on you," the guy said.

Faroe checked the Caller ID on her cell. "It's my agent," she said. "He's not going to give up on me."

"Smart guy."

And did he just flirt? Faroe looked into his eyes, liking what she saw there. The phone continued to ring, and she was amazed at how she hadn't heard it before and now it was so damned annoying.

"You an actress or something?" the guy asked.

Shaking her head, Faroe said, "No. I'm an artist."

"Explains the sketchbook."

A middle-aged man with gray in his beard and white, cottony hair shoved his head into the stairwell from below. "Hey, Gunn, are you ready? You gonna flirt or are you gonna fight?" the man asked.

Gunn grinned at Faroe and jerked a hand toward the gym area. "I got a fight."

"Grudge match?" Faroe asked, knowing she had no business flirting with the guy. There were too many things going on in her career at the moment, and Lenny Thomas, her agent, was probably calling to remind her of all of them.

"No," Gunn said. "Just a guy I scheduled a session with. I'm a . . . a detective. Like to keep myself in shape."

"I can see that." *Okay,* Faroe said, *time to check the hormones.* Her face felt hot. *Now who's embarrassed?* She tried to cover. "I mean, why else would you show up at a boxing gym?"

"Gunn," the man called, "we're burning daylight here."

Gunn nodded and rolled his eyes. "Daylight was over hours ago. See you around maybe?"

Tell him no, Faroe thought. Instead, she smiled and said, "Maybe."

"Great." Turning, Gunn trotted down the stairs and almost tripped.

Faroe covered her mouth with a hand and gazed down at the sketchbook so he wouldn't catch her laughing. She listened to his footsteps recede, then glanced back up to watch him walk out to the main gym area. Sighing, she turned her attention to the ringing phone and tapped the answer button. "Hello?"

"Faroe?" Lenny Thomas said in a worried voice. "Where the hell have you been? I've been calling for five minutes and there hasn't been an answer. I was starting to get worried."

"I had to find the phone. You know my studio is a mess."

"Yeah, I figured it was something like that. You're working?"

"A little," she admitted, and hated the guilt that came crashing down on her. Lenny didn't understand that lately she felt more creative than ever. She needed to work as an outlet for all the pressure building inside her.

Lenny, however, seemed to thrive on pressure. "Starting on a new project at this point might not be feasible. I thought we discussed that."

Faroe sighed. "We did, Lenny, and I tried to explain to you how I feel about my work. It's not just something I do. It relaxes me and brings me a sense of . . . of . . ." *Of what?* She'd often wondered that, but there was no way she could find words to express how it made her feel. Maybe a writer could. And somebody who got the same kind of feel from their work or their art, or whatever the hell they wanted to call it, probably already knew without being told.

Lenny was an agent.

Faroe hoped that some agents understood. Then she felt guilty for thinking about him in such a bad way. Lenny Thomas had been good for her. He'd had confidence in her work long before she'd ever believed it, and now his own confidence was shaking a little because her career was rocketing.

"You know what," Faroe said before he could say anything else, "I'm closing up the sketch pad and putting it away. It'll keep till after the gallery showing."

"That's my girl," Lenny said, and she could hear the smile in his voice. "We'll concentrate on this gallery showing, then I guarantee you that you'll have a lot more time to paint worry-free when we have all the deals in place."

With some reluctance, Faroe closed the sketch pad.

She also pushed thoughts of the young boxer from her mind. Gathering her markers and the empty Evian water bottle from the steps, she turned and headed up the stairwell. She listened to Lenny talk as she entered her studio.

The smells of the gym—the sweat and the soap and the astringent disinfectants—stopped at the doorway. Inside the studio, all she could smell was paint. Canvases lined the four walls of the spacious room. She'd even pulled the sleeper-sofa she used for a bed toward the center of the room to allow more wall space. Her art never looked natural till it was up against a wall.

Aerosol cans lined the two secondhand tables she'd purchased from a local flea market. Disposable plastic cups held fistfuls of markers and charcoal. Sketch pads lay everywhere, on the worktables, on the small foldout table covered over with take-out cartons from the nearby Chinese restaurant, on the bed that she hadn't folded back into a sofa, and on the scarred hardwood floor.

She glanced up at the skylight, surprised to find that the smog was clear enough that stars could be seen against the sable night. Crossing the room to the small apartment-sized refrigerator, she took a fresh Evian bottle from inside, twisted off the top, drank, and listened to her agent talk.

"I was thinking," Lenny said, "that for the interview we do with Conan O'Brien—"

As she drank the cold water, she spotted a shadow flitting across the skylight.

"—we could rent you a studio," Lenny went on.

"I have a studio." Faroe put her water bottle down and

crept under the skylight. Was it her imagination, or was someone really up there? Over the past few days, she'd gotten the impression that someone was watching her. Part of that had been due to the attention Lenny Thomas was getting her, though.

"Then we'd need to hire a crew to clean the one that you have," Lenny told her.

If she hadn't been creeped out by the shadow, Faroe knew she'd be angrier about Lenny's inference about her cleaning habits. Instead, she strode to the sofa bed, crouched down, and reached underneath for the Smith & Wesson .38 revolver she kept there. She left the water bottle on the floor by the bed. Maybe Lenny thought her cleaning habits were lacking, but he had no clue about the pistol.

"I like my studio the way it is," Faroe said, watching the skylight and raising the .38 in front of her in both hands. Goose bumps danced across the back of her neck.

"We've got to think about your image here, darling," Lenny said.

"Don't call me darling, Lenny," she warned, pacing around the room and keeping an eye on the skylight.

"Sorry, sorry," Lenny said. "I forgot. Mea culpa."

"And you're not Italian either."

"Am I calling at a bad time?"

Probably, Faroe thought, but she didn't want the phone connection broken. "It's me. I'm just a little nervous about the gallery opening tomorrow."

"Don't worry about that. I've got everything covered there. You'll have a great time. Everybody will love you. It'll be—"

The shadow returned to the skylight, and this time it didn't just flit along the edges. It threw itself forward and dropped like a rock, smashing through the glass panes and plummeting into the studio below.

Faroe dodged back from the falling glass, throwing an arm across her face to protect it from the spinning shards. Even then, some of them got through, nicking her face and arms. Her first thought was for her eyes. Eyes meant everything to an artist.

The shadow stood in the center of the studio. Clad in a wind suit, the man could have passed on a street in the neighborhood and never been looked at twice—except for the demon's face he wore. His skin tone was as orange as a pumpkin, and black shading marked his eyes and mouth. He had no nose. Four spiky ears—two on each side—twitched and moved like satellite dishes.

Demon! Faroe's mind screamed. She'd seen demons and vampires before. Growing up in the streets of L.A., a lot of people did. Not everybody survived that experience. *Get the gun up! Get the gun up!* The weapon felt like an anvil in her hands as she fought to bring it up. Her face, neck, and arm burned from the cuts she'd gotten from the falling glass. But she thrust the .38 out at the demon as he rushed at her. Her artist's mind took in details immediately, noting that the demon was grinning in spite of the weapon she held, and that he only had a thumb and three fingers on each hand.

She fired at point-blank range, squeezing off all five rounds in the pistol as fast as she could pull the trigger. The .38 bounced in her hands with bruising force.

Two or more of her bullets slammed into the demon's

face, jerking his head back. Amber-colored blood flew as he stutter-stepped to a stop.

For a moment, Faroe thought she had killed him.

"What was that?" Lenny demanded over the phone connection. "Was that a gun?"

Then the demon raised his head. Though the face was a ruin of torn flesh, he grinned and cocked his head. "Not so easy to kill. Not so easy at all. But that hurts like hell. You're going to have to pay for that." He reached for her again, moving with impossible speed.

"Faroe!" Lenny yelled over the phone.

The demon closed his hand, gripping her sweatshirt.

"Send help," Faroe called. "Send help, Lenny!" But she knew it would be too late.

The demon had her.

Chapter One

"If I told you I was interested in something tall, steaming, and sordid, would you be the man I was looking for?"

Even after two hundred and fifty years of an adventurous life and unlife in some of the roughest parts of the world, the question caught Angel by surprise. He shifted his attention from the man he was watching to the woman who had stepped to his side.

Her pale green eyes regarded him with playful challenge, but Angel saw potential darkness waiting in there as well. The black silk-and-satin gown molded itself to her body, concealing and exposing every dangerous curve, while the plunging V-neckline revealed considerable cleavage. Silver combs sporting dark emeralds held her dark hair from her face, pulling it back just enough to let Angel know it would shake loose in an instant. Though the bracelet on her right wrist looked simple, Angel was willing to bet it hadn't come with a simple price tag. She was in her late fifties, but she took care of herself. A good plastic surgeon had taken twenty years off her age, but Angel's practiced eye saw through that.

Several of the men sitting at tables in the bar watched her with obvious interest. Angel had noticed her earlier as well, but he was in the tavern on a job that required his full attention.

The woman didn't belong in the bar any more than did the man Angel was there to watch. Located between Beverly Hills and the downtown convention area, where sections of blue-collar L.A. citizens worked and lived to service the glittering image the city sold to the world, the bar was an upscale dive. Black-and-white photographs and fight cards of old-time boxers, Jack Dempsey and Joe Louis and others, littered the walls. In the old days, the place had been a sports bar staged below three floors of hotel rooms for reporters in town to cover fights at the Forum. Canned jazz issued from the PA speakers mounted on the walls.

Striking a pose, one hand to a generously rounded hip thrust out toward Angel, the woman arched her eyebrows. "You do speak, don't you?"

Seated on a stool at the bar that occupied one corner of the tavern, carefully out of the way of the large mirror that reflected the glowing neon lights but not him, Angel said, "Yes."

"And you do speak the language?"

"Yes."

The woman waited with obvious expectation.

Angel waited as well, glancing past her and checking on the man he was there to watch.

Eddie Ashford was an actor under contract with Nova Studios, the client Angel Investigations was working for at the time, on a three-picture deal that was supposed to skyrocket him to fame as an international action star. The studio exec Wesley was in contact with insisted on comparing Eddie Ashford to Mark Wahlberg and Freddie Prinze, Jr. As DaShio Mercury, intergalactic bounty hunter turned hero of the hard-pressed Frexian Federation warring against the evil Sneddark Alliance, Nova Studios considered Eddie Ashford a bankable commodity for investment. The studio execs wanted Ashford protected.

Unfortunately, Ashford seemed to have an unhealthy interest in risky living. Red-haired and good looking, dressed in gangsta rap threads that were as far from an intergalactic bounty hunter's look as they could be, Ashford leaned into the platinum-haired woman he sat at the table with. He whispered something in her ear and she laughed, grabbing the back of his head and pulling him closer.

"Do you have a thing for movie stars, handsome?" the woman asked.

Angel hesitated, not sure what to say.

"I see you've noticed Eddie Ashford," the woman said.

"Is that who that is?" Angel asked. "I thought I knew him from somewhere. But I was thinking maybe it was a guy I worked with or something."

The woman smiled. "The magic of Hollywood. You see somebody up on those big screens, you feel like they're your friends." She glanced at Ashford. "Of course, a lot of fans would be really surprised to see how their heroes and heartthrobs actually live. Eddie Ashford's just an accident waiting to happen."

"What makes you say that?"

"Look at him," the woman said, gesturing at the movie star. "He's down here slumming, thinking he's have a great time by risking his career. But inside, he figures he doesn't deserve the success he's getting, so he's going to sabotage it."

Angel looked at the woman with more curiosity. "Are you a psychologist?"

She laughed, and the plunging V-neckline did amazing things. "No, I'm not."

"But you know Eddie Ashford?"

"He's been in a few times." The woman glanced with disdain at the movie star. "He's not my cup of tea."

Angel nodded. "So what type is he?" Nova Studios suspected that Eddie Ashford had some kind of problem and had put studio security on him. Ashford had lost the security guys whenever he wanted to, which was why the studio executive had approached Wesley and offered the job to Angel Investigations. Wily and clever with lots of practice, Ashford would have lost Angel too if it hadn't been for his vampire senses and past experiences at tracking prey.

"You're not here looking for a good time, are you, handsome?" the woman asked.

Hesitating, feeling a little bad because the woman had approached him and now knew it wasn't going anywhere, Angel shook his head. "No."

"Are you a reporter?"

"No."

"I'd expect a reporter to be following Eddie Ashford around," the woman said. "Especially one of those *Corner of the Eye* tabloid people. They seem to have been especially lucky catching stars in their—" She paused. "Let's just say, *indelicate* positions."

Angel knew that. Wesley and Cordelia were already working on discovering the reasons for *Corner of the Eye's* phenomenal luck at getting dirt on stars and movie studios. That was the other assignment Nova Studios had given them.

Cordelia hadn't had any visions in the last few days, and business had been slow. Wesley, always wanting to make a go of things he was involved in, had been working on redefining how Angel Investigations was perceived in the public eye. When the job offer came from Nova Studios, Wesley had agreed to it.

"If you're not a reporter, then what are you, handsome?" the woman asked.

Taking one of the cards Cordelia had made when she'd first joined him in the agency from the pocket of his trenchcoat, Angel slid it across the bar.

The woman took the card and read it. "Angel Investigations? You're a detective?"

Angel nodded. It still felt strange to say that when he was working a straight case instead of an assignment from the Powers That Be.

"What's your name, handsome?" the woman asked.

"Angel."

Her eyebrows lifted in surprise. "You run your own business?"

"My friends and I do."

"It doesn't say Angel and Friends Investigations on the card."

"It should," Angel said.

Moving with casual grace, the woman slid onto the stool next to Angel. "You're here checking up on Eddie Ashford?"

"Yes."

"The studio's worried about him?"

Angel smiled and shook his head. "I can't talk about a client."

The woman chuckled. "Oh, and you're a Boy Scout, too. Aren't you just a peach?"

Glancing back at Eddie Ashford, Angel saw that the man was still involved with the woman he'd been hitting on.

"Like I said," the woman told Angel, "Eddie Ashford is a disaster waiting to happen."

"What does he do when he comes in here?" If this was a routine with the movie star, Angel wanted to know about it. Nova Studios was interested in where Ashford disappeared to in case they had to do damage control.

The first movie in the three-picture deal was going well in theaters, the second movie had been shot, and they were in the planning stages of the third. DaShio Mercury was, as Wesley had said the studio exec had put it, fast on its way to becoming a solid franchise. Nova Studios didn't want to lose that franchise and hoped to leverage that success into greater things.

"Buy me a drink, handsome," the woman said, "and I'll tell you everything I know about Eddie Ashford. That's worth at least a drink . . . if nothing else."

Angel flagged the bartender down, dragging the man's attention from the Mohammed Ali–Joe Frazier rebroadcast on the television in the corner of the bar area. The woman ordered a strawberry daiquiri, and Angel stayed with the beer he'd ordered as a cover.

"You do much work for the studios?" the woman asked.

"A little," Angel said. Despite everything else he did, there had been a few jobs in the entertainment business. "It's hard to be in this town without bumping into it."

The woman nodded and sipped her drink. "Wish I'd have had a Boy Scout watching over me back in the day. Maybe I'd have been in television longer than I was."

Angel looked at her, trying to place her face. Cordelia would probably have known in a heartbeat.

"You don't know me, handsome?" She showed him a sad frown. "Damn, I must really be getting older than I think. I'm Fanny Amore. At least, that was my name after my agent and the studio got through with me. I played Concho the Panther Princess in *The Adventures of Jungle Mann* back in the sixties. I was the leopard-skin bikinied sidekick. That was back when Julie Newmar was vamping the small screen up as Catwoman in the *Batman* series. Probably before your time."

Angel made no reply, turning his attention back to Eddie Ashford.

"Ah, your assignment," Fanny said. "You're diligent, too."

"Yes," Angel replied.

"Eddie comes here to pick up women."

"Any favorites?"

"No. He doesn't much care to play in the same sand-box twice."

Angel glanced around the room. "What's so special about this place?"

"You can find women of . . . *different* persuasions here."

15

"How different?"

Fanny stuck a finger in her drink and swirled it. She captured a strawberry chunk between her thumb and forefinger. "How long have you been in L.A., handsome?"

"Some days," Angel said, "it feels just like forever."

Grinning, Fanny nodded. "Then you've noticed that everyone here isn't exactly . . . human?"

Angel nodded. "Eddie's interested in demons?"

"Eddie's got a serious jones for demons," Fannie said. "At least, that's who I usually see him with."

"How many times have you seen him here?"

"Three or four times. I don't keep count. I find him unattractive. Oh, he looks good on the outside, but once he opens that big mouth of his, that sexy, debonair image goes right out the window." Fanny laid a hand on Angel's wrist. "He's not like you at all, handsome.

"I've thought about vampires," Fanny continued. "I spend hours at the gym to keep my figure, and I pay a king's ransom to plastic surgeons to keep me looking good. But some people tell me one crimson kiss from a vampire will give me back my youth."

She blinked at Angel, looking almost innocent. Her hand was warm against the back of his wrist.

"Do you suppose that's true?" she whispered. "Could I find one I can trust?"

"The price would be too high even if you could," Angel told her.

Bitter disappointment shone in Fanny's eyes. "And you'd be the expert?"

"In this," Angel said, "yes."

Fanny stirred her drink again, looking away from Angel. "You're not the first I've asked."

Angel hadn't supposed that he was, and he wasn't quite sure how the woman had pegged him as a vampire. But if she knew about Eddie Ashford's own interest in vampires, maybe she'd developed an eye for them.

"The others I've talked to," Fanny said, "only laughed at me."

"Don't talk to them," Angel said. "They'll kill you and leave you where you fall. Not everyone the vampires kill come back."

"They laughed at me," Fanny said. "Taunted me. It made me feel old. I don't like feeling that way, and no matter what I do, how I make myself look, I know that I am."

"Sometimes," Angel said, "just being yourself isn't easy."

"I know." Fanny's voice was hoarse. "There's just so many things I'd change if I could go back. Or if I knew I had enough time ahead of me."

"Not many of us get the chance."

"I suppose not." Fanny took her hand from Angel's wrist, breaking the connection she had with him. Sadness and resignation darkened her eyes. She nodded toward the other side of the room. "You'd better be on your toes, handsome. Looks like your baby-sitting job is about to go big."

Looking back at the table where Eddie Ashford had been, Angel spotted a tired cocktail waitress lifting her tip and the empty glasses from the tabletop. He glanced through the crowd and saw the platinum-haired woman holding onto Ashford's shirtfront as she led him through the crush of tables and chairs. They entered the arthritic elevator with dented chrome kick plates. Eddie Ashford smiled and took the woman into his arms as the doors drifted together. The floor indicator arm above the elevator doors lifted and began ticking off the floors.

"They'll be on the fourth floor," Fanny told Angel. "Eddie always takes the girls to the top floor when he's slumming."

"Thanks," Angel said, reaching inside his shirt pocket to leave money for the drinks and a tip. "And keep the card."

"I plan to, handsome. Anybody who offers to 'help the helpless' might be someone I'd want to call someday. You hurry on now, and save the tattered remnants of Eddie Ashford's innocence so Nova Studios doesn't lose their multimillion-dollar baby."

Angel turned and left, thinking how much he really didn't want this job. Saving Eddie Ashford for a night was possible, but somebody had to save the guy from himself. Wesley might be running the detective agency now, but Angel lived for the moments when he battled the darkness that he'd once been part of.

There was only the one elevator. Angel stood in front of the doors and waited for it. The doors opened with a weak ding, and he scanned the mirrored back wall of the cage. No one was inside. The mirror's reflection didn't show him, of course, but it showed Fanny asking the bartender for a light at the bar and the people at the tables.

It didn't show the men that came at Angel from behind until they were almost on top of him.

The only warning Angel got was a too-fast rustle of

clothing, a shoe scraping the linoleum floor, and a tingle at the back of his neck. The tingle didn't have anything to do with his being a vampire; it came from years of being the hunter as well as the hunted.

Angel turned around, taking his hands from the pockets of his trench coat.

Three Garlock demons closed on him. All of them were as big as football players in full uniform, with lead-gray skin and smooth heads that looked like oversized bowling balls. Their tiny features looked pressed-in. They wore slacks and turtlenecks, hats and wraparound sunglasses, as well as thick gold chains.

"Hey," Angel said, "maybe I'll wait for the next cage. I'm not in a big hurry."

The lead Garlock placed a three-fingered hand in the center of Angel's chest and pushed him back. Even though the effort looked like a child's push, Angel slammed against the mirrored back wall and shattered it. Gleaming shards tinkled down around his feet as the three demons crowded into the elevator cage. Angel felt like he'd been hit in the chest by a bulldozer. A human might have died from the impact alone.

"We'll take this one," the Garlock demon said.

Angel was surprised they all fit into the cage, but it was wall-to-wall Garlock demons while they were there.

One of other demons tapped the elevator keypad. The doors wheezed and whined closed. With a jerk, the cage started up.

Angel glanced at the thick gold chains the demons wore. "Is there a Run DMC concert playing somewhere tonight?"

The lead demon stared at Angel with fiery eyes. "You were following Eddie Ashford. I want to know why."

Angel shrugged. "I wouldn't say I was following him. More like we share an interest in elevators."

With blinding speed, the demon backhanded Angel. The only reason he didn't fall to the floor as his senses swam was that the demon caught him by the shirt with one huge hand.

This is going to be trouble.

Chapter Two

Cordelia Chase sat in the lumpy chair in the small waiting room and sighed. It was one of those sighs she'd been working on for the O Heavenly Dog Biscuits commercial audition that was being held in a week. If she had to say so herself, the sigh was quite good. Maybe one of the best artistic things she'd ever done. She repeated it.

As expected, the receptionist glanced at her over a tiny metal desk covered with fast-food containers and old tabloids. The woman was ninety if she was a day, and her flour-white skin was wrinkled as a prune, framed by windblown iron-gray hair cut shoulder length.

Marking her place in her book with a gnarled finger, the woman took the unfiltered cigarette from her lips, knocked the inch of gray ash into an empty soda can, and stared at Cordelia. The receptionist wore rubber galoshes and stained, white coveralls that had JOE'S PIZZERIA embroidered in red over the left breast. The name STAN was embroidered over the right breast.

"That's a lovely shade of lipstick you're wearing," Cordelia offered. Compliments won favors.

"Not lipstick," the ancient receptionist said. "Chili." She wiped her mouth with her sleeve. Most of the deep red color left her lips and smeared the sleeve.

Okay. Cordelia tried another winning smile. "This is the home office of *Corner of the Eye* publications, right?" Cordelia asked. "Because that's what it says on the door." She pointed at the door in case the woman had forgotten—or never noticed—what the block lettering on the pebbled glass pane showed.

"Yeah."

"Then I'm in the right place."

"And you're looking for a job?"

Cordelia nodded. "That's the story." Actually, it was the cover Wesley had dreamed up to get her into the tabloid's office. She was there to investigate the blackmailing ring that seemed to have sprung up from the tabloid.

The receptionist took a red handkerchief from her pocket, blew her nose loudly, and replaced it in her pocket. "You a reporter?"

Cordelia blinked. Although the application she'd filled out had requested a job history, she hadn't felt that she'd needed to claim that she'd been a reporter. After all, it hadn't exactly come out and asked. Of course, she didn't put down that she was a detective with Angel Investigations either, which probably would have sounded like she'd already done a lot of snooping. But Wesley had pointed out that such a background probably wouldn't entice interest. The tabloid had been sued a number of times, though only a few suits were successful.

"I can be a reporter," Cordelia said. "*Corner of the Eye* is really like a lot of gossip. Gossip I can do. I promise, I dish with the best. And back in high school, nobody could keep a secret from me. I'm like, a living, breathing lie detector in designer clothing." She straightened the hemline of her dark blue halter dress, then patted the French braid she'd put her long dark hair into. "Oh, and I'm like a secret magnet. You just can't hide things from me."

"This ain't just gossip," the receptionist said. "The people who work for *Corner of the Eye* get breaking stories about celebrities involved in all kinds of craziness."

The door behind the receptionist's desk opened and a bald man with glasses dressed in jeans and a yellow turtleneck stuck his head out. "Miss Hepplemeyer?"

Cordelia sat silent for a moment, noticing the receptionist giving her a strange look, then realized the Hepplemeyer name was the one she was using. She held up a hand and smiled broader. "Hepplemeyer. That would be me. Don't I look like a Hepplemeyer?"

Concern filled the bald man's round face. He opened the door wider and waved Cordelia into the office with her application. "This way, Miss Hepplemeyer."

Gathering her bag, Cordelia stepped into the room beyond the receptionist's area.

The next room wasn't much bigger than the receptionist's area. Two metal desks covered with computer equipment lined up head to head. Without skirting or modesty plates on the desks, the thick coils of wires that went to the computers were visible. Someone had used Safe-T ties to bundle them together.

Framed copies of *Corner of the Eye* hung on the walls. Track lighting illuminated the room, and moonlight stained the dark world outside the room's only window. Low book-shelves occupied two of the walls, filled to capacity with books and magazines.

So okay then, Cordelia thought as she looked around, *they're not using the blackmail money they scam on décor.*

The bald man stepped in behind Cordelia, pointing to a small folding chair in front of the two desks. "Please. Sit."

Having no choice, Cordelia sat. "Thank you." She smoothed the dress's hemline again. Two of the people in the office with her were male. No matter what else was going on, Cordelia knew about the effect that she had on men. She smiled and placed her hands primly in her lap for the benefit of the woman. It was her fresh-faced innocence look, and it was always a hit with older guys. The effort was probably going to be a wash on the woman, though.

The woman was in her early twenties and conscious of her own effect on men. Cordelia could tell that from the way she sat in the office chair. The woman wore her hair two-toned, harvest gold spritzed with carmine red on the ends. Her long nails, metallic blue and black, drummed the desktop and screamed impatience. She wore a red corset-back blouse with shirred sleeves, a Spandex micro-miniskirt, and combat boots that were all about attitude.

"I'm Buck Davis," the bald guy said. He pointed to the woman. "That's Cassi."

"Short for Castigation," the woman said, holding up a finger. "One name. One attitude. If you've read my pieces in the paper, you know I'm heavy into severely punishing those people who deserve it. Especially stars and studios who think they're holier-than-thou."

"Sure," Cordelia said, though she couldn't remember who had written the articles she'd read.

"And that's Roger Cadenasso."

"Hey," Roger said, flashing Cordelia a peace sign. Thin and tall, he had wheat-colored hair sporting a skater cut, a jutting chin beard that made him look like a billy goat, and cat's-eye glasses so thick they made his eyes look huge. He wore a beige-and-cream silk print shirt and bright orange slacks.

"You're here about a job," Buck said, walking over to the desk that sat by itself.

"Yes." Cordelia leaned forward on the edge of her chair and looked interested but just short of pathetically desperate.

Buck looked over the neat application Cordelia had turned in. "And you want to be a reporter."

"I want to be where the action is," Cordelia said. "Busting people who have secrets to hide. Exposing sordid histories of film and television stars. You know, that kind of thing."

"How much experience have you had in that field?" Cassi asked.

"Oh, tons," Cordelia said. She pointed to the tabloids framed up on the walls. "You do a lot of demony stories. I'm really good with demony things. Most people have a tendency to lump all demons into one category, but there are actually a number of demons. I could specialize in demony stories."

"And you've got experience with demons?" Roger asked, taking up a pencil from the cup in front of him and running it between his fingers.

"It's not something I like to brag about," Cordelia said. "I've got a really good friend who's a demon and runs a karaoke place. Great place to go to for a business lunch, by the way."

The three *Corner of the Eye* editors swapped glances. Then Buck glanced back at Cordelia. "Miss Hepplemeyer—"

"Eunice," Cordelia said, and tried not to gag. She even had ID with her picture and that name on it.

"Eunice," Buck said, "we're really not open to taking on a new reporter at this point."

"We've got professional talent handling things," Cassi said. "The last thing we need is an amateur in here mucking things up."

Cordelia held back the immediate scathing retort that came to mind. She even gave them a sweet smile and reminded herself that Nova Studios was paying a big retainer to Angel Investigations to find out how *Corner of the Eye* was getting all the dirt on the Hollywood scene. "What about a receptionist, then? While I was waiting out in the, uh, waiting room, I couldn't help but notice the lady out there lacks a little in the social skills department."

"She's supposed to lack in the social skills department," Cassi said. "Stan keeps people away from us. That's how we like it. We don't want to be bothered. We have work to do."

A knock sounded on the door, and before anyone could say anything the ancient receptionist stepped into the room. She carried a plumber's helper slung over one shoulder like a militiaman's rifle. A cigarette hung from her lip. "Got a pipe backed up down in Six-C. I'll put the 'Out To Lunch' sign on the door. Be back quick as I can."

In disbelief, Cordelia watched the woman pull a grimy cap from her back pocket, snug it over her head, and shuffle back out of the room. The door closed with a bang.

"Besides that," Roger said, "we own the building and lease office space. Stan does janitorial work."

"And plumbing," Buck added. He peered at Cordelia. "We could use another plumber. The pipes in this building are really ancient."

"Gross," Cordelia said before she could restrain herself. "No way." Even the mention of such a prospect triggered her need for candles and a bubble bath.

"Then I guess we're through here," Cassi said, folding her arms across her chest. "Now we can get back to the real work we do."

Cordelia headed for the door. Before she reached it, a loud, gurgling, belching grunt echoed through the room. An obnoxious stench, like burning onions dipped in bleach and sulfur, filled the room. She looked at the three other people in the room.

"That was the pipes," Buck said, looking a little embarrassed.

"Backing up," Cassi said.

"That will burn your nose," Cordelia said, grabbing her own nose in self-defense as tears filled her eyes. "How do you people stand to work here?"

"Probably more than just Six-C," Roger commented. "Not to worry. Stan will fix it."

"Ewwww," Cordelia said, and opened the door to escape. She kept her hand in place over her nose as she headed through the waiting room, but her mind stayed busy. Maybe she didn't get the job as a reporter for the tabloid as Wesley had hoped, but she had more information. The three tabloid people could say backed-up pipes all they wanted to, but she knew a demon when she heard one.

And smelled one. That putrid vapor had held a definite demony stench.

The gunshots threw Charles Gunn's timing off as he boxed his opponent in the gym. His right glove skidded off his opponent's ribs instead of making solid contact, and the punch pulled him off-balance, leaving him open for the guy's left hook response.

Gunn's skull, despite the protective headgear he wore, seemed to explode and jump off his spine when the guy hit him. *Damn. Feels like he had a brick in there.* He staggered and brought his hands up, knowing the guy was going to be all over him.

Less than two minutes into the first round, Gunn knew the guy that had arranged the fight had set him up. Gunn attended the gym every now and then, going up against club fighters to maintain his edge. He'd been fighting vampires on the streets long before he'd met Angel and the others. Fighting in the shadows didn't allow for practice; he lived or died by his skills. The occasional workout at the gym kept him finely tuned.

There were no other shots after the five he'd heard fired.

A dozen other boxers who were gathered around the ring in the center of the gym cheered them on. Some rooted for Gunn and some rooted for DJ Pain, which was what the other boxer called himself. None of them seemed to have heard the shots, or maybe they just didn't figure it was any of their business.

Gunn held up his hands. "Break," he said, having trouble speaking the word around the mouthpiece between his teeth.

"Break hell," DJ Pain snarled, juking his hands and advancing. "I ain't had enough of you yet."

The other boxer was lean and wiry, heavily muscled in the chest and shoulders. Although the guy that had organized the fight had promised DJ Pain wouldn't be any bigger than Gunn, DJ Pain had at least a thirty-pound advantage. Scars from bullets and knives and burns advertised the harsh life he'd lived in twenty years. Maybe DJ Pain had a coach now, but the street had been his teacher. He popped a flurry of punches at Gunn's head, still counting on him being dazed from the earlier shot.

Gunn fielded the punches with his raised hands and stepped back. Who the hell had been shooting inside the building? He got irritated at the young boxer for not backing off. DJ Pain lived to hurt people.

"Break, Wally," Gunn called out to the old man that owned the gym. He danced back out of DJ Pain's reach.

Wally was short and heavy, his skin the blue-black color of anthracite. Gunn hardly remembered a time when Wally didn't have a cigar stub tucked into the corner of his frowning mouth and wasn't wearing a clean dress shirt, slacks, and suspenders. The gym owner reached over and rang the bell on the table beside the ring.

The bell's tone sounded clearer than the gunshots had, but Gunn was certain he'd heard the shots.

"Ain't no bell gonna save you," DJ Pain promised. "I want you. Ain't gonna stop till I get me alla you I want. My manager told me you was somethin' else. Told me you was gonna stomp my butt. That's BS, homey, 'cause we gonna see who get the stompin'." He fired a big left hand straight out from his shoulder at Gunn's head.

Gunn swatted the blow away, then blocked a flurry of them. Even though none of the punches hit him solidly, the sheer onslaught the young boxer offered drove Gunn backward.

"Watch out for the ropes," Wally called out in his gravelly voice. "He gonna get you up against them ropes and work you good if you don't watch your ass."

DJ Pain wasted breath cursing Gunn, calling him every foul thing he could think of. Gunn ignored it, focusing on the rhythm and move of the fight. He could have gone with Cordelia and Wesley to investigate the offices of *Corner of the Eye*, but doing straight jobs that Angel Investigations took on didn't interest him. Gunn had signed on to fight monsters like the one that had killed his sister. And maybe he could have gone with Angel and shadowed the movie-star guy, Ashford, but there had been zero interest in that as well.

With nothing happening on the street at the moment, Gunn had figured on a severe workout at the gym, a few bruises, dinner at one of the Chinese places he liked, then crashing. The weekend was coming up. He figured there would be plenty of demon activity going on by then.

Of course, the way DJ Pain was acting, Gunn wasn't going to make it to the weekend.

The insults and cursing continued. Less than a minute had passed since Gunn had called for the break, but it had been enough time that he felt certain DJ Pain should have exhausted himself. Instead, the boxer kept on coming, acting tougher and stronger than ever.

Steroids, Gunn thought. *Man, it's gotta be freakin' steroids.* The presence of those in the boxer's body made him uncontrollable, and maybe to a degree invulnerable.

Then the woman's scream reverberated through the gym.

The sound distracted Gunn and he didn't pull back in time to prevent DJ Pain from landing his huge right fist into the middle of his face. Black spots swam in his vision and he tasted the metallic copper of blood.

DJ Pain crowed in triumph as Gunn battled to stay alive, just able to knock aside the next avalanche of blows. The woman's scream made him think of the woman he'd met in the stairwell earlier. Wally had told him about her. She was Faroe Burke, some kind of artist who had rented one of the upstairs studios.

The woman screamed again, drawing the attention of some of the men around the ring now, but DJ Pain focused on Gunn and threw sledgehammer blow after sledgehammer blow. Setting himself, Gunn dodged to the left, gliding under the boxer's fists, holding his upper body almost parallel to the mat, then pulled back into DJ Pain, hammering him with an elbow to the side, digging into the man's short ribs.

DJ Pain squealed in agony, but threw another blow.

Gunn batted the blow away, came up coiled and compact, took a step back, and drove the heel of his shoe into his opponent's forehead, snapping his head back. Before the boxer could react, Gunn kicked him in the crotch like a punter going for long yardage.

Whimpering, DJ Pain crashed to the mat and curled up into a fetal ball.

By the time the big boxer went down, another scream sounded from upstairs and Gunn was in motion. He vaulted the boxing ring ropes and landed by Wally. Thrusting his gloved hands out, he said, "Cut 'em off."

Wally flicked a straight razor out of his pocket and opened it. The keen edge sliced through the strings.

"Was that Faroe?" Gunn asked as he shook the gloves off onto the floor.

"I think so."

Gunn looked up the stairwell in the corner of the gym. "Top floor?"

Wally nodded. "At the back. Can't miss it."

Not with all that screaming, Gunn thought. He grabbed his nylon shirt jacket from one of the benches in front of the ring, then sprinted up the stairwell.

Somewhere above, a demon roared.

Chapter Three

The Garlock demon shoved Angel through the door to the building's rooftop.

Catching himself, Angel stumbled across the rock and pebble rooftop surface but didn't fall. His head still rang from the demon's earlier blow. He glanced back at the Garlock demons as they followed him out onto the rooftop. He knew they weren't there just to scare him off. They wanted blood.

Angel backed away from the trio, giving himself time to recover from the sucker punch. Warm wind spilled down over the San Gabriel Mountains east of L.A. and fought back the cooling effect of the Pacific Ocean. Angel smelled the thick, sour smog in the night air, but there was a trace of chaparral as well. Horns honked in the streets below, the sound floating up with strains of music from car audios as well as nearby apartments with the windows open. For most people, it was just another night in the city.

The three Garlocks strode toward Angel, their confidence evident. It became even more evident as they took pistols and camp axes from under their jackets.

"Put the pistols away, boys," the lead Garlock ordered. "This is a vampire. You can't kill them with bullets." He smiled, and the tiny face embedded in the bowling ball head looked obscene. He hefted the broad-bladed camping axe in his other fist, twisting it so it caught the moonlight and the ambient light streaming from the street below. "But you can chop them into pieces and burn them in direct sunlight."

"Sounds like it beats burning ants with a magnifying glass, Tuez," one of the Garlocks said.

"Maybe we could talk about this," Angel suggested. He reached the rooftop's edge and peered down. Traffic passed in bright blurs in the street four stories below, then the traffic lights at the intersection changed and another tide of cars surged forward.

"As long as I find you amusing," Tuez said.

"What's your interest in Eddie Ashford?" Angel asked.

"The pretty boy you were following around?" Tuez asked.

"Yeah." Angel watched the three Garlocks in a semicircle before him. The other two wouldn't move until the biggest one moved first. Garlocks grouped and acted like a wolf pack, centering on an alpha male.

"My girlfriend decided she liked the way he looked," Tuez answered.

"You don't work for *Corner of the Eye*?" Angel asked.

The cherub's face on the huge bowling ball head wrinkled in disgust. "No way. Wouldn't use that crap to line a birdcage."

Angel nodded. At least that took some of the threat

out of the Garlocks' interest in Eddie Ashford. That left their only reason for being there as some kind of demon business. "I'll bet you're not exactly Oprah's Book Club material either."

Tuez frowned. "I'm not amused, vampire."

"You're planning on introducing Eddie to your girlfriend?" Angel asked. "Get his autograph? Something like that?"

"My girlfriend is feeling domestic these days," Tuez stated. "She wants a baby."

Memory struck a chord in Angel's mind, but it was elusive and vague. He couldn't hang onto it, and the near-thought was gone like breath on a foggy morning. There was something about the way Garlocks had children.

"I told her we could take one off the streets," Tuez continued, "but Ranyel wants us to have one ourselves. I was thinking, you know, that's just a lot of trouble, but I really like her a lot and she's not gonna take no for an answer. We've gotten into that demanding phase of the relationship, you know. Real pain in the ass if you ask me, but what am I gonna do?"

"You might ask yourself if you're ready to be a father." Angel sized the three demons up, striving to find the weakest link so he could exploit it if he had to.

"Ranyel's gonna take care of the kid," Tuez said. "I just gotta be there for the naming ceremony."

Angel walked to his left along the rooftop. The Garlock there moved to cut him off, letting him know he had no choice but to stay put or try to go through him. "What does your girlfriend wanting a baby have to do with Eddie Ashford?"

"Everything," Tuez said. "Ashford's gonna be the donor."

When Angel recalled the lore about the Garlocks' reproductive cycle, everything clicked. Female Garlocks had the ability to morph their shapes to look human or animal or demon; whatever it took to draw out the third party necessary to conceive a child. "The blonde woman with Ashford is your girlfriend?"

A proud grin split Tuez's tiny face. "Yeah. Ranyel. She's a hottie, ain't she?"

"Ranyel's with Eddie Ashford now?" Angel asked. He felt strong and his head seemed clear. From the way the Garlocks slowly crept in, he knew it wouldn't be much longer before they attacked.

"Yeah. You ain't gonna be able to stop her."

Angel shrugged. "Eddie's no friend of mine. I was just watching him for somebody."

Tuez grinned. "Good. Then you won't mind him having my girlfriend's baby. It was Ranyel's idea to have the donor be somebody famous. After we found out Eddie Ashford hung out around here sometimes, I thought it'd be a good idea to look him up."

"How did you find out about Eddie Ashford?"

"Some guy Ranyel met a few days ago." Tuez hefted his camp axe again.

"If I were you," Angel said, "I'd worry about your girl."

"Nothing to worry about there. She could take Eddie Ashford with one hand tied behind her."

"I wasn't talking about that," Angel said. "When she changes herself to look like a human, she takes on the desires and interests of that form as well. Eddie Ashford is an attractive guy."

Tuez's face wrinkled in angry perplexion. "What are you trying to say, fangface?"

"Maybe Ranyel will get caught up in the moment, find Eddie Ashford a little too attractive."

"Ranyel would never cheat on me."

"Maybe not in her demon form, but right now she isn't exactly the Ranyel you think you know." Angel shrugged and put a tone of doubt in his voice. "But, if it's any consolation, you're probably right. You know her better than I do."

Tuez cursed and drew the camp axe back. "Time's up, vampire. You gotta die now."

Cordelia met Wesley Wyndham-Pryce two floors down in the shadow-filled stairwell. He'd been waiting there in case she ran into any demon trouble she couldn't handle.

Tall, lean, and immaculately dressed in a black suit and turtleneck, wearing glasses and looking every inch the erudite university professor—which meant he totally looked out of place in the section of inner L.A. they were currently in—Wesley looked up at her at once. "Well?" he asked in his pronounced and terribly correct British accent.

Shaking her head as she joined him on the landing, Cordelia said, "It was a wash. They're not hiring."

"For anything?"

Thinking briefly of the plumber's helper that Stan had been carrying, Cordelia said, "No. They're full up. But I was thinking."

Wesley stared at her with interest.

"Maybe we could wait for Angel," Cordelia suggested, smiling at the thought of her own brilliance. Her plan was so simple. Wesley always liked to complicate things. "Angel could go into the office and throw somebody—preferably Cassi—through a window. People don't seem to have a problem keeping secrets when Angel starts throwing people through windows."

Wesley crossed his arms over his chest and placed one hand against his cheek. "That's not exactly a circumspect method, now is it?"

"At this point," Cordelia said, "I'm not all about being circumspect."

"And Angel doesn't like to take that tack unless it's made evident that it's the only way to go."

"It's the only way to go," Cordelia said. "They turned me down and didn't hire me. I found the whole ordeal amazingly insulting. I mean, can you believe not hiring me?"

Wesley just looked at her in a manner Cordelia found way too reproachful.

"Anyway," she said, ignoring the reproach assault—which Wesley should have known didn't really work well those few times that she was wrong about something—"they're the bad guys."

"I see. I gather they did something to you that made you angry at them."

"Duh." Cordelia still felt humiliated from the way the three editor/reporters for *Corner of the Eye* had treated her. "They made me feel awful. Like they wouldn't even trust me to sharpen their pencils."

"Those people do have a lot of secrets in that office, Cordelia," Wesley explained. "Or somewhere."

"They're not very good at keeping secrets. That's why they end up on the front pages of the magazines."

"I'm talking about the ones they keep back to blackmail celebrities and studios with," Wesley pointed out. "Remember? That's why we're here. Because of the blackmailing, not the fact that they're plastering everyone's dirty laundry in their nasty little periodical. And chief among those secrets is the source, or sources, of all the stories they're getting."

"They don't need a source for a lot of stuff that they do," Cordelia argued. "Just a couple of pictures, some really good computer graphic software, and an imagination. I mean, did you see the picture of the alligator-man on the cover of this week's issue? That wasn't—"

"That was a Moldaryan demon," Wesley said.

"Stalking the cast members of the *Partridge Family*?" Cordelia shook her head. "Maybe the demon was real, but there was no way it ever got that close to David Cassidy. Even the hotel room they were supposed to be in looked fake."

Wesley frowned at her. "Perhaps not. At any rate, we knew going in that there was a chance those people wouldn't hire just anyone."

"I'm not," Cordelia corrected, perhaps a little louder than necessary, "just anyone."

"Exactly," Wesley said. "You have a certain charm and edge to you that I thought they would recognize as the consummate muckraker. If they wouldn't hire you to be a reporter, it's evident that they wouldn't hire anyone."

"Thank you. I think."

Wesley waved her thanks away. "I would have much

preferred to slip you into their ranks as a reporter. It would have made this whole thing feel much more clandestine, like a true covert operation."

"Sometimes you get into playing Boy Detective too much, Wesley."

"Perhaps. But that is our edge, Cordelia, and we should never lose sight of it. We are the champions, the force for good, and we should never stoop to the level of operations put forth by our chosen enemies."

They didn't offer you a job cleaning toilets, Cordelia thought. There was no way she was going to work in bathrooms that might have been covered in demon poop.

The thought reminded Cordelia of what she'd heard in the office. "They have a demon."

Interested in her again, Wesley asked, "What kind of demon?"

"Big. Stinky."

"There are a number of larger and odoriferous demon species," Wesley said. "Perhaps you could narrow the options."

"Haven't got a clue. But it sounded really big. It's in the office behind their private office. Or maybe it's in the walls. I'm not sure. It gave off this putrid, gurgling, demony stink."

Wesley checked his watch.

Cordelia glanced at him. "I didn't get the job. I didn't know we were on some kind of time frame here."

"I'm waiting for Plan B."

"Plan B?"

Wesley nodded. "I thought perhaps getting you aboard *Corner of the Eye* as a reporter might not work."

Exasperated, Cordelia put her hands on her hips. "If you had Plan B, we could have skipped Plan A. I didn't need to have my ego torn up and tossed back at me."

Lowering his voice, Wesley whispered, "I wasn't really happy with Plan B."

"Why?"

An uncomfortable look flashed on Wesley's face. "Because Plan B is sneaky, underhanded, and duplicitous. It's not my style at all."

"I guess," a familiar voice whined, "Plan B would be me."

Turning, Cordelia glanced at the flight of stairs leading down to the next floor. The pale-blue glow of a bug zapper screwed into the wall there highlighted the approaching demon's mottled and bumpy skin. His bald head looked too big and too elongated for his thin body. He had a lizard's cold orange eyes and pointed teeth.

"Merl?" Cordelia said, recognizing the demon at once.

Merl was a demon Angel used as a snitch in the underworld community. Sometimes Angel paid Merl in exchange for favors and sometimes he had to threaten him. Despite the fact that his services were available, whether for money or to save his own neck, Merl wasn't what Cordelia thought of as dependable. He owed Angel Investigations no loyalty.

Cordelia looked back at Wesley in angry disbelief. "Plan A, involving a degradation of my self-image, is only a step up from Plan B, which is *Merl*?"

Wesley held his hands up and took a step back as Cordelia approached him. "Now, Cordelia, it's not like that."

Cordelia pointed at the demon as he joined them on

the stairwell landing. "It's *Merl*, Wesley. It's exactly like that."

Wesley opened his mouth, but nothing came out.

When Cordelia turned her attention on Merl, he stepped back and looked away. Cordelia felt like she was going to explode. She looked at Wesley. "Thank your lucky stars there are no windows handy right now."

"You know," Merl said, "maybe I came at a bad time, but I could have sworn you told me to be here now."

"Actually," Wesley said, making the attempt to straighten his tie and gather his aplomb, "you're twenty minutes late."

"You already had Plan B waiting?" Cordelia fumed.

"Cordelia," Wesley protested, "it was Plan B. I had to have Plan B waiting."

"Hey," Merl interrupted, "you mean I wasn't first choice for this job? I didn't agree to do this just to pick up somebody else's slack."

Cordelia whirled on him. "You're not picking up anybody's slack." She drove her words home by stabbing her forefinger into the demon's chest.

"Sure." Merl rubbed his bruised chest. "I'm not picking up anybody's slack. In fact, now that I've had time to think about this and realize that you didn't exactly tell me what's going on, I'm out of here." He turned to go.

"I have money," Wesley said.

Merl waved without looking back. "Keep it. I got something else working tonight. I was just doing you guys a favor when I showed up."

Wesley looked at Cordelia. "Cordelia, please. We need him."

"I'm not apologizing," Cordelia said, holding her hands up. "That's just so not happening."

"I wasn't asking for an apology. You carry a certain threat level that I can't maintain with Merl."

Feeling slightly mollified, Cordelia smiled. She raised her voice and put steel in it. "Merl."

Halfway down the stairs, Merl jerked, letting her know he'd heard her, but he kept walking.

"Tonight," Cordelia told the demon, "would not be the night to make me come after you."

Merl halted and his shoulders slumped. He turned and started back up the stairs. "Man, I hate you guys. How come none of you people can ever just ask a guy nicelike? How come you always gotta threaten to beat me up?"

"I believe I offered money," Wesley said.

Merl shoved a hand out. "Okay. That helps. A hundred bucks, right?"

"Oh," Cordelia said, "and Plan B was getting paid?"

"You are a partner in the agency," Wesley pointed out. "In a sense, you're already getting paid for tonight's performance." He took folded bills from his inside jacket pocket.

Cordelia plucked the money from Wesley's hand before Merl could get it. "Then, in that same sense, this is my money too."

"Now I'm not getting my money?" Merl protested, glancing at Wesley.

"You'll get the money," Wesley promised.

"But only if you succeed," Cordelia said, meeting Wesley's gaze. "Otherwise, we're saving our money. I've got my eye on a new dress that would help the office décor."

Before Merl could say anything further, Wesley took him by the elbow and headed up the stairs. "I hate you guys," the demon called back.

"How do you feel about cleaning toilets, Merl?" Cordelia asked.

"Toilets?"

"Something was said about backed-up pipes while I was in the offices earlier," Cordelia said. "Maybe you can get a job cleaning toilets."

"If they provide gloves," Merl said, "maybe."

Wesley got him going again. "Cordelia, you'll find a fire alarm on the wall there. If anything goes wrong while we're up there, I'll call you on my cell phone." He held it up to show her, then replaced it in his pocket. "If I should call, pull the fire alarm. It should cause enough of a distraction to allow Merl and me to get out of there."

"Is this going to be dangerous?" Merl protested. "You didn't say anything about dangerous. For dangerous I charge a whole lot more than a measly hundred."

Standing on the stairwell landing, Cordelia felt satisfied. There was no way Merl was going to succeed where she hadn't. Before she had much time to enjoy that happy little thought, pain slammed through her skull and knocked her from her feet.

Chapter Four

The door to Faroe Burke's art studio was locked, but Gunn heard the sounds of a fight inside. Ferocious thumps followed blistering curses, from masculine voices as well as a feminine voice. He took that as a good sign as he gazed back along the hallway he'd followed at the top of the stairs. None of the other men in the gym had hurried to follow him.

Solo, Gunn thought as he glanced at the door and examined his options. *Not surprising. Gunshots. Demonic howling. That'll clear the room. Especially in a neighborhood like this.*

Being solo was fine. Gunn had lived most of his life on his own except for his sister. These days, there were only three people he'd trust his back to, and even then only grudgingly.

The woman screamed again.

She was still alive. It was still a good sign, but there was no guarantee that she'd stay that way. Glass shattered inside the room. Demonic growls and curses echoed out in the hall.

Gunn shrugged into his nylon jacket. He kept stakes in the pockets to use against vampires. Work through Angel Investigations or his own hunt through Los Angeles made encounters with those demons a regular experience.

Glancing down the narrow hallway that led to the four studios at the top of Wally's building, Gunn knew he'd have recognized the woman's studio even if Wally hadn't told him which one it was. Graffiti artwork marked the door in neon colors, a moving image of a small girl standing before a mountain that had stretched out a hand shaped like a boulder for her to stand on. While the mountain held her, the small girl painted trees and clouds to crown the mountain.

Was the message a proclamation of innocence or defiance?

Gunn had seen Faroe around the gym a couple times before, but he hadn't gone out of his way to speak to her until tonight. Faroe was a beauty, tall and slim-hipped and easy on the eyes. Gunn had been more than a little interested in her before without knowing anything at all about her, but after Wally had noticed, ribbed him about it, and said that she was an artist, Gunn had taken a pass on any small talk. He had his mission, and nothing got in the way of that. A woman like Faroe Burke, he knew, could cause a guy to reconsider what he considered to be his calling in life.

Spotting a red fire extinguisher hanging on the wall and incorporated in the design around the doorframe, Gunn ripped it from the wall and stepped back. He lifted a leg and drove it into the door, immediately feeling like he'd broken his foot.

The damn door was reinforced.

Gunn stepped in again and used the fire extinguisher like a battering ram, slamming the bottom of it against the door below the locking mechanism. On the fourth attempt, the locking mechanism shattered, spewing machined parts into a bouncing chaos on the hardwood floor. Without hesitation, Gunn threw his shoulder into the door and went through.

Moonlight streaming through the skylight above framed the struggle in the center of the room. Faroe Burke rammed her head into the face of the demon holding her, then followed up with a handful of fingernails that almost caught the demon's eyes.

The demon cursed and jerked away, releasing her for a moment. "Get her!" the demon yelled.

"Don't let her get away," another demon yelled as he staggered against one of the tables covered with art supplies. "She gets away, we don't get paid."

Gunn registered the conversation and filed it away. There wasn't much time to think. A demon that had been guarding the door, the only way out of the studio, reached for him out of the shadows.

Whirling, holding the fire extinguisher in both hands, Gunn slammed the heavy cylinder into the demon's head. The hollow, ringing bong let Gunn know he'd made solid contact.

Dazed, the demon staggered back against the wall and cradled his head in his hands. He cursed in his own language as well as English.

Not relenting, Gunn stepped up and delivered two more blows, battering his opponent back against the wall.

Sheetrock cracked and fell in chunks, taking pieces out of the graffiti murals that had been painted on the walls. Gunn felt bad about the destruction; Faroe had gone to a lot of trouble to make the studio homey.

The demon dropped to the floor and quivered.

Gunn knew he hadn't killed the demon, but it was seriously decommissioned for a moment. Breathing hard, blood throbbing at his temples, he turned to the two demons bearing down on Faroe Burke. Gunn raced across the floor and altered his hold on the fire extinguisher, pulling the safety pin, then gripping the handle and the nozzle.

The demon closest to the woman reached for her again.

"Hey, ugly," Gunn called, lifting the fire extinguisher.

The demon turned around, a grin pasted across his fierce face. His four ears twitched and turned toward Gunn.

"Must be hell when you get an earache," Gunn said. Then he squeezed the fire extinguisher's trigger. A chemical snowstorm belched from the nozzle, coating the demon's head and shoulders in white powder.

A coughing fit swept over the demon, doubling him over as he tried to claw the chemical from his eyes. He screamed in pain as the fire-retardant powder burned his eyes, nose, and mouth. Large blisters popped up on the demon's exposed skin.

Jaakel demons were sensitive to chemicals in fire extinguishers, Gunn realized. He wondered if Wesley knew that. But that was only a momentary thought that ran through Gunn's mind amid the self-preservation program already running. Survival was all about learning on the fly. He slammed the fire extinguisher into the demon, knocking him back.

The third demon straightened, revealing the carnage his face had become. The long tears in the orange flesh offered mute testimony regarding what the gunfire had been about. Throwing his head back, the demon bayed like a wolf.

"Check out the battle cry," Gunn taunted as he took a fresh grip on the fire extinguisher. "Is that supposed to scare me?"

The demon smiled through the ruined flesh of his face. "No," he said in a hoarse voice. "That was to call in a couple of friends."

Gunn watched a shadow slide across the moonlight. It heeled like a kite and dove straight for the broken skylight.

This has absolutely got to be the stupidest act I've ever committed, Wesley Wyndham-Pryce told himself as he watched the deadpan expressions of the three *Corner of the Eye* editors. Still, there was a certain merit to the plan because it was slimy and disgusting, and Merl certainly fit the bill in those requirements. Wesley nervously drummed the briefcase in his lap, caught himself, and stopped. He breathed in, choosing to present confidence and hoping none of the embarrassment showed.

However, perhaps Merl's supposed role was a tad beyond what the three were willing to believe him capable of.

"A gigolo," Buck Davis repeated, leaning back in his chair.

"That's right," Merl said. He licked his fingertips and ran them across the ridges above his eyes where brows would normally be. "I'm telling you, once human women get a taste of me . . . well, they never go back to human again."

Roger Cadenasso leaned forward, a pencil balanced between his fingers, interest showing on his face as he gazed at Wesley. "And that would make you his pimp?" Roger asked.

Wesley cleared his throat. "Not a pimp."

"Oh?" Roger asked. The pencil lead penetrated his fingertip with a pop. He withdrew it, gazed at the bead of blood that formed there with fascination, then licked it off. "Then what do you call yourself?"

"Geez," Merl complained in his whiny voice. "What do you call anybody you ain't married to that gets twenty-five percent of your take?"

All three tabloid reporters gazed at the demon.

Merl snorted with laughter. "Come on." He spread his hands in supplication. "He's my agent. Work with me here. Can't you tell he's sensitive about the work I do?"

Cassi smiled and popped her gum. "He looks like he just climbed up out of a sewer."

"Hey, hey, hey," Merl protested, smoothing his wrinkled orange leather slacks and crushed purple velour shirt. "This look doesn't come easy. This is chic. Grunge, baby. It's coming back."

And Merl's dress is only one of the problems with this plan, Wesley thought. Still, he wasn't exactly sure how one properly dressed a gigolo.

Cassi opened her mouth, stuck her finger down her throat, and made gagging noises.

"That's not called for," Merl said. He turned to Wesley. "You're my agent. Tell her I'm not here to take abuse."

Straightening his shoulders and his tie, praying that they got out of the situation alive, Wesley said, "My client is not here to take abuse." He slid his hand along the pocket that contained the cell phone. He had Cordelia's number on quick dial. One push of the button and she'd be there to mount a rescue attempt. At least, that was the plan.

"Too bad," Davis commented. "Demon abuse stories by major film stars and political figures could be a big story."

"However," Wesley said, "if a fair offer is made and limitations set on the abuse that won't disfigure or otherwise harm my client, we'll take it under consideration." He tapped the briefcase across his knees with an air of confidence, as if the case contained boilerplate contracts for that very thing.

Merl looked at Wesley in disbelief. "What?"

"We've got plenty of abuse stories," Cassi said. "This guy is telling it like he's every woman's dream."

"Every human woman's," Merl said.

Something gurgled behind the door at the rear of the office room. An ill odor immediately followed the noise.

Definitely demonic, Wesley told himself as he took a kerchief from his pocket and pressed it over his mouth and nose. *Probably a Gorgranian from the stench of it.* That particular species of demon explained why *Corner of the Eye* operated as it did. He struggled to keep the contents of his stomach under control.

"The pipes," Davis said, noticing Wesley's discomfort although he didn't appear to be in any distress himself.

"They keep backing up," Roger added, then licked at his wounded finger again.

"Stan will get them clear," Davis promised.

"Stan?" Wesley echoed. "The elderly lady manning the secretarial desk?"

"She just reads romance novels there," Cassi said, "while she's waiting for the pipes to back up."

"She doesn't get much reading done," Davis said.

Wesley supposed not. Gorgranian demons were simply horrible on disposal pipes.

"Getting back to you," Cassi said to Merl.

"Here I am," Merl said, flipping his hands out. "I am my own favorite subject."

"Of course you are," Cassi said, unimpressed. "Why did you come here?"

"I'm a gigolo, babe," Merl said. "You wouldn't believe the women I've offered companionship to. I'm here to sell my stories."

"Do you have pictures?"

"Sure I do," Merl lied. "Dozens of them. Hundreds of them. I got pictures those women don't even know I have. And I got autographed ones, too."

"We might be interested in your pictures," Cassi said.

Behind the safety of the kerchief pressed over his mouth and nose, Wesley relaxed a little. Perhaps the plan was going to work after all.

"Sure," Merl said, rubbing his hands. "But they don't come cheap."

Wesley removed the kerchief and stoutly endured the

horrid stench that had filled the room. "Might I remind you that we're not just here to offer my client's past conquests? We're also prepared to offer potential liaisons between my client and other entertainment stars."

"Which you want us to help set up?" Davis asked.

"Yes," Wesley said. By doing so, the editorial staff would also expose their network of resources. Nova Studios feared they had people within their organization that were selling them out. Finding out if that were true would mean a lot to the clients.

"And you expect us to believe your"—Cassi raked Merl with a withering glance—"*star* has the equipment to catch these women in compromising positions?"

"Yes," Wesley said, and he was able to keep a straight face because he was scared and because he was British.

"Show me," Cassi challenged.

Cold dread filled Wesley. "Excuse me?"

Looking at him, Cassi said, "I'm a human female, and right now I'm feeling in no way predisposed to your client. Let's see if he can start my engine."

"Start your engine?" Wesley couldn't believe it.

"Sure." Cassi didn't even crack a smile.

Shoving a finger inside his collar to loosen it, Wesley also reached inside his pocket for the cell phone. He glanced at Merl. "Show her."

Merl blinked at Wesley with frightened lizard eyes, then licked his lipless mouth.

"Go on," Wesley said. "Don't be shy."

"Consider it an audition," Cassi said.

"An audition?" Merl shook his head and acted offended. "No way, toots. If I play, you pay."

Reaching into her blouse, Cassi took out a roll of money. "Sure," she said, peeling off a twenty and placing it on the table between them. She added another bill, and another, keeping the pile nice and tight.

"That's money," Merl said, eyes focused on the bills.

"Bust a move," Cassi said.

Licking his lips, the greed evident on his face, Merl pushed out of his chair and stood. "I need some mood music."

Cassi reached into her desk and took out a Discman with detachable speakers. She pressed PLAY and one of Rod Stewart's greatest hits started playing.

"That's the best you can do?" Merl asked as strains of '70s rock filled the office, punctuated by more gurgling behind the door and the foul odor.

"That's it," Cassi replied. "I've paid. Now play."

Wesley closed his hand over the cell phone in his pocket. *Cordelia is only one phone call away.*

Then, just when Wesley was about to press the button, Merl began to move. The demon didn't exactly dance, but the gyrations he performed were certainly suggestive as he popped his body back and forth.

"Take off the clothes," Cassi suggested.

Merl hesitated only a moment, then the woman added another twenty to the stack on the table. "Whoa, baby!" Merl shrieked as he tore off his shirt. "I hope you're ready for something like me! I'm gonna bend you! I'm gonna warp your mind!"

Oh . . . god. . . . Wesley cringed. Maybe it wouldn't be so bad if he closed one eye.

Merl whipped his shirt off, then pulled it between his

legs and bucked his hips like he was riding a horse in slow motion.

Wesley didn't even want to ask where the demon had learned the moves. With the stunned fascination of someone watching a train wreck in progress, Wesley swallowed hard. When he'd considered, created, and crafted Plan B, he'd never once thought of Merl getting so much into the act.

Unable to take it anymore, not knowing how far Merl was going to go because Cassi tossed another twenty onto the pile and still seemed to have a big roll left, Wesley pressed the button on the cell phone. He couldn't endure any more of Merl's show without losing every shred of decency and dignity he had. He only prayed that Cordelia pulled the fire alarm in time.

But Rod Stewart's song continued and Cassi tossed another twenty onto the growing pile.

The fire alarm didn't go off.

Wesley began to get worried, thinking that something might have happened to Cordelia. He shouldn't have left her alone in the stairwell. This was not a safe building or a safe neighborhood. Anything could have happened.

Merl stripped and tossed his underwear at Wesley.

Nothing this bad could have happened to Cordelia, of course, Wesley thought as he dodged the demon's boxers. He placed his briefcase on the floor beside him, preparing himself to move quickly.

"Okay," Cassi said, "I've seen enough."

Merl grinned, standing with his hands on his hips. "Got your motor revved up, don't I?" he asked. "Some chicks really dig demon."

Picking up the money from the table, Cassi brought up a pistol and pointed it at Merl's groin. "No." She glanced at Davis and Roger. "I told you after we had Little Miss Prom Queen in here earlier that these guys were probably fakes." She gestured with the pistol. "There's your evidence. What little of it there is."

Wesley pressed the cell phone button again, but the fire alarm remained silent. *Where is Cordelia?* Surely she hadn't gotten angry enough to leave.

"What do want to do with them?" Davis asked.

Cassi smiled. "Torture them. Find out who sent them. Then kill them. What we usually do with snoops."

Anxious nausea swept over Wesley. Being threatened with death was one thing, but being found in a Dumpster with Merl's nude body for company was too horrid to contemplate. There really was a fate worse than death.

Where the hell was *Cordelia?*

Chapter Five

The Garlock on Angel's left rushed him, screaming and raising the camp axe high above his head.

Angel waited to meet the threat, centering his mind, balancing his purpose, retreating to the void where nothing existed and from which a true warrior took all his or her strength. When the approaching Garlock was close enough, Angel struck, his body uncoiling like a released spring. And the dark demon that fueled the violent impulses that constantly moved within him howled with glee, anxious to be set free.

Moving to the side to avoid the descending camp axe, Angel slapped the demon's left elbow to throw him off balance. Setting his right foot, Angel twisted and executed a back kick, driving the heel of his left foot against the demon's bowling ball head and getting all of his weight behind it. When the kick landed against the demon's stony hide, Angel still thought for a moment that he'd broken his foot.

Despite his size and weight, the Garlock toppled over

the rooftop's edge. He screamed, realizing too late that only a four-story fall waited to catch him. "Tuez!"

Unable to recover his balance because it had taken such a big kick to dislodge the demon, knowing Tuez was closing in on him, Angel dropped and went sprawling across the pebbled rooftop. He caught himself on one arm, going into an automatic tuck and roll that brought him back to his feet in front of the third demon.

"Tuez! He's over here!" The Garlock swung his axe at Angel's head.

Whirling, morphing at the same time, and going into full vampire mode, Angel dodged again. By the time he turned back to the Garlock, Angel wore his own demon's face. He felt the smile tighten his face and put a gleam in his eyes.

The Garlock swung again, pulling the blow from his off side and trying to cut Angel in a horizontal arc. Taking advantage of his full vampire's strength and speed, Angel placed both his hands on the demon's thick wrist as he flipped, driving both feet into his opponent's tiny face. The huge bowling ball head rocked back.

Recovering his balance in a single synaptic muscle twitch, Angel landed in a crouching position on his feet. The dark fury writhed within him, wanting to bring more of itself to the surface.

"Tuez!" the other demon yelled. He slashed at Angel again.

The demon's skill with the axe was lacking. Timing the blow, Angel blocked the Garlock's hands with the bottom of one foot, slowing the blow but not stopping it. The demon's hands seemed to float by him as he plucked the camp axe from them. Still on the move, Angel spun and swept the Garlock's legs from beneath him. As the big demon slammed against the rooftop, car horns blared out on the street below, punctuated by the shrill chirp of a car alarm.

The rooftop shivered when the demon hit. Cracks opened up beneath the Garlock. Before the demon could get up, Angel split his skull with the camp axe. The demon's stone skin grated and sparked, but didn't hold against the axe's keen edge and Angel's vampire strength.

Thumping footsteps and three dancing shadows caused by streetlights and stemming from a single point warned Angel of Tuez's approach. Yanking the camp axe free of the demon's corpse, he used the weapon to block Tuez's attack. Metal screeched as the blades met.

Tuez reached for Angel's head with his free hand.

Knowing he'd have real trouble if the demon managed to grab hold of him, Angel backed away.

"Come here, you stinking vampire!" Tuez roared, charging after Angel.

His mind working at a furious pace, knowing that he didn't have much time to manage the save for Eddie Ashford and Nova Studios, Angel sprinted for the small brick structure that housed the door back into the building's maintenance room. He kept himself just out of Tuez's reach, knowing the demon would lock into the chase.

Closing on the maintenance building, Angel never broke stride. He raised his leg and ran up the building, coming around in a back flip that put him in the air.

Tuez ran underneath him, saw the maintenance building, and couldn't stop. His huge feet tore patches of pebbles and tar from the rooftop as he put the brakes on, but he slammed into the maintenance building like a wrecking ball. Tuez's loose weight crashed through the building, then dropped like a rock down the stairwell that led up to the maintenance door.

The bloodlust still on him, Angel landed on his feet, then hurried forward and dropped through the huge hole in the roof where the small building had once been. He dropped, landing in a ready crouch within arm's reach of Tuez's body.

The demon was dead or knocked out. Angel didn't know which, and it didn't matter. With effort, he pulled the demon back into the small place within where he kept it, then morphed his features back into human.

Angel tossed the axe he held onto Tuez's body, then turned and looked down the dimly lit hallway that led to the upstairs apartments.

He didn't wait. Eddie Ashford was in danger, and if he didn't move fast, the movie star was toast.

Taking a step back, listening to Faroe moving somewhere in the art studio behind him, Gunn glanced up and saw a winged Toolian demon glide through the skylight. If it hadn't been for Wesley's constant barrage of information about all things demonic, Gunn would never have known what the creature was because he'd never seen one. The Jaakels were familiar to him because they often hired out as mercenaries.

The Toolian demon stood two feet high on the ground, but had a wingspread of nearly a dozen feet. The leathery wings were used more for gliding on thermals than actual flight, but they were quick and dangerous. Possessing humanoid bodies and the ability to morph into the avian shape, Toolian demons usually passed as little people. In their avian forms, they lost most of their humanoid facial features because the skull reformed, pushing out into a long, chitinous beak under elongated eyes less than an inch apart. The narrow skull didn't look like it held a spoonful of brains.

Gunn braced himself, drawing the fire extinguisher back.

"Move," an angry feminine voice commanded. Then Faroe was beside Gunn, bumping him aside with her hip as she slid the last cartridge into the .38 she had. She flipped the cylinder closed with a practiced move and brought the pistol up like a cowboy in an old Western movie, but slid her off-hand under her wrist for support.

The .38 spat flame five times as quickly as she could pull the trigger. Gunn noted that the woman had locked her elbow, causing the revolver to rise with each shot, instead of keeping her grip loose and relaxed.

Not that he could have complained. Two of the five rounds cored into the Toolian demon. One of them slammed into the elongated beak only an inch or so in front of the close-set eyes, and the other punched through the creature's narrow skull.

Motor control gone, the Toolian demon dropped like a rock. The heavy beak struck the hardwood floor, ripping a huge gash in the polished surface.

Gunn stepped to one side, hooking an arm around Faroe's slender waist and throwing them both from the path of the dead or dying demon. They tripped over the open sofa bed behind them, landing amid the tangled sheets as the Toolian slid across the floor and took out the nearby worktable.

Paints and supplies thudded to the floor in a cacophony of noise. Some of the aerosol paint cans lost their nozzles and spewed neon colors over the floor as they spun and rolled. The sudden release of compressed gas sent the cans shooting across the floor.

Gunn landed on top of Faroe. Despite the tension of the moment, he was definitely aware of the womanly curves beneath him. He gazed into her brown eyes. *Defiance*, he thought, a smile twisting his lips. *This lady's all about defiance.*

The Jaakel demon roared an oath. "Man, you want something done, you gotta do it yourself."

Faroe gazed into Gunn's eyes. "Get up," she said.

"Right," Gunn replied, but he felt genuine regret at breaking the moment. He rolled from the sofa bed, getting momentarily tangled in the sheets. Her perfume, something he couldn't place and something he knew damn well he was never going to forget, filled his nostrils. Then he landed on his butt on the floor.

Faroe rose from the bed, breaking the .38 open and dumping loose brass. The smoking empties tinkled against the floor as she ran toward an open chest of drawers that had jewelry and accessories scattered across the top. There was also a box of .38 ammo.

Who the hell is this woman? Gunn wondered as he fought the sheets. He got free of them, then watched as two more Jaaekel demons dropped into the room through the broken skylight. After a quick glance at their leader, they took up positions in front of the door. The remaining Toolian demon that had invaded the room swooped down from the shadows crowding the high ceiling.

"Kill the man," the Jaakel ordered, "but I want the woman left alive."

Gunn dodged as the second Toolian demon sped at him. He lifted the sheets, drawing the flying demon into it. Wrapped in the sheets and unable to see, the Toolian crashed through the big windows lining the back studio wall. Caught by the window frames but driven by the demon's weight and speed, the wings cracked as bone splintered. Outside the window, the Toolian dropped like a rock, headed for the street three stories below.

Faroe grabbed a fistful of shells from the box, turned, and started trying to jam them into the open cylinder. Despite her determination and bravery, her hands shook and bullets spilled to the floor.

The Jaakels started forward, baring lockback knives.

Gunn cursed the demons. Part of their heritage and ritual demanded blood sacrifice—not their own, of course, but of their prey. The blood had to be let by knives, not firearms. At least, Gunn thought as he ran toward Faroe, they had that to be thankful for.

He reached the woman and grabbed her arm, tugging her into motion. "Let's go."

Faroe tried to yank away from him but Gunn tightened his grip.

"Stay here and you die," Gunn told her.

"You die," she said. "They want me alive."

63

"With a Jaakel demon," Gunn said, "dying is easiest." He pulled at her again and got her moving.

"I've got a gun," she told him, brandishing her weapon.

"Might as well be a paperweight against Jaakels," Gunn said. "For them, you need silver. Or rowan wood." Still on the move, he grabbed a stool with his free hand and whirled it into the feet of the two Jaakels pursuing them.

The stool caught the demons at the ankles and sent them tumbling to the floor. It took them a moment to get back to their feet.

While their pursuers were delayed, Gunn guided Faroe to the broken window and peered down. The street was three stories below. The sheet-draped body of the Toolian demon hung in a treetop. From the weak fluttering it managed, Gunn knew the Toolian was no longer a threat.

"Damn, but that's a long way down," Gunn said. He reached down and patted the foot-wide ledge that jutted out from the building. "Does this go all the way around?"

"We're not going out there," Faroe said, drawing back from him. "*I'm* not going out there."

Gunn shoved his head out the broken window and looked to the right. The way he had it figured there was another studio only a few feet farther down. He glanced back over his shoulder. "Maybe you want to stay and entertain the riffraff."

Faroe lifted her pistol and pulled the trigger. Only a series of clicks answered her efforts. None of the chambers held a fresh cartridge.

Gunn stepped up onto the ledge and eased out of the window. The chill air slammed into him, given a little more edge by the sweat-drenched clothes from the boxing match earlier. He reached back for the woman.

"Come on," he coaxed, holding out his hand, trying to ignore the two Jaakel demons up and running for them.

Faroe glanced at the demons, at the street three floors below, then at Gunn. "If you let me fall," she threatened, "I'm taking you with me."

Gunn grinned. "You're a tough lady."

She turned and threw the pistol at the demons, causing both of them to duck while the Jaakel with the bullet-riddled face roared at them to get the woman. She reached up, caught hold of Gunn's hand, resisted for a moment as he tried to pull her out onto the ledge, then went.

Surefooted as a cat and no stranger to high places throughout Los Angeles having stalked his demonic prey there on several occasions, Gunn backed away in quick steps. The woman followed him, as surefooted as he was in spite of her reluctance, and he loved how she followed his movement with a natural skill. For a moment, a brief flicker in all the chaos spreading around them, he wondered what it would be like to take her out onto a dance floor.

Then the Jaakel demons reached the windows and tore through the remaining glass. They turned their pumpkin-orange faces toward the woman.

Faroe started to look back.

"Don't," Gunn cautioned. "Just look at me. They haven't reached you. They're not going to."

"You're not watching where you're going," she protested.

"Got plenty of ledge here," Gunn said, slipping his foot back while maintaining toe contact to guide him. "I got four more windows before I run out of room." He'd counted even as he'd stepped out onto the ledge. He kept turned in, the left side of his chest bumping into the building every other step or so.

"How do you know that?"

"Anybody ever have to tell you what color to use when you paint?"

"No."

Gunn smiled, watching as the two Jaakel demons stepped out onto the ledge with obvious trepidation. "This is what I do." He shook his jacket sleeve, freeing the small throwing knife he had hidden there. Catching the smooth handle in his hand, he whipped his arm back and forward, not letting the demons know it was coming.

The knife flipped twice, splintering the weak moonlight, then caught the lead Jaakel demon in the neck, pinning his Adam's apple to the back of his throat.

The demon reached for the knife, gurgling in pain, standing up straight too suddenly on the ledge. He bumped into the demon behind him and fell, almost taking the demon behind him as well.

"Was that silver?" Faroe asked, watching as the demon crunched into the sidewalk below in front of a pizza delivery guy. The pizza cartons hit the sidewalk just after the demon did, then the delivery guy was streaking for his double-parked compact station wagon like an Olympic sprinter.

"No," Gunn said. "But I bet it hurt like hell."

Her eyes widened in horror. "Look out!" she screamed.

Glancing over his shoulder, Gunn spotted the other Jaakel demon gliding toward them. The demon's legs morphed into an eagle's hooked claws, ready to rend and tear flesh as it closed on Gunn.

Lying on the cold linoleum floor of the stairwell, Cordelia trembled and quaked in the throes of the vision. Most of the time when the visions came on, she hated them. She'd never endured such blinding headaches like them in her life.

And she never knew what the visions were going to show her.

She felt the cool linoleum against her cheek, smelled the faint stink of disinfectant, but maybe that was just wishful thinking on her part. Probably nothing clean had touched the floor in years.

Strident ringing filled her ears, but she thought it was part of the vision attack. It couldn't be the phone, could it?

Then the vision pulled her into it.

Cordelia lost sight of the stairwell. Fluorescent lights flickered into her skull and lit the scene. She saw an African-American woman walking through some kind of storage building.

The woman was pretty, dressed in designer clothes. She walked through the storage area and gazed at the pictures on the walls.

No. Wait. Those aren't pictures. They're paintings.

Something else was there, something that hunted the woman. The thing slithered along the ceiling, coiling and uncoiling its body, stalking the woman without making a sound.

And there, against the wall, reflected in glass covering one of the paintings, was a name: YRELLAG TRA EDAJ EZNORB.

The vision started to fade.

Cordelia held on, knowing the brutal treatment she was going through was almost over. She had the information she needed. Although she didn't know the name of the person, she knew the place and she could describe—

A blinding rush of pain splintered Cordelia's thoughts as another image filled her head.

The second vision showed a child playing with multi-colored blocks at a table. He sat in a chair facing Cordelia, tongue hanging slightly out of his mouth as he stacked yet another block on the tower he was building. The child had blond hair and blue eyes. Although Cordelia wasn't good at guessing the ages of children, she knew this one couldn't be more than three or four. He was walking and maybe talking a little, but he was interested in stacking blocks, not playing video games.

He sat at the table in a child's room. The bed in the far corner of the room was an antique four-poster affair scaled down to kid-size. A mobile, ducks with outstretched wings, hung idle above the bed. Toy trucks and carved animals occupied the big toy box in the far corner of the room.

There were no mirrors in the room.

For some reason that fact seemed important to

Cordelia. She watched the room flash through her mind again, still locked in and watching the boy stack blocks. Calliope music reached her ears now.

A creature slid into the doorway behind the boy.

At least a dozen tentacles hung down from the demon's head and thorax, and the closest thing Cordelia could think of that it looked like was a squid. Only this squid wasn't all loose and squishy the way squids are. This one had the ability to walk—or, rather, glide—on its tentacles. It seemed to take little tiptoe steps, but it covered ground quickly, rushing up to the boy.

The squid-thing's head split open, revealing a multi-jawed parrot's beak filled with sharp teeth. Bending down, the demon opened its jaws wide.

Cordelia could suddenly see again, but only the lonely dark of the shadow-filled stairwell surrounded her. She took a wipe from her purse and mopped her face. The cool clean of the medicated tissue made her feel better immediately, but the headache throbbed and threatened to split her skull.

Images of the woman and the boy flashed through her mind. Somehow they were connected. She hadn't seen how, but she knew it was true. *Angel,* she reminded herself. *Gotta tell Angel.*

She reached into her purse and took out her cell phone. When she touched the keypad, she saw that she'd missed three calls. A quick trip through the menu showed her that all the calls had come from Wesley's cell phone, and they had come in rapid succession.

Please let him be all right! Cordelia summoned her flagging strength and pushed herself up. Dizziness swept over her, and if the fire alarm had been one step farther away she might not have made it.

She gripped the fire alarm, then yanked it. For a second she thought nothing was going to happen, then the harsh, jangling noise of the alarm filled the stairwell and echoed through the building above her. She leaned against the wall and breathed, trying to push all the pain away. She didn't know if the alarm had been in time or not.

Grimly, Cordelia punched in Angel's number and started up the stairs, leaning heavily on the railing.

Chapter Six

The fire alarm blared into the offices of *Corner of the Eye* and caught the three tabloid editors by surprise. Cassi looked at the door, unconsciously dragging her pistol sights from Merl's groin.

The gurgling beyond the office door at the back of the room intensified, and more of the foul stench than ever filled the room.

Wasting no time, Wesley strode forward to the desks where Cassi and Roger Cadenasso sat. He lashed out with his foot, pushing Cassi's desk as hard as he could even as she brought the pistol to bear on him.

The report of the shot trapped inside the office was deafening, and for a moment Wesley thought there was no way the woman could have missed him at the close range. He watched as Cassi went over backward, barreled over by the desk as Merl came tumbling off altogether and splatted on the floor.

Surprised that he hadn't been hit, that in fact Cassi's bullet had struck Buck Davis and knocked him to the floor, Wesley remained in motion. He still held Merl's pants, which he flung into Roger Cadenasso's face as the man rose.

"Merl," Wesley commanded as he launched himself at Roger Cadenasso, "get the weapon."

"Where are my pants?" Merl demanded.

Wesley doubled his fist and slammed it into Roger Cadenasso's face, driving the man backward into the wall. Roger's head smacked against the wall, knocking some of the framed copies of the tabloid to the floor. Glass shattered.

Ripping the demon's pants from his opponent's head, Wesley threw them at Merl. "Get the gun. Now!"

"Yeah, yeah, yeah," the demon said. "Keep your shirt on."

"You should be talking," Wesley said, then hit Roger again.

Without a word or much of a struggle, Roger sank to the floor, unconscious.

Wesley turned, knowing the biggest danger in the room was Cassi and the pistol. He looked at the woman just as she closed her hand on the weapon and tried to bring it around. Merl, hopping around like a madman and trying to pull his pants on, fell and landed on the woman's gun arm, trapping it beneath his body. The pistol blasted again, spouting flame, but the bullet dug into the desk.

Throwing himself forward, Wesley grabbed Cassi's gun arm, struggling as much with Merl rolling around on the floor as with the woman trying to kill them. Cordelia walked in in the middle of that.

Cordelia stared at Wesley wrestling with Cassi and Merl still trying to pull his pants on. She blinked and held up a hand. "You know, I'm not even going to ask. I'm in no mood for even a ha-ha funny."

From her pale and haggard appearance, Wesley guessed that she'd had a vision. He redoubled his efforts to pry the pistol from Cassi's hand, finally succeeding in wresting it away at about the time Merl got both feet into his pants. Unfortunately, both feet went into the same pants leg and it tore.

"Awww, man," Merl said, extricating himself.

The gurgling in the building grew louder.

"Something demony, right?" Cordelia asked.

Breathing hard, Wesley stood above the woman, who curled up into a fetal ball and snarled curses. "Yes," Wesley said. "Unless I miss my guess, it's a Gorgranian demon these people have summoned from a demon world that lies adjacent to our own."

"Does it have tentacles or look like a squid?" Cordelia asked.

Wesley shook his head. He checked Buck Davis, but there was no help for the man. Cassi's shot had taken him in the heart. Davis's dead eyes stared up at nothing.

"No," Wesley said, turning his attention back to Cassi, who was pummeling a screaming Merl without mercy. "Gorgranian demons are more on the order of snails. Big blobby masses of putrid pus that can scarcely get around under their own steam."

"Gross," Cordelia said.

"Gorgranian demons are meddlesome," Wesley said as he pocketed the pistol and walked toward his briefcase by the chair he'd been seated in. "Fortunately, few of them choose to travel into this world because transportation is a big issue with them. However, once they are here, Gorgranians can be very effective instruments of terror and blackmail. They can sniff out secrets and exploit personality defects and weaknesses. The Nazis used Gorgranians extensively back in World War Two." He popped the latches on the briefcase and flipped it open.

"What are we going to do?"

Wesley slipped the double-bitted battle-axe from the briefcase. Flicking a small button on the side of the metal handle, he watched as the handle telescoped to three feet, seven inches. Perhaps it wasn't mired in antiquity and a history redolent of past wars, but it was a serviceable weapon.

"Would you care for something?" Wesley asked, looking over the supply of cutlery he'd brought along. From the beginning he'd believed *Corner of the Eye* had allied itself with demons of some sort. Too many of the tabloid's stories had centered around demons for there not to be some kind of connection.

"No thanks," Cordelia said.

Pushing his glasses back up his nose, Wesley said, "Gorgranian demons can be quite large. I'd rather have someone at my back that I know can defend herself should a more direct approach to our quarry be necessitated through circumstance."

"I'll take something," Merl said, coming up behind Wesley while pulling his shirt on.

"You?" Cordelia challenged.

"Hey," the demon protested. "You wouldn't believe what these people had me doing in here."

"And I'd like to keep it that way," Cordelia responded.

Merl looked offended, but being half-dressed, the look didn't quite come off as well as Wesley knew the demon wanted.

"I'm due some payback against that thing," Merl said.

The gurgling behind the door rumbled louder and the foul stench increased.

"Of course," Merl said, glancing at the door, "maybe I can leave revenge and retribution in the hands of you guys. You're the experts at that sort of thing."

Wesley took a war mallet from the briefcase. The head held a flat surface on one side for dealing blunt damage, and the other side tapered into a pick designed to pierce armor and skulls.

"A hammer?" Merl sounded like he couldn't believe it. He jerked a thumb over his shoulder at the gurgling noises coming from the other side of the office. "Doesn't sound like we're driving nails in there."

"That's a fourteenth-century French mallet," Wesley said. "And it's one of Angel's favorites. If I were you I'd take very good care of that mallet," Wesley continued. He took an ironbound truncheon from the briefcase and handed it to Cordelia. "Someone other than Merl at my back, if you please."

Cordelia took the truncheon and swung it experimentally.

"Are we set?" Wesley asked, closing the briefcase and standing. "With the clamor of the fire alarm, I don't think we have much time before the fire department arrives."

"I'm good," Cordelia said, but her face was pasty and pain still flickered in her eyes.

Wesley took off his tie and shoved it into his jacket pocket with the pistol. He crept past Cassi, who continued rocking herself in a fetal ball and making humming noises. Davis remained dead, and Roger remained unconscious.

"What's her story?" Cordelia asked, pointing at the woman.

"Symbiotic link," Wesley said. "Gorgranians use them to keep their minions under control. Obviously the Gorgranian we're about to confront has decided to take her to task for failing to protect him."

"Working for demons doesn't exactly net you a lot of job bennies," Merl said. "Or even much security. One day you're a henchman, the next day your boss has been staked or turned to goo or banished back to another dimension by some know-it-all vampire do-gooder."

"This way," Wesley said, stepping back and driving his foot into the door. The lock sheared with a metallic screech and the door popped open.

Gunn turned away from the flying Toolian demon but knew they wouldn't be able to remain on the ledge of the building and avoid the slashing claws. He shielded his head with an arm as he threw himself into the window at his side.

Inside the room on the other side of the window, an old woman dressed all in black sat at a small round table and held the hand of a young woman who seemed intent on her every word. The room was lit only by two candles that reflected in the crystal ball between the two women.

The glass in the window shattered when Gunn struck

it. He gave silent thanks that the building wasn't up to code or that the impact-resistant glass usually installed in buildings of suicide height wasn't in place. Keeping hold of Faroe Burke's arm, he dragged her after him.

Both of them hit the ground rolling. The Toolian demon drew up short of the building and didn't follow them inside.

Gunn shoved himself to his feet, reaching down for Faroe and pulling her up as well. He glanced back at the broken window as a Jaakel demon reached it.

"They're in here!" the Jaakel demon shouted.

Grabbing an empty chair from the table where the old woman and her client still sat, Gunn said, "Excuse me, ma'am." He turned and threw the chair at the window, watching as the Jaakel dodged back.

Gunn glanced at the room, taking in the stuffed ravens and bookcase filled with ancient books. Incense hung heavy in the air, so strong it made his eyes water. A beaded curtain separated the small office from the rest of the studio.

"Madame Njemile," Faroe said.

The name clicked into place in Gunn's mind. Madame Njemile was Wally's oldest renter. She ran a sports-book gambling operation and a fortune-telling business on top floor.

Madame Njemile released the young woman's hand and looked at Faroe. "What the hell do you think you're doing? Come busting in here like that, you like to have give me a heart attack."

"The door," Gunn said. "Now."

The old woman stood up, her wrinkled face a mask of

fury. She took a cell phone from the pocket of her black robe. "I'm gonna call nine-one-one, get the Five-Oh down here to bust a cap in your ass is what I'm gonna do."

The Jaakel stepped forward on the ledge and dropped into the building. Snarling, the demon lifted a pistol and pointed it at Gunn.

Faroe grabbed Gunn by the shoulder and pulled him after her as she ran through the beaded curtain. The pistol banged and the bullet burned by Gunn's face. He ran, following Faroe through the beaded curtain and into the rest of the studio.

Behind them, the bullet fired twice more. Gunn glanced back long enough to make sure that Madame Njemile and her client had taken cover.

The Jaakel charged after them, tearing at the beaded curtain, ripping it down over him. He cursed and growled, and two other demons bumped into him, nearly sending them all sprawling.

"This studio's laid out like mine," Faroe said, pushing off a wall and running through a narrow corridor between modular walls that snapped into the floor. "She just added all the walls. The door's at the back."

"Shouldn't it be the other way?" Gunn asked.

"Mirror image," Faroe explained. "Studio's laid out like mine, only backward."

They ran through a living room area equipped with a computer, entertainment center, and recliner. A spotted cat's head popped up by the recliner's arm. The cat's eyes grew large as Gunn and Faroe sprinted across the room, then it yowled and leaped from the chair.

"There," Faroe said, pointing at the door ahead.

Before Gunn could respond, the modular wall behind them came crashing down, driven forward by the rampaging Jaakel demon that had knocked it down. The demon rode the wall down, slamming on top of a coffee table and collapsing it. A bowl of popcorn that had been sitting on the coffee table shot into the air and rained down like confetti.

The demon behind the one that had brought the wall down raised a knife and charged through.

Gunn seized a heavy glass candy dish from a small table beside the recliner. He whirled, flipping the candy like a Frisbee into the demon's face.

"Come on," Faroe said, yanking the door open.

"Right behind you," Gunn said.

She led the way out into the hallway, coming out between her own studio and the stairwell leading to the lower floors and the gym. Without hesitation, she ran for the stairwell.

"You do this kind of thing often?" Gunn asked as he paced her.

"What?"

"Running from demons."

"No," Faroe responded, breathing rapidly. "I must be a natural."

Gunn grinned. "Brave and a sense of humor. I like that."

Faroe shot him a glance. "Didn't know I was here to meet with your approval."

Before Gunn could think of a response, the Jaakel demons tore through Madame Njemile's door behind

ANGEL

them. Gunn turned the corner and started down into the
stairwell, then spotted the railing just inside the doorway.

"Keep going," Gunn said, stopping and clambering up
on the railing where he couldn't be seen.

The woman didn't seem to have a problem with that.
She never broke stride as she ran, taking three and four
steps at a time.

Gunn stood at the top of the railing, hidden by the
stairwell frame. He breathed out, trying to control the
pattern and make sure he got plenty of oxygen instead of
building up carbon dioxide. And he waited.

Faroe Burke had turned the corner at the landing of
the first set of stairs by the time the three Jaakel demons
put in their appearance. They didn't hesitate, descending
the stairs and glancing over the side to see the fleeing
woman.

"There she goes!" one of the demons yelled.

"Where's that other guy?" another asked.

Moving silently, Gunn stepped off the railing and back
to the top of the stairwell. A quick glance showed him no
one else was in the corridor. "Here," he said.

The three demons lining the stairwell turned to look at
him.

Gunn brought his leg up and around in a roundhouse
kick, putting all his weight and strength into it. His foot
caught the demon at the top section of the stairs full in
the face, lifting him from his feet and sending him crashing back into his companions.

The falling demons turned into an avalanche that
bumped and thumped down the stairwell. Bones broke.

Knowing he'd only succeeded in buying a little more

time for himself and the woman, Gunn grabbed the stairwell railing and heaved himself over. He dropped, managing to land safely on the next set of stairs below without breaking or twisting an ankle. He vaulted through the next set of stairs as well, reaching the woman just as she ran around the final turn and out into the gym area.

Gunn followed her, getting up to speed now, impressed by Faroe Burke's own skills. He stretched out, putting more leg into the run, making the two or three inches he had on her count. Otherwise he'd have never caught her.

No one was in the gym and the ring stood vacant under the halogen lamps.

In seconds, Gunn trailed Faroe out onto the dark street, staying a dogged half step behind her. They ran under the tree that held the broken corpse of the Jaakel demon. The lamp near the tree painted the demon's shadow against the broken pavement of the sidewalk. People gathered out on the street moved away from them. If someone was running, someone was chasing him or her. No one wanted to get in between hunter and hunted.

Glancing ahead, Gunn figured Faroe's destination was the small parking garage in the next block. "You got wheels?" he asked.

"Yes," she replied.

"A place to go?"

"Yes."

Gunn glanced over his shoulder and saw the Jaakel demons rush out of the gym. "That's good, because they aren't giving up."

Faroe didn't say anything, putting all her strength into running. She ran past the young garage attendant flipping through a Daredevil graphic novel, and to the second row of cars.

The parking garage had low ceilings mined with dim fluorescent bulbs that had burned out in several places. The yellow stripes marking the spaces had faded over the years, and oil patches stained several of them. A mixed miasma of gasoline fumes and petroleum products pervaded the garage.

Faroe dropped down beside a new yellow-and-black Mustang hardtop, slid a magnetic key box from underneath, and opened the car door. She slid in behind the wheel and started the engine.

"Hey." Standing beside the car's passenger door, Gunn rapped on the window.

Faroe looked at him. A small trickle of blood leaked from the left corner of her mouth.

Gunn didn't know when that had happened, but if that was all she'd come out of the encounter with, they were both lucky. He pointed at the door. "Door's locked."

"It's staying locked," she told him, putting the sports car into reverse. The tires spun as she backed out of the space.

Gunn kept pace with her with difficulty. "Hey? Is that any way to be? I saved your butt."

"And I saved yours a couple times back there, too," Faroe said. "If you don't figure we're even-up, send me a bill."

"To who?" Gunn couldn't believe she was just going to leave him like that, just drive right out of his life like he was nothing.

"If you know Wally," Faroe said, "he knows me." She slammed the sports car into first gear. Putting her foot down on the accelerator, she released the clutch. The Mustang's rear tires shrilled and the car fishtailed for a moment before they caught hold.

Helpless, Gunn watched her go. The Jaakel demons stepped into the mouth of the parking garage just as Faroe reached it. She didn't even touch the brake, punching through them and sending them flying like tenpins.

Impressive, Gunn thought as he watched the ruby taillights screech out into traffic and narrowly avoid a collision. And just like that, she was gone.

Wesley followed the broken door into the room behind the main office of *Corner of the Eye.* He kept the battle-axe raised and at the ready.

Inside the room, filing cabinets lined the walls and guttering candles lined the cabinet tops, offering only weak illumination that filtered through the accumulation of candle smoke and shadows. The room had no windows.

In the center of the room, a huge thousand-gallon aquarium as large as a waterbed and much deeper sat on the floor. Murky water filled the aquarium. It was surrounded by a dozen rows of thick candles. Piles of personal items like combs, watches, jewelry, baseball cards, toothbrushes, intimate apparel, and photographs occupied the space between the candles.

"This place is a rat's nest," Cordelia said as she followed Wesley into the room.

Wesley stepped cautiously among the candles. "It's not a rat's nest," he said. "This is the warren of the Gorgranian demon. You see, Gorgranian's feed on fear of someone they control. As owner of *Corner of the Eye,* with all the sources the demon accessed, the Gorgranian was obviously in position to blackmail dozens of people. Perhaps the tabloid people profited from the ransom money the victims paid, but the Gorgranian lived on the fear they generated."

"But once a story was known," Cordelia asked, "what was there to fear?"

Glancing around the filing cabinets, Wesley said, "The tabloid reporters didn't tell every dirty little secret they knew. They told just enough to create a dearth of fear in the victims they blackmailed instead of exposed."

"Then all the stories in the filing cabinets are all still secrets," Cordelia said.

"Yes." Wesley surveyed the murky water in the aquarium.

"Cool," Cordelia said. "I bet if I had a quick peek at some of those files, I could get a few acting jobs."

Something roiled in the aquarium's murky water as Wesley crept closer. The Gorgranian demon had to live there at least part of the time due to its aquatic needs. "Don't think like that, Cordelia."

"It's kind of hard not to," Cordelia said.

"The Gorgranian demon feeds on thoughts like that," Wesley explained. "The same way it feeds off all these personal items it demands as tribute from its victims. It draws its strength from fear and greed and lust."

Wesley leaned forward, one hand resting against the

aquarium glass while he carried the battle-axe in the other. The dank water made the glass reflective, showing Cordelia and Merl behind him, both of them looking unsure of themselves as they cradled their weapons.

"Terrific," Merl said. "I'm half-dressed and Cordelia's in the room. You know that Gorgranian's gotta be picking up on lust."

Cordelia turned on the demon and drew the truncheon back. "If you so much as think about me that way, I'm going to leave your brain on the floor for the demon to eat."

"It doesn't actually eat brains," Wesley said. "That was a popular misconception about the demon during the twelfth century."

"Whatever," Cordelia said.

"Your time might be better spent looking through those files," Wesley said. He felt vibrations from the aquarium glass against his palm. Something moved inside the container. "See if you can find the Nova Studios files."

"Do you think it would be filed under Studios, then sub-filed under Nova?" Cordelia asked. "Or just under Nova Studios?" She started pulling filing cabinet drawers open.

"I wouldn't know," Wesley said. Then he heard a cell phone keypad beeping. He turned and glanced at Cordelia, who had her cell phone out. "What are you doing?"

"Calling Angel," Cordelia replied. "I had a vision he needs to know about. I couldn't get him earlier because he wouldn't pick up. You know how he is about these phones, but that's no excuse. He knows it's us. I mean, who else has the number?"

"Find the files," Wesley said. "Quickly, please." He glanced at Merl and saw that the demon was going through filing cabinets.

"Nova Studios, you said?" Merl asked.

"Yes."

"They must have deep pockets if they hired you guys." Merl opened another cabinet, leaving the wreckage of files strewn over the floor at his feet. He paused to look at a photograph. "Wow."

"Put that back," Wesley commanded. "We're not here to snoop through every dirty little secret contained in those files."

"Right," Cordelia said, holding the cell phone to her ear. "We'd be here for days. Weeks, even."

Reluctantly, Merl dropped the file folder to the floor. "Isn't Nova Studios the ones with the new SF picture? The DaShio Mercury guy?"

"Less talk," Wesley suggested. "More work." The vibrations inside the aquarium grew stronger, drawing his attention. He glanced back at the container and spotted three bulbous, crimson eyestalks pressed against the glass. Unable to stop himself, he jumped back from the horrendous sight. He yelled and went sprawling, knocking over candles that rolled across the floor.

Some of the rolling candles reached the piles of paper Merl had dropped on the floor. As soon as the flame touched the papers, they caught fire.

"Hey!" Merl shouted. "Hey, hey, hey! I did *not* do that!"

"Put it out," Wesley ordered, grabbing the battle-axe and scrambling to his feet just as the Gorgranian demon surged up out of the aquarium.

The demon looked like a four-foot-tall jalapeño pepper with two spindly arms and the consistency of gelatin. The three eyestalks jutted up from its rounded head more than a foot, bobbing and weaving as they turned in different directions. The tubular body moved as if boneless, swaying one way and then the other.

"Leave my things alone!" the demon shrilled in a high-pitched voice. "Put those back!"

"Jeez," Merl called derisively, stomping at the flaming papers scattered across the floor, "and don't he look fierce. And the manly voice on that guy. Wow."

Without warning, the Gorgranian demon swelled to three times its size. The increased bulk ruptured the aquarium and spilled the murky water in all directions. With a lithe leap that belied its huge bulbous bulk, the Gorgranian demon leaped from the wreckage of the aquarium and seized Wesley around the throat.

Chapter Seven

Down the hallway from where Tuez had crashed through the maintenance doorway and the rooftop, Angel threw open the first door he came to. The rooms above the sports bar weren't dwellings, just flops where business was done. His vampirism didn't act to keep him outside. A cloud of dust from the debris behind him fogged the corridor.

"Get out of here!" a scantily-clad woman yelled at Angel, pulling the sheet up to cover herself in bed.

The half-dressed man standing in the room wasn't Eddie Ashford.

"Sorry," Angel apologized, backing out of the room and slamming the door closed as the man started for him.

Back in the hallway, Angel glanced at the other three closed doors. The next one opened onto an empty room, but the one after that held a guy with a shoulder-rigged professional camcorder pressed up against the wall.

The guy was young, dressed in chinos and a black T-shirt that had a word balloon encapsulating "Doh!" on it. His hair was razored in a skater cut and piercings flashed on his left eye, nose, and cheek. A tattoo of a purple-and-crimson gecko lizard wrapped his neck. A frightened look filled his face as he looked at Angel.

Angel figured the cameraman wasn't there to take pictures of the cracked plaster and chipped paint. He stepped toward him.

"Hey, man, who the hell are you?" The guy didn't even think to remove the camcorder from the wall.

Crossing the room, Angel yanked the guy from the wall and tossed him onto the bed. The dropped camcorder smashed against the floor.

"Hey, dude," the guy complained, "you can't just come in here and start trashing my stuff. That's expensive equipment."

"Sue me," Angel said, spotting the hole cut into the wall.

"Are you a cop?" the man demanded. He started off the bed. "Because if you are, this is police brutality and I'll have your badge."

"No, I'm not a cop," Angel replied, placing a hand against the man's chest and shoving him back onto the bed again. "And trust me, things haven't even started to get brutal."

Peering through the hole in the wall, Angel saw Eddie Ashford standing near the bed in the next room. He held the blonde woman in a frantic embrace. Clothing was coming off with astonishing speed.

"Do you know what's going on in there?" Angel asked, backing away from the wall and searching the room.

The guy on the bed cowered and stayed put. "This is

just a job. What goes on between two consenting adults—"

"One of those consenting adults is a demon in disguise," Angel said. "And she's about to execute Eddie Ashford to birth her baby."

Surprise widened the cameraman's eyes, but the emotion was followed by excited avarice. "No way."

"Way," Angel said. "Only I don't think the people who sent you here realized that." He hefted the camcorder, thinking it was heavy enough and solid enough that it might do the job.

"Get outta here," the man said. "This was just a gig. Catch Eddie Ashford slumming. Pays the bills and maybe kids find out that DaShio Mercury is not a guy to look up to. Nobody said nothing about killing nobody. But, man, nobody's ever filmed a male movie star giving birth to a demon baby." He paused. "Eddie Ashford *is* a guy, isn't he? That could be a really cool twist."

"You work for *Corner of the Eye*?" Angel asked.

The man hesitated, then nodded. "Freelance. But don't go off on me about being a peeping Tom. We're talking First Amendment rights here. People got a right to know about people. If Eddie Ashford has got some serious kinks, that's not my fault. I didn't put 'em there."

"But you don't mind exploiting them."

"I'm getting paid."

"Did you have anything to do with the woman in the room with him?" Angel backed away from the wall. Surprise was the key when dealing with a female Garlock demon.

"No. I was just told to show up here, shoot pictures of Eddie Ashford and whoever he ended up with."

"Some job," Angel said. He ignored the ringing cell phone in his jacket pocket.

The cameraman looked offended. "Hey, man, at least I don't go around terrorizing people."

"Sure you do," Angel said. "I just do mine more out in the open." He drew the camcorder back. "By the way, you need to get a new job. *Corner of the Eye* is going out of business." He stepped forward and threw the camcorder at the wall.

The camcorder smashed through the wall, tearing through cheap plaster and garish wallpaper. After it passed through the wall, the camcorder slammed against the wall on the opposite side of the next room, drawing the attention of Eddie Ashford and the female Garlock.

Angel tore through the hole after the camcorder. On the other side of the wall, he streaked for Ashford as the movie star and the woman turned to look back at him. Shoving Ashford with one hand, Angel knocked the half-dressed man into the air and back onto the bed.

The female Garlock wheeled on Angel, the clothing barely concealing the generous feminine curves that had led Ashford from the sports bar only minutes ago. Her eyes blazed with electric fury.

"What are you doing here?" she demanded.

"Taking care of Eddie," Angel said. "I don't want any trouble, Ranyel." He remembered the demon's name from his conversation with Tuez on the rooftop.

The woman cocked her head. "How do you know me?"

"I talked to Tuez."

"You know Tuez?"

Angel hesitated. "We met. Recently." Even across the six feet of distance that separated him from her, he felt the restless anxiety that filled her. "It was a short conversation."

Pain wracked her beautiful features. She glared at the hole in the wall that Angel had walked through. "Eddie's mine," she said.

"Yeah," Ashford called from the bed. "Eddie's hers." His voice was thick enough and slurred enough that Angel knew Ashford had been drinking or using while he'd been in the bar below. The movie star tried getting up from the collapsed bed.

"Stay," Angel said, taking a step in between the female Garlock and Ashford.

"Did the studio send you?" Ashford asked.

"Yeah," Angel said, but he didn't take his eyes from the demon.

"Tell them they can mind their own business," Ashford instructed. "And stay out of mine. They pay me for work I do. They don't own me. I'm entitled to a little fun."

"This woman isn't a little fun, Eddie," Angel said.

"Damnit," Ashford swore. "Do you have any idea who I am?"

"Yeah," Angel said, eyes never leaving the Garlock demon's. "A guy about thirty seconds from being dead. This isn't a woman. This is a Garlock demon. She's gravid. She's about to have a child," Angel said.

Ashford stared at the blonde. "No way. Look at that figure."

"She's a demon," Angel said. "She changes the way she looks."

"Don't listen to him, Eddie," Ranyel said. "Call up security and get this guy tossed out of here."

Angel shrugged. "Tuez and his two buddies tried tossing me out. Didn't work for them."

Concern flickered across the demon's human face. "Where is Tuez?"

"Dead," Angel said, even though he didn't know if it was true.

"Who the hell is Tuez?" Ashford asked.

With an inarticulate cry of rage, the female Garlock launched herself at Angel. Her speed caught him by surprise, allowing her to get a hand around his throat and start squeezing. If he'd been human, his neck would have snapped like dry kindling. As it was, pain throbbed in Angel's vision and threatened to shut out his senses. Struggling, he watched her morph from the blonde siren to the bowling-ball-headed creature that she really was.

"Son of a bitch!" Ashford yelled, backing away, pressing against the wall in the corner of the room.

"Damn you!" Ranyel screamed. "You've ruined this! Tuez was supposed to live to watch his son being born!" She lifted Angel from his feet, pressing him back against the wall. Then she stutter-stepped, almost dropping to her knees as the labor pains took her.

Angel fought to break free of her grip, but her pain and the excitement of the impending birth made her stronger than ever. Before he knew what she was going to do, she twisted and threw him toward the room's window.

Flipping end over end once, Angel sailed through the window, breaking glass and scattering gleaming shards. He stuck out both hands and barely managed to grab the window frame with one hand. Maybe the fall wouldn't have killed him, but the time he took to return to the room would have cost Ashford his life.

Screeching precariously, the window frame held and Angel's flight came to a sudden stop. Caught by one hand, his body flipped on the impromptu axis and slammed him against the brick side of the building. Feeling as though his arm had been pulled from its socket, Angel pushed his feet against the side of the building and pulled himself back up to the window.

Drawing even with the window, Angel peered through, watching as Ranyel caught up with Ashford running for the door. The female Garlock seized Ashford by one shoulder and carried him back to the collapsed bed. She threw him down onto the bed, then flung herself on top of him, trapping his body with hers.

Ashford fought and screamed, but he couldn't move her off him.

Leaning forward, the Garlock demon's body morphed again. A spigot of concrete-gray flesh shoved out from her abdomen as she leaned forward and thrust her stomach toward her prey. The cocktail dress she'd been wearing hung from her massive body in shreds. The tendril of flesh formed a tube that coiled and searched for Ashford's face.

"Come on, movie star," Ranyel taunted in her gravelly voice. "Open up. It will only hurt till it kills you."

Recognizing the ovipositor sliding across Ashford's throat, Angel kicked his feet against the wall and pulled himself back into the room. Garlock demons reproduced like insects. Once pregnant, the female carried the egg till it was ready to be born. Near the end of the birth-cycle, the female either let herself be consumed by the birth of her young, or deposited it into a host through the ovipositor to be consumed.

"No!" the demon roared as she saw Angel sprinting toward her.

The ovipositor moved with a mind of its own, probing for Ashford's mouth. The flesh was thin enough that Angel could see the dark shape of the young demon the size of a tennis ball in the tube. Ashford wouldn't survive having the ovipositor rammed down into his lungs.

Ranyel reached for Angel, but she was hampered by the ovipositor seeking out its victim. Ashford screamed, but he kept his mouth closed so the noise came through his nose, and kept twisting his head from side to side as he tried to bury his face in the bedclothes.

Angel dove at the woman, slamming into her as the cell phone in his pocket started ringing again. Despite the Garlock female's size and strength, he dislodged her from Ashford and knocked her to the floor against the wall. Together, they fell in a tangle into the small break-fast table and two chairs. The furniture shattered.

Pain blazed through Angel as he tried to push himself up. Something tugged at his stomach. Glancing down, he saw that a long sliver of wood from one of the chairs pierced his side and jutted out four inches.

"Missed your heart, vampire," Ranyel growled, rolling to her knees in front of Angel.

The ovipositor from her abdomen probed him, bouncing across his chest, but at the touch of his dead flesh, the organ jerked back as though flame-broiled. Vampires couldn't be used as incubators for the demon young because their touch killed them.

Angel reached for the demon, seizing her bowling ball head in both hands. He groaned in pain as Ranyel yanked the wooden splinter from his side and fisted it like a dagger.

"I won't miss," she threatened, drawing the splinter back.

Knowing he couldn't dodge the blow in time and that she was strong enough to drive the wooden shaft through his heart and dust him, Angel twisted her head and snapped her neck. Her blow came at him, but her aim was off and the wooden splinter ripped across his ribs instead.

Putting a hand to his side, Angel released the demon's corpse and staggered to his feet.

Even after her death, the birth-cycle tried to continue. The ovipositor retreated within the demon's body, then she was consumed by an internal combustion. Flames leaped up from the demonic corpse as flesh and bone burned. The fire scorched the wallpaper and curtains as well, catching the room on fire.

Angel backed away from the flames, watching as the Garlock demon's body became a whirling inferno. The young demon didn't survive either.

The cell phone continued to ring.

Frustrated and hurting, Angel dug in his trench coat pocket and pulled the phone out. He flipped it open and said, "What?"

"Well, and aren't you bright and cheery," Cordelia said.

"I'm kind of busy here," Angel said.

"Are you hurt?" Cordelia asked. "You sound like you're hurt."

Angel stepped back farther from the swirl of fire climbing the room's walls. They were already eating into the textured ceiling. "I'm fine. And I'm busy."

"We're not exactly having a day out at the beach here," Cordelia said. "Wesley's being throttled by a Gorgranian demon and Merl has set the building on fire."

"Maybe you should help him," Angel suggested, glancing at Ashford and seeing him grabbing loose clothing. The phone connection also delivered painful grunts, gasps, and choking sounds, as well as the insistent and strident rings of a fire alarm somewhere in the background. He glanced at Ashford. "Stay there."

"Stay there?" Cordelia asked.

"Not you," Angel said. "Ashford."

"Oh, you saved him?"

Angel looked at the flames consuming the room. "Yeah," he answered, because he didn't want to explain. "And I didn't mean you should help Merl. I meant that you should help Wesley."

"Merl's helping Wesley. After all, he's Plan B and we are, technically, in the Plan B phase of everything."

Angel listened to more painful grunting and groaning, recognizing Wesley's voice as well as Merl's. Neither of them sounded like they were having a good time.

Holding his clothing, Ashford crept toward the door.

Angel went after Ashford, catching the man by the ear before he got out into the hallway.

Ashford bleated in fear and pain and outrage.

"What's that?" Cordelia asked.

"Ashford," Angel said.

"Is he hurt?"

Angel took the man by the elbow and squeezed hard enough to get Ashford's attention without breaking the arm. "Not yet, but he's resisting rescue. Hurting him is becoming an attractive possibility."

"Is that the studio?" Ashford demanded, grabbing hold of Angel's hand and trying to pull it from his ear. "If it is, tell them my lawyers are going to be all over them. Farragut and Marsh will march a microscope of their collective—"

"Shut up," Angel ordered. Then, knowing how Cordelia's mind worked and the fact that she was listening, he added, "Not you, Cordy."

Ashford fell silent as they passed Tuez lying stretched out in the hallway.

"You called for a reason," Angel prompted. He hated cellular phones, and he was already starting to hear white noise over the handset as he went down the steps.

"I had a vision," Cordelia said.

"Cordelia," Wesley called over the phone, sounding stressed and far away.

"Was that Wesley?" Angel asked.

"Yeah," Cordelia said. "Plan B isn't working out so well. Although I think the fire is turning out to be a good thing because it looks like it's going to destroy all the blackmail files *Corner of the Eye* had on the premises. There are so many files that we couldn't get them all out of here. And we haven't found Nova Studios' stuff yet. By the time the firemen get here, there probably won't be anything left. It should be another job well done."

Or at least flame-broiled, Angel thought.

"Cordelia!" Wesley called again, sounding exasperated.

"Wesley hasn't fought a Gorgranian demon before, has he?" Angel asked.

"I didn't ask. He knew what it was, but when it swelled up on him faster than boiled rice, he really looked surprised. I don't let things like that bother me as much anymore."

"Salt," Angel said, maintaining his hold on the movie star's ear and guiding him through the door into the sports bar. People were starting to come up through the stairwell now but they stepped back when they saw him herding Ashford, clothes still clasped to his chest, down.

"What?" Cordelia asked.

"Salt," Angel repeated. "Find some salt. That's a Gorgranian demon's greatest weakness."

"I thought they lived in saltwater. This guy was in an aquarium when we found him. Her. It."

"The aquarium is filled with fresh water," Angel said.

"Ewww. Gross. That is definitely not fresh water. We're talking slimy barf-water here."

"There's no saline content," Angel said. "Find some salt."

"Cordelia!" Wesley yelled.

"Be there in a minute," Cordelia promised in a cheery voice. "Anyway, back to the vision."

Angel guided Ashford through the bar's small kitchen and out the back door. Cats leaped from the garbage bins lining the alley. Only a little farther ahead, Angel's black Plymouth Belvedere GTX convertible sat dormant and silent.

"The place is called the Bronze Jade Art Gallery," Cordelia continued. "There's a woman there, and some creepy, tentacled, demony-thing is there waiting for her."

"Bronze Jade Art Gallery," Angel repeated.

"Yeah. I called information and got the address." Cordelia gave it.

"Did you get the woman's name?" Angel asked. Sometimes the visions came with names, which made saving the people involved easier.

"Just of the gallery."

Merl screamed in the background.

"Okay," Cordelia sighed. "Gotta get back to the slime-fest. How come I only feel needed when somebody's up to their eyeballs in demons? Call if you need anything."

Angel folded the cell phone and slipped it into his pocket as he shoved Ashford to the convertible's rear. He brought out his keys.

"This your ride?" Ashford asked.

"Yeah," Angel replied. He fit the trunk key into the lock and twisted, popping the trunk lid.

"Cool wheels," Ashford said, a drunken glaze shining in his bloodshot eyes.

"I like to think so," Angel said.

"Would that demon really have impregnated me with her kid?"

"Yeah."

"So you saved me."

"Pretty much," Angel said.

Ashford looked into the convertible's trunk yawning before them. "I guess I'm not riding up front, huh?"

"No," Angel said, and shoved the movie star into the

big trunk. He took an axe from the armory he carried there, thinking if he was going up against a demon with tentacles it might be a good idea to chop a few of them off. Unless, of course, two grew back for every one that got lopped.

Shifting gingerly among the weapons, Ashford lay down. "I feel sick."

"Don't even think about it," Angel advised. He slammed the trunk lid and climbed behind the steering wheel. Looking over his shoulder, he floored the accelerator and shot out into the street. He cut the wheel hard, narrowly missing a taxi that zipped through the streets and the arriving fire truck.

Skidding and straightening the wheels, Angel shoved the transmission into first and tapped the accelerator again, shooting into the flow of traffic. Horns honked behind him, and he could hear Eddie Ashford screaming the Twenty-third Psalm.

The gallery wasn't far away, but usually the visions Cordelia got didn't leave much time to act.

Chapter Eight

"What the hell are you doing there?"

Pacing the darkened storage room to the Bronze Jade Art Gallery, Faroe Burke looked at the pieces stored there that were going to be on display for the opening tomorrow. God, it was hard to believe it was already Friday. Her heart still beat way above normal, hammering at her ribs.

Her footsteps echoed in the stillness of the storage room. The ceiling was twenty feet above her, crossed by naked steel girders. Pods of fluorescent lights hung between the girders and supports. Crates, boxes, cylinders containing rolled canvases, and stacks of chairs covered almost half the warehouse floor.

"Lenny," Faroe said in the calmest voice she had left to her after the last half hour of craziness. She held the cell phone close to her mouth, listening to the connection fade in and out as the structure of the building interfered with signal reception.

"You could have been killed," Lenny Thomas, her agent, yelled, interrupting her.

"I know," Faroe said. "I kind of got that between nearly getting my face ripped off and nearly taking a header off the fourth-floor ledge when I was outside the building."

"You were *outside* the building?" Disbelief filled Lenny's voice.

Faroe sighed. She hadn't told him everything that had happened at the studio. "Only for a little while."

"What were you doing out there?"

"Dodging demons," Faroe said. She paused in front of one of the canvases she'd come to see. Using care, she took the white cloth from the painting. Even in the dim light provided by the storage room's security lighting, the neon reds, turquoises, and apple greens stood out like they were electrified.

"You never said why they were after you," Lenny pointed out.

"That's because I don't know why." The painting only came up to her chin. Faroe was used to seeing her work up high. Squatting, she peered up at the painting, but it wasn't the same. She'd grown used to working on larger canvases, too.

"Do you owe anybody money?" Lenny asked. "Is that what this was about?"

Faroe blew out her breath and forced herself to remain calm. "No. I'm clean. You know that. I've never done drugs. I don't gamble. My only addiction has been painting. And you helped me find a legal way to do that, so I'm not even in trouble with the police."

"I don't get it. Then why were they after you?"

"Lenny, listen to me. I don't know why they were after

me." Faroe surveyed the painting. The design was one of her best scenes of the street, copied from the wall she'd first drawn it on.

On the canvas, a uniformed policeman lay in a pool of blood in an alley while a trio of cats that were nothing more than hairy sacks of bones looked on. The policeman's gun lay just out of his reach. A little girl in a too-big L.A. Lakers uniform top was kneeling beside the policeman, taking a single fragile dandelion from the pistol barrel.

"That's insane," Lenny said. "If there's no reason for them to be after you, then they shouldn't have been after you."

Faroe stood and glanced back at the paintings waiting to go on display in the morning. It was no use. Usually there was some amount of solace that she got from looking at her work. Tonight there was none. She'd removed eight protective sheets, all with the same results.

"Have you stolen anything?" Lenny asked. "I mean, if that's what it is, we can fix it. I've got lawyers on retainer that can take care of stuff like this. And if you needed money, you should have just told me. I've got a good feeling about this showing. You're going to make some money."

And, in turn, that meant Lenny Thomas was going to make some money when he recouped the advances he'd given her as well as his percentage. Faroe knew her agent was more worried about the gallery showing than she was. Even if the show didn't take off and get the acclaim or the audience that Lenny hoped it would, she felt certain that she'd have a career that would take care of her and let her paint. They were already turning down work.

"No," Faroe said, and she let him hear some of the steel in her voice. "I haven't stolen anything since I gave you my word that I wouldn't."

"Faroe—"

His tone told Faroe that the agent wasn't completely buying her story.

"Faroe—"

"No," Faroe said, cutting him off as she paced again. "You back off just a damn minute, Lenny. You're my agent, and you better damn well act like it right now. I've been through enough tonight without listening to you trying to guilt me. We both know the kind of trouble I came from, and I know I'm not going back there again. That's what these last two years have been about. You either trust me, or you walk away."

For a moment, Faroe thought she'd lost the signal and didn't know it.

"Faroe," Lenny said at length, sounding worn and tired, "why didn't you just go to the police and report this?"

"The history I've had with law enforcement?" Faroe said. "I don't think so. Maybe I'm not in trouble with them at the moment, but that doesn't mean I'm buying into the whole 'Mr. Policeman is your friend' song and dance."

"Then what are you doing there?"

"I've got to relax."

"At the gallery?"

"It was the only place I could think of to go." That wasn't true, though. The first place Faroe had thought of was the inner-city area where she'd grown up on the streets. Some of her graffiti work was still there; pieces that had allowed the Lenny Thomas Agency to parlay her crimes into art that garnered national attention. "I wanted to be somewhere that I could paint."

"Paint?"

"On canvas, damn it. Lenny, the walls are safe here." Faroe walked to the worktables at the back of the storage room. She'd stretched a canvas to fit a frame and had laid down some charcoal. She resented the small space she had to work on. It felt better, more natural, to work big.

"You don't need to be painting," Lenny said. "You should be resting. Tomorrow's a big day."

"Painting helps me relax. I'm so wired right now that I can't sleep." Lifting an aerosol can containing carmine red, Faroe sprayed two whirling lines of paint on the canvas. Lenny and others had tried to get her to use an airbrush when she worked, but nothing had felt as comfortable as an aerosol can in her hand.

"If your studio was vandalized . . .," Lenny began.

"It was more than vandalized," Faroe said. "There are dead demons in my studio."

"Demons." Lenny still wasn't buying the demon angle.

"Forget it," Faroe said. "The police will probably just write it off as a break-in. Nobody human died."

At least, she hoped the guy—Gunn, she remembered—hadn't died. A twinge of guilt still ached within her when she thought of the way she'd just driven away and left him there in the parking garage. But she hadn't known him except for the gym, and that was no reason to trust him. In fact, these days she found few reasons to trust anyone.

"If you don't want to go back to your apartment," Lenny said, "I can at least put you up in a hotel."

"They won't let me paint there." When she'd first starting improving her lifestyle and had ended up in a hotel, she'd learned the ban against painting quickly. Hotel security had arrived, certain she was huffing paint fumes. That had required a call to Lenny to get everything straightened out.

"You could do charcoal," Lenny said. "You know you can work with charcoal at the hotel."

Faroe pressed the button on the aerosol can, laying down more lines. "Charcoal isn't the same as working with paint." She didn't know how many times she'd told him that over the last two years.

"You're not safe there."

"Lenny, if those guys came after me in my studio, they could come after me in a hotel room." Surveying the lines of paint as they ran across the canvas, Faroe felt some of the tension leave her body. There was nothing in life that was like painting.

"Then let me have the police meet you there and put you under guard."

"Lenny," Faroe said, choosing a can of bright blue paint, "I really need to paint."

She kept boxes of aerosol cans in the back of her car, and some days it was hard to pass blank building walls by. Depressing the release button, she added circular shapes, not really knowing where she was going for the moment, but trusting her subconscious. Sometimes images came out in the paintings, and sometimes it was only emotion. Tonight she wanted to play with light and dark, see how the mix between them sorted out.

"You shouldn't be there by yourself," the agent replied.

"I can paint better by myself." That was how Faroe could remember best painting: by herself and by the glow of a flashlight in the middle of a night, anticipating dawn so she could return and take a look at her handiwork. Of course, that was also how she'd been caught those times she'd been caught.

"Paint some other time."

That was another point of disagreement they had. Faroe couldn't explain the burning need she had to paint these past few days. Between the meetings Lenny had set up, she'd felt certain that she'd painted herself into exhaustion only to rise again early the next morning and start painting.

"I can't," Faroe said. "I need to paint now." *More than anything else in the world.*

She reached for an aerosol can of daisy yellow, dropping the lid at her feet, adding another line of paint before the lid hit the concrete floor. She could see the image in her head—almost. But it came across like a half-remembered melody to a favorite song, and was as elusive as hell.

"Faroe," Lenny said in a quieter voice.

"What?"

"You don't have a key to the gallery's storage area. How did you get in there?"

Faroe thought quickly, but there was no way around it. "I let myself in."

She'd learned to let herself into other places when she'd been growing up on the streets. Sometimes she'd needed food or a place to crash, but mostly it was to get paint, which she could never get enough of.

"Damn it!" Lenny swore. "That's breaking and entering."

Dreamily, lost in the painting, Faroe said, "Do you really think Taylor Rawley or any of her staff is going to press charges against me when they've been advertising my gallery opening for the last six months?"

"*Our* gallery opening," Lenny said automatically.

Faroe grinned and reached for a can of orange paint, something to soften the yellow she'd used. "*Our* gallery opening."

"No," he admitted, "I don't think she would. As long as the walls are left intact."

"They are, and they will be," Faroe said. "Although the urge to leave Taylor an original is way too appealing for me to—"

A door slammed at the back of the storage room.

Chilled by the streak of fear that ran down her spine, Faroe turned from the painting toward the back of the storage room. Thick shadows cloistered the area.

"Faroe?" Lenny asked.

"Quiet," she whispered.

"What?"

"I think someone just broke into the storage room."

"I'm going to put you on hold," Lenny said, "then I'm going to call nine-one-one."

Faroe strained her ears, trying to hear, but there were no sounds. Had someone entered? Or had it just been the wind? She could remember closing the door, but she didn't know if she'd picked it locked again.

"They're on their way," Lenny said a moment later.

Clutching the can of spray paint, Faroe flattened against a line of boxed art that was shipping out for another gallery in the next few days. Her heart exploded in her chest. *I shouldn't have come here. I should have gone to the police. Or to a hotel room.*

"Faroe?" Lenny called over the cell phone.

"Yeah," she whispered, her voice hoarse and dry as the desert.

"Just hang tight and talk to me till the police get there. Can you do that?"

"Yeah," Faroe replied. It felt like there wasn't enough air in the storage room to breathe. She also couldn't stand still. Cautiously, she edged toward the rear of the building, staying within the shelter of the stacks of crates.

Only a few steps farther on, she stopped beside the crates at the end of the row fronting the worktable area. Heart in her throat, she turned and looked toward the door she'd picked the lock on earlier. Damn it, she should have picked the lock closed. An open door like that was an invitation to thieves. Her problem was she didn't think like a thief, and when she'd been doing it, she hadn't stolen as a thief either. That was why she'd gotten caught.

That was why whoever had slipped into the storage room with her had been able to get inside.

Leaning forward, afraid of what she would see, Faroe peered around the corner of the crate and looked at the door.

The door came open again as she watched. Caught by the wind, the door slid open for a moment, let in a shifting rectangle of light from the security light in the alley behind the art gallery, then banged shut again.

The sound echoed throughout the building.

"What was that?" Lenny demanded over the phone. "That sounded like a gunshot."

Sighing with relief, Faroe said, "It was just the wind. I left the door open." Feeling a little more confident, she forced herself out of the shelter of the crate and crossed the floor to the door, intending to pick it locked so she'd be alone. At least, she'd be alone until the police arrived.

I won't get any painting done, though.

Reaching the door, Faroe pulled it closed, listening to the latch click closed. The sound was loud inside the storage area, but it was also reassuring. Nothing could come in now, and she'd be—

She froze as the sensation of being watched flooded through her. It wasn't her imagination.

"Faroe," Lenny called over the cell phone. It was strange how far away he sounded over the device. "Faroe."

She turned and found herself face-to-orange-face with a demon like the ones that had invaded her studio.

"Surprised?" the demon asked, smiling.

Faroe's voice locked in the back of her throat. She couldn't scream, couldn't run. Beyond the demon, she saw three more step from the shadows.

Then someone dropped from the naked beams running across the storage center ceiling.

Faroe watched the new arrival land without effort behind the demon standing in front of her. The man was tall and good looking, but his expression was cold and hard. His dark eyes glinted. Dressed all in black, he carried a long-handled axe in his hands.

"Hey," the guy said in a soft, nonthreatening voice.

The demon turned around, stepping to the side.

Uncoiling in a blinding arc of speed almost too fast for Faroe's eyes to follow, the man swung the axe and sliced the demon's head from his shoulders. Stunned, Faroe watched the garish orange head bounce away while the body stood its ground and bled only a little at the amputated neck area.

"Silver," Faroe said, remembering what the man had told her earlier at her studio. "It takes silver to kill them."

"Yeah," the man said as he grabbed the headless demon's body by the arm and flung it to one side. "Problem is, I didn't bring any with me."

The decapitated body slammed into a crate and bounced from it. Stretching its arms out and dropping to its knees, the body began searching for the missing head while the head itself called out directions to find it. However, the body didn't have any ears, so the head's efforts were primarily lost. Under other circumstances, though Faroe had no inkling of what they might be, she was certain she'd have thought the sight of the headless body searching for its head would have been hilarious. Any chance of hilarity disappeared as more demons emerged from the shadows.

Faroe ran, heading for the door, leaving the man behind her fighting the demons.

Angel fought without restraint, setting the demon inside him free. He felt his face change, and felt the superhuman speed and strength fill him. Setting himself, he worked the axe, using the head as well as the long shaft to batter the encroaching demons back.

"Get him!" a demon yelled.

"Forget him," another demon growled. "Our orders are to get the girl."

"She's getting away!"

One of the demons broke free of the pack and started for the door.

Fighting the grip of the demon holding him, Angel drove the axe handle up, slamming the creature's mouth shut and breaking teeth. Angel lifted his foot and kicked into the demon's chest, propelling him back into two more demons. The three demons fell, tripping over each other.

Taking two long strides forward, too quick for the other demons to pursue, Angel brought the axe around and a swift, vicious curve of explosive force. The axe blade cleaved the demon's head from crown to chin, knocking him down to his knees even though the cruel blow and savage wound wouldn't prove fatal. Angel yanked the axe free of the demon's skull, stepped onto his opponent's shoulder, and hurled himself at the open door.

Out in the parking lot behind the gallery, Faroe Burke had reached her car.

Angel took a fresh grip on the axe and faced the gathering demons. "Okay, guys, who wants to get hurt first?"

"Stay out of this, vampire," one of the demons warned.

Angel shook his head. "Can't."

"Then you're going to get yourself staked." The demon started forward, holding a wooden shard from a broken crate in one hand.

Moving quickly, Angel shifted to the side. The axe came around in a blur, lopping off the demon's hand. The amputated hand hit the floor, released the wooden shard, then scuttled away.

"Not by you," Angel said.

In the parking lot, Faroe started her car, powered into a tire-eating reverse skid, then fishtailed out of the parking lot. Her undercarriage scraped the street as she shot out onto it, scattering sparks. Horns blared, but none of the other vehicles on the street collided with her. Her taillights flared and she disappeared.

"Another time," the demon with the missing hand said. He bent down and picked up his hand, fitting it to his bloody stump. He gestured to the other demons, waving them away.

Angel stood his ground, knowing he couldn't pursue them and hoping to question one of them.

A scuttling noise sounded overhead.

Looking up, Angel spotted a man dressed all in black standing on one of the beams across the ceiling. Angel didn't know if the guy had been there when he'd broken into the gallery or if the guy had just arrived.

The man stared back at Angel, his black eyes widening in startled recognition. His voice, when he spoke, was only a whisper, but Angel's keen hearing heard him.

"Angelus," the man said in a hoarse voice.

Despite the misshapen features and the bulbous growths on the man's face, Angel recognized him. "Gabriel," Angel whispered in disbelief. The man was human and should have been dead a long time ago. Then Angel raised his voice. "Gabriel Dantz."

Without a word, the man in black—the man who might have once been Gabriel Dantz and should have been dead a hundred years ago and more—reached up and caught the edges of the open skylight. Even as Angel started forward, the man in black hauled himself up through the roof.

Angel followed, leaping up onto stacks of crates and clambering to the skylight. On top of the building, he stared around at the shadows littering the night but saw no sign of the man in black. Gabriel Dantz, Angel mused as police sirens sounded in the distance and grew closer. He remembered when he'd first met the man. That had been in Venice, and Angel had been with Darla then.

Chapter Nine

Venice, 1815

"Do you think they'll kill him, Angelus?" Darla asked in her softest and sexiest voice.

Angelus grinned at the sight of the two rugged men holding a third man who was built slender and almost half a head shorter than either of them. The two big men had the smaller man draped over the side of the bridge railing, one man holding each of the smaller man's legs while he flailed helplessly for the bridge.

Even suffused as it had to be with blood, the hanging man's face looked pale and feverish. He glanced down at the slow-moving water below him. Provided he could swim, the twenty-foot drop wouldn't kill him. The canal water looked dark and turgid, and at this time of night Angelus knew the rats would be out scavenging through the sewers that emptied into it. Since arriving in Venice only a few days ago, he'd heard that the rats sometimes attacked anyone unlucky enough to fall into the canal.

He'd seen no evidence of that and guessed that tales of a drunken man's death were made more interesting by embellishing an attack by predatory, flesh-eating rats.

The candle in the streetlight back along the sidewalk Angelus had come down illuminated the scene only a little more than the moonlight streaming down over them. Against the dark of night, the alabaster brick and stone that made up the buildings in the city looked white as bleached bone. A cool breeze drifted in from the lagoon to the east of the main part of the city, but it also carried the stench of the city's waste that flooded into the canals. That stink, Angelus knew, was worse in the summer months, but they wouldn't be there by then.

"Well you know, love," Angelus drawled, never taking his eyes from the bizarre scene before them, "that what you see here be an improper way to divest a man of his riches and wherewithal. Holding him upside down by his boot heels, you see, would guarantee that whatever rolled free of his pockets would vanish into the canal this night. Perhaps these men are amateurs at their trade, but from the look of them, I'd not think that long. I'd wager they've already emptied his pockets, and I don't think they just intend to rob their victim."

"Please," the dangling man said. "You can't let them do this."

Darla covered her mouth in mock horror and stood stock-still on the bridge. "Oh, my. Then they do intend to kill that man."

Angelus glanced at Darla and had trouble keeping the smile from his lips. Dressed in the flowing evening gown and outfitted with jewelry they'd stolen in Paris less than a month ago and intended to sell as they needed to finance their trip to Venice, she looked like a proper young lady of standing squired about on the arm of her man.

The two men holding the third over the bridge railing glanced at each other. They were both dressed in breeches and blouses that had seen better days, but the swords at their sides showed frequent care and much use.

The man with the scar bisecting his right eyebrow said, "You best be shoving off, mate, for you surely don't want none of this." His accent marked him as English, and that alone turned Angelus against him.

"Oh, now," Darla said, "you shouldn't have gone and put it to him like that. Angelus doesn't much care for threats." But she kept her hand on his wrist, holding him back for just a moment.

"Oh, an' he don't care for threats, does he?" the man asked. He glanced at his companion. "You got this damn fool, James?"

The second man grinned and took a firmer hold on the dangling man. As he turned his head, Angelus saw the huge birthmark that marred half his face, which had been hidden in the night's shadows. "Aye, an' I do, Will."

"Then hold what you got," Will advised. "I'll be back in just a moment." He stepped toward Angelus, shifting his broad shoulders and emphasizing their size as well as his apparent strength. His rolling gait identified him as a sailor by trade, and the various knife and rope scars on his hands and arms bore that out.

Darla looked at Angelus. "Well, aren't you going to protect me? That brute took a threatening step in our direction."

Angelus only grinned, warming to the idea of the fight

118

even though his opponent was only human and no real challenge at all.

"Aye, an' it's gonna be more than a threatening step I'll be taking in yer direction if'n ye don't just pull that big nose of yers back outta business what's our'n," Will warned. He dropped his hand to the sword's hilt, curling his fingers around the scarred metal pommel.

Angelus reached into his pocket and took out a scented handkerchief. He dabbed at his nostrils, cutting the stench of the canal water for a moment. Turning to Darla, keeping the sailor in his view, Angelus said, "This is their business, and we are interfering in it."

Darla stepped over to the bridge's side and peered down at the man. She smiled at him. "Oh, look at his face, Angelus. Do you see the innocence and fear there? Why, he's little more than a child."

"And still no business of ours," Angelus said.

The sailor watched them, puzzlement spreading over his battered, weather-roughened features. By rights, if they were part of the genteel crowd that came to Venice on holiday, they should have been frightened out of their minds.

Darla gazed down at the young man. "Are you in any pain?"

"A little, dear lady," the young man answered. "I fear my ankle may be near to breaking, and my head pounds as though it may well explode at any moment."

Looking to James, the sailor who held the young man's leg, Darla said, "Perhaps you could try to hold him in a more favorable position."

The man stared at her in slack-jawed surprise. "I think not. The man who hired me for this little set-to, why he wanted this fella in as much pain as we could muster."

"Angelus," Darla said, looking back at him and acting very much put off by her conversation with the man, "please remember that this oaf has been very rude to me."

"Oaf?" the man exploded. "Oaf then, is it?" He took another hold on the dangling man's leg and gave a vicious yank.

Darla leaned over the bridge again. "Are you in pain, sir?"

"Considerable, lady," the man replied in a strained voice. He groaned. "Forgive me for carrying on about my own problems. Perhaps you should go on. I don't think your delicate ears shouldn't hear the agony I'm liable to give vent to. I'm not a very brave man."

"I don't know how you can say that," Darla said. "You've managed very bravely so far."

Angelus was irritated. "Darla," he said, seeking to put an end to it, "this is really none of our business. As this man has pointed out."

"But I'm curious, dear Angelus, and you know how I get when I'm curious," Darla protested.

Curious was a dangerous place for Darla to be. Angelus knew that from past experience. When she grew interested or curious about someone, she sated that curiosity. If the experience didn't live up to her expectations, the person or persons who disappointed her died horribly. If she decided to let that person or persons live, others died much sooner or for less than she usually allowed.

Angelus looked at the sailor standing near him. "She's curious," he explained.

Will scowled. "Ye'd best be served by gettin' her on out of here."

"Probably," Angelus agreed. "But she can be quite contrary. She's very high-spirited."

"It's been me own experience," the sailor offered, "that a high-spirited woman can be gentled by a man with a hard, quick hand. An' I can warrant ye that course of action will be a lot less wearin' on you than hangin' around here much longer."

Angelus sighed, knowing the whole affair wasn't going to end prettily.

"You seem to have vexed these men mightily, sir," Darla called down.

"Yes," the man replied, trying again to reach the bridge but failing. He groaned in pain.

"How have you vexed them?" Darla asked.

"They claim that I owe them money."

"And do you?"

"No. I was paid for a job that I did fairly and well. In fact, I was dramatically underpaid for the service that I rendered."

Beside Angelus, Will harrumphed in displeasure.

A gondola floated beneath the bridge. The gondolier halted the long, slow movements of his pole as the four passengers in the boat stared up at the man dangling from the bridge. Lanterns at the front and back of the boat created a yellow bubble of light across the dark water and against the dark night.

"I suppose you no longer have the money they seek to get from you," Darla said.

"Spent," the young man replied sadly.

"Wisely, then?"

"On wine, women, and song, dear lady. And painting supplies. No one realizes how much good brushes and paints cost."

"You're a painter?" Darla asked with animated interest.

"Dear lady," the man said, "I am no painter. I am an artist of the first water."

"Do you do portraits?" Darla asked.

"Some of the finest in all Europe," the young man answered. "You can find my work in some of the finest houses in England, Italy, France, Austria, and Switzerland. That they don't hang in houses other than in those nations is only because I've not yet ventured there."

"Sir," Darla admonished, "you seem to have no lack of confidence in your abilities."

"None whatsoever."

"And if I should get you out of your present predicament," Darla asked, "could I persuade you to do a portrait of me in return?"

"Gladly, lady."

Darla straightened and looked at Angelus. "I should like very much to have my portrait painted."

"You've had your portrait painted before," Angelus said. As a vampire, Darla could no longer look in a mirror, a glass, or the smooth surface of a fountain or pond to see her likeness. Angelus didn't care about the lack of the experience, but Darla possessed a streak of vanity.

"That was a long time ago," Darla said. "And, besides, I've not had occasion to see that portrait in a long time. Nor did I especially care for it."

"You did at the time."

Darla looked petulant. "I only told you that because you paid for it, and because it was a gift from you."

Over the years, living as vampires sometimes on the run and hunted by slayers as well as other groups that organized to track down and kill demons, Angelus and Darla hadn't always been able to keep their belongings together. They were always predators, moving from one hunting ground to another as the prey became less plentiful or learned to fight back.

"I want my portrait painted, Angelus."

Sighing, Angelus turned to the big sailor. "How much does he owe?"

The sailor shook his head. "Were it in me power, perhaps I'd dicker with ye. But it's not. The man what set me on this path, why he demands money as well as satisfaction."

"Satisfaction?"

"He wants the hand of the artist that defamed his wife."

The dangling man started swinging wildly. "You're going to cut my hand off? Oh god, you can't mean that! That's not only un-Christian, but that's cruel!"

The sailor rolled his eyes. "Now ye've gone and upset him. After we'd killed him, we could have taken the hand all quiet-like. This didn't have to be messy."

Angelus was intrigued. Taking body parts was nothing new to him, but the defamation of the man's wife was at least passably interesting. "What did this man do to the wife?"

"His painting of her was ugly," the sailor said.

"Ugly?" the dangling artist roared. "That was a

damned good painting! Why, if you wanted to see ugly, all you had to do was look at that wife!"

"The man who hired him," Will said, "offered to just take his money back. Of course, this fool didn't have it An' to make matters worse, the wife was sitting for the portraits an' wanted to see the work that was goin' on. The first couple of paintin's she didn't see. But she saw the last one. That's when we was told to kill him and bring back his hand."

"He ran?" Angelus asked.

"Like a hare before a huntin' falcon," Will said.

"Maybe we could work out an arrangement," Angelus said.

The sailor stepped away and the moment of commonality they'd shared while gazing at Darla evaporated. "No, sir. The man I'm workin' for, why he's a feared an' powerful man, he is, an' I'd lief as not give him no reason to set men to huntin' me."

"But it's a hand," Angelus said. "Surely, any hand would do."

"That man's hand is known," the sailor said. "When the wife saw her picture, she attacked the artist, cut him across the palms with a letter opener before he got away. Gettin' out of the room, he landed in paint. He's got purple and green tattooing that took in them cuts."

Angelus crossed to the bridge's railing, not happy that everything was becoming even more complicated. He gazed down at the dangling man. "Let me see your palms."

"Sir," the sailor holding the artist said, "there's probably not enough light—"

The artist held his hands palms up. Even in the wan streetlight and moonlight, Angelus's vampire eyes saw the purple and green streaks plainly.

"I see them fine," he said, turning from the artist in disgust. He regarded Will. "That tattooing could be faked as well."

"An' ye'd cut off an honest man's hand to set this man free?" Will sounded as though he couldn't believe it.

"Yes," Angelus answered without hesitation. Making Darla happy had its attractions, and they were there in Venice on holiday. "Getting him away from you would only free him for a short time. If the man who sent you decided to send other men."

"Aye, an' he would, I can warrant ye that. He's some fierce piece of work, an' a vengeful man besides." The sailor rubbed his bewhiskered chin and shook his head. "Nope. There ain't no way around it, ye see. Me an' James, we got to kill this here man and take his hand back with us."

Angelus turned back to Darla, scanning the area around them and making sure there were no other passersby.

Darla batted her eyes at him. "Angelus, I want very much to have my portrait painted."

"Lady," Will butted in, "if'n ye don't mind me sayin', this here's Venice. There's any number of painters livin' an' workin' here. Why, I bet ye'd be able to find one what would be more'n happy to paint yer likeness. If'n I had a callin' for it, I'd be happy me ownself to spend days lookin' at ye and paintin' ye."

A radiant smile broke across Darla's pale face. "Why, what a clever tongue you have."

"Thank ye, lady." Will looked as though he actually blushed.

"But I'm afraid that won't do," Darla said. "I want an artist who is true, one that will have a care more for his work than for the coin that he's paid in."

Will's face hardened and he glanced at Angelus. "Sir, I'm only gonna ask ye to remove her once more. Else I'm going to do it me ownself."

Angelus smiled. The thought of the gruff sailor trying to force Darla to do anything was amusing.

Leaning over the bridge railing again, Darla asked, "Would you paint my portrait if I get you out of this?"

"Yes," the man replied, but he didn't sound as though he believed that she could do it.

"And you'll be able to start soon? I've no idea how long I'll be in Venice."

"This very night if you so will it, lady," the artist promised.

"Here now," Will barked, "an' I've had me just about enough of this tomfoolery. That wretch, why he ain't goin' nowheres 'cept that there canal after me an' James has killed him and taken his hand." He stretched out a hand to grab Darla's shoulder.

Out of sight of the man below, Darla morphed her face, letting the demon within her surface. Looking like evil incarnate, she snapped her fangs at the man's hand.

"God's blood," the sailor swore, yanking his hand back only an instant before Darla's fangs could pierce his flesh. He reached for the sword at his side.

Drawing his own rapier, listening to the razor-sharp edge glide free of the sheath, Angelus snapped the sword out parallel to the ground. Spinning, he brought the blade around in a glittering arc that decapitated Will in a spray of bright, crimson blood.

The headless corpse collapsed to its knees on the bridge. The sword jerked in the dead man's hands for just an instant before the body toppled and lay still.

In motion now, knowing the other man's death was necessary as well, Angelus stepped across the corpse, pausing only long enough to pick up the decapitated head by the hair and fling it into the canal. Venice's canals had all held dead men before. With luck, the current would take the corpses out to the lagoon by morning and no one would know for sure where they had come from.

The other sailor released the artist's leg, but before the man had time to drop more than a few inches, Darla seized his foot. Her vampire's strength proved more than equal to the task of supporting him while he screamed in fright.

Angelus watched as the man drew his blade, eyes wide with consternation as he watched Darla holding the would-be victim with such ease. Moonlight silvered the blade for a moment.

Smiling in anticipation, Angelus saluted the man with the rapier, cutting the air with liquid swishes as he gathered the tails of his jacket out of his way. "Are you any good with that thing, then?" he asked.

"I've taken men's lives before," the sailor answered. "I won't hesitate to gut you."

Cutting the air with quick strokes, Angelus advanced, driving the man back as steel rang on steel. The man's grip was strong, his bladework steady. For a moment, Angelus enjoyed the workout, giving himself over to his training. Although he hadn't learned much in the way of formal martial arts and swordplay before Darla had turned him in Galway, he'd devoted part of his long life since then to it.

"Angelus!" Darla complained. "I need help. I can hold him, but I can't get the leverage I need to pull him back onto the bridge."

"I'm busy," Angelus said, focusing on his opponent.

"Someone's coming," Darla insisted. "And how would it look if I were caught holding this man?"

"Damn it," Angelus swore in irritation. Darla was always so demanding. Without warning, his foot slipped on blood covering the bridge. Before he could recover, the man lunged forward, following his sword point, penetrating Angelus's guard and sinking the blade through his chest just left of center.

Pain filled Angelus as the steel shot through his heart. He howled with the pain of it, then stared into the unbelieving eyes of the sailor.

"You're not human," the sailor gasped.

Blood ran through Angelus's fingers as he placed his hand over the wound in his chest. Despite the liquid fire that filled him from the puncture, he made himself grin. "No," he croaked, "not in a long time."

The sailor tried to withdraw his sword but Angelus held onto it. Concentrating, letting the demonic rage fuel him, Angelus stood. He'd carry the wound for a time, but he could already feel it knitting. The blood flow shut off, leaving him hungry again.

"Demon!" The sailor shoved the blade forward, sinking it entirely through Angelus's chest.

But the demon rage forced Angelus to remain standing even against the renewed pain and the sailor's strength. Giving in to the fear that filled him, the sailor abandoned his sword and turned and ran.

"Angelus," Darla said impatiently.

Fisting the sword blade, Angelus glanced over his shoulder and saw a torch carried by a small group of pedestrians that walked toward the bridge. Pushing all thought of the coming pain from his mind, Angelus yanked the blade from his chest, withdrawing a foot of steel. He gazed at the sailor, who had gained the other side of the bridge.

Drawing his arm back, trusting his skill and his strength, Angelus threw the sword. The weapon flipped once, then caught the running sailor in the back, point first. The blade sank to the hilt, knocking the sailor forward across the narrow sidewalk at the other end of the bridge and pinning him against the side of the building. The sword hilt quivered.

"Angelus," Darla called.

Looking down at his chest, Angelus knew there was no hope for the shirt. Crimson had spread across the white silk, wrecking it beyond repair even if the tear could be darned.

"Damn it, Darla. We'll have to go by that clothier again tomorrow evening."

"It's all right. I'll send one of the hotel staff to fetch you a new one."

Angelus joined her at the side of the bridge, caught hold of the man's leg, and pulled him to safety.

The man was so weak that he couldn't stand. His knees

buckled and he would have gone down if Angelus hadn't kept hold of him. They were so close Angelus couldn't help smelling the rich nectar that pulsed within the man. The dark hunger that filled him barely remained within his control. He felt his human features starting to slip as the demon's tried to take over.

The man looked up at Angelus with anxious eyes. His gaze locked on the crimson patch showing against the white of Angelus's blouse.

"You're injured," the man gasped.

Angelus smiled. "Trust me. It looks much worse than it is."

The man had dishwater blond hair and pale features from staying inside. His eyes were almost colorless, either a light gray or a pale blue with black pupils. They were eyes that belonged on a wolf. His thin, aquiline nose split his face into quadrants and kept him just this side of being nondescript. It was a plain face, but with the impressive nose, Angelus knew it would be a face that he would remember.

Darla helped the man to his feet.

"I thank you for my life," the man said.

Angelus crossed to the decapitated body, picked it up, and heaved it into the canal. The body made a terrific splash when it struck the water, but it went under at once. When he glanced back at the artist, Angelus watched the man shudder.

"He was dead?" the man asked.

"Yes," Angelus replied.

Without another word, the artist leaned over the bridge and threw up. Darla made soothing noises and offered comfort by massaging his shoulders and neck.

Angelus grew irritated with the man and with Darla. Here he stood, with a gaping hole in his chest, and she hadn't even concerned herself over how he might be. "Haven't you ever seen a dead man before?" Angelus asked.

"Of course I have." The man wiped his lips with a lace kerchief that Darla handed him. "I've painted the final portraits of lost loved ones for families to ease their grief. I've sat with two men in Newgate Prison and finished painting their likenesses only hours before their executions."

"He's sensitive," Darla said. "I've heard that's a good quality in an artist."

"I wouldn't know about that," the man said, mopping at his mouth with the lace handkerchief. "I only know that I've never before caused the death of a man."

Angelus walked to the other end of the bridge, drawing himself up and trying hard not to stagger or stumble from the pain. He grabbed hold of the sword pinning the second dead man to the wall. The stones turned loose of the sword blade with shrill protest. He caught the dead man by the jacket before he tumbled to the narrow sidewalk, then wheeled and threw the corpse into the canal.

"We've got to go," Darla said, looking back at the approaching group. She looked at the artist. "Where do you stay?"

The man shook his head. "Lady, I've not found a place yet. There's an alley where I keep my easel and paints, but I've yet to secure work that would allow me to rent a room."

"Well," Darla said, "for the time you can stay with Angelus and me."

Angelus wanted to protest, but a glance from Darla quieted him. When she got interested in something like this, it was better to humor her or go find something else to do for months. Perhaps her interest in the artist and the portrait, as could be arranged for the artist himself, would be short-lived.

Darla took the young man by the hand and started leading him from the bridge. "What's your name?" she asked.

"Gabriel," he replied. "Gabriel Dantz."

Chapter Ten

Almost two hours after the confrontation at the Bronze Jade Art Gallery and after Eddie Ashford had been delivered to the Nova Studios security personnel, Angel arrived back at the hotel where the agency had set up shop. It had taken only a year to outgrow the small office he'd started with when he'd first arrived in Los Angeles. Questions about Gabriel Dantz ran rampant in his mind as he let himself into the building, but after he'd dealt with the demons and the woman at the art gallery, Angel had found no trace of the man.

He's not a man, Angel reminded himself as he stepped through the hotel foyer. The last time he'd seen Dantz had been nearly two hundred years ago. Nothing human could have lived that long. In fact, the last time Angel had seen Gabriel Dantz he would have sworn the man had died within minutes.

As always whenever he entered the hotel, Angel briefly recalled the time he'd first lived there in the 1950s. The world had been different back then, and the hotel had been a successful venture. He'd been on the verge of finding himself, of finding a way to make peace with the tortured soul the gypsy curse had bequeathed to him. But he hadn't made that peace then. Now he was making his life a successful venture and the hotel had closed.

Wesley sat on one of the couches in front of the main desk area. The ex-Watcher looked worn and exhausted, and he was covered in greenish goo.

Gunn, definitely not according to custom, sat at the desk and scrolled through screens of information on the computer. Rips showed in his clothing, and Angel detected the smell of gun smoke.

"Rough night, guys?" Angel asked.

"I've definitely had better," Wesley replied morosely.

Gunn didn't say anything.

Angel made a stop at the huge weapons rack against the wall. He knelt and searched through the bottom drawers for the first-aid kit.

"Where's Cordy?" Angel asked.

"In the shower," Wesley replied. "She called first dibs. I, knowing how much she would have caterwauled had I not let her go first, relinquished any such claim on the facilities."

"There are other rooms," Angel pointed out.

"Somehow, it seems more homey to wait. Plus, there is the matter of this demonic goo." Wesley slicked a finger along his arm, leaving a shiny trail on his skin. "It doesn't seem to come off very well. I thought perhaps I'd wait and see if Cordelia enjoyed any success in removing it."

"Cordy found salt?" Angel took out industrial-sized rolls of gauze and adhesive tape. Being a vampire meant his wounds were going to heal and not kill him, but they remained noticeable for awhile, as well as painful.

"Yes, and thank you for that." Wesley pulled chunks of goo from his face and hair, dropping them into a wastepaper basket between his feet. "I'd not read about using salt on a Gorgranian demon. Their usual method of dispatch is to chop them up."

"You could have done that. It would have taken longer."

"Yes, well the salt was terribly impressive. Gorgranians have the ability to dramatically add to their size. The salt causes them to swell even more, and uncontrollably so. I thought we had a problem of gargantuan proportions on our hands till it exploded."

"I know."

"Oh, that's true. Since you knew about the salt, it only stands to reason that you knew about the other."

"I've fought them before." Angel crossed the large open area to the desk.

Gunn glanced up at him only for an instant, then returned his attention to the computer screen.

"I thought you took the night off," Angel said, laying out the supplies. He glanced at the stairs leading up to the other floors. The hotel offered a lot of room for all of them to stay without tripping over each other.

"I did," Gunn said. "Worked out at the gym. Whacked a few demons."

"Busman's holiday."

"No joke."

Angel ripped his shirt off. The blood had crusted over the buttons and buttonholes, and the tear was too large to leave the shirt salvageable. It was a shame, because he'd liked the shirt and it had been a gift from Cordelia.

"What are you doing?" Cordelia demanded. "I just got that shirt for you a couple weeks ago."

"I know," Angel apologized, turning to her and seeing her standing in a bathrobe, her hair tied up in a towel. Green goo still showed in her eyebrows. "And I liked the shirt. I didn't count on getting stabbed tonight."

"That wasn't a work shirt," Cordelia said, approaching the desk and picking up the bloody rags the shirt had become, not even interested in the wound in his side. She sniffed the shirt. "And is that smoke?"

"There was a fire," Angel admitted.

"You can't wear silk around smoke," Cordelia said. "That material just inhales it. There are some things in this life that still need to breathe, you know."

"Yeah."

Cordelia threw the tattered, bloody shirt at the wastepaper basket between Wesley's feet. She missed and the shirt fell over Wesley's foot, spreading blood over his shoe.

Wesley gave her a reproachful glance, but the effort didn't pay off with all the green goo sticking to his face.

"I can't get that demon out of my hair," Cordelia complained as she unwrapped the towel from her head.

"Use peanut butter," Angel suggested.

Cordelia glared at him through her goo-stained hair. "Peanut butter?"

"Yeah."

"Is this some kind of trick?"

"Do I look like I'm in the mood?" Angel pointed to the wound in his side.

Cordelia looked at him. "You do look kind of broody. Did you find the little boy I saw?"

"He wasn't there."

"Did you look?"

"Everywhere," Angel said.

"What about the woman?"

"She was there."

"And?"

"Saved."

"So where is she?"

Angel grimaced as he probed the wound, wanting to make sure it was clear of any residual splinters that could slow down the healing process. "She left in the middle of me fighting the demons that went there for her." The image of Gabriel Dantz's feverish face popped into Angel's head. The woman hadn't been the only one to leave.

"Was the tentacled thing there?" Cordelia asked.

"Never showed," Angel said. "But I'm fine. Thanks."

"I didn't know if the tentacled thing would be there," Cordelia mused. "When I saw the little boy and Mr. Tentacles, they looked like they were in a house. Were there any houses near the art gallery?"

"No."

"You checked?"

"I looked." Angel cleaned his wound. "The gallery is situated in a business sector. There are no residences."

"Would you like some help?" Wesley asked. "That looks very painful."

"It is," Angel said. "And I would."

Wesley got up from the couch and came around the desk. Taking a pair of disposable surgical gloves from one of the desk drawers, he pulled one on with a snap.

Angel flinched.

"What's wrong?" Wesley asked.

"Nothing," Angel said.

"No, it's something," Wesley said. "I definitely detected apprehension in your eyes when I started to help you."

Gunn took a chocolate chip cookie from a small takeout bag beside the keyboard. "It's the whole rubber glove thing, Wesley. Some guys just never adjust to that."

"I'm not even going to dignify that with a comment," Wesley said. He took an antiseptic wipe from the carton on the desk and started vigorously cleansing Angel's wound.

"Owww," Angel groaned, moving away from Wesley. "That hurts."

"What?" Wesley asked innocently. "I barely got started. And it only stings a little."

Angel grimaced but lifted his arm, baring the wound. "Let's get this done. Just—just take it easy."

"Peanut butter?" Cordelia repeated.

Trying not to cry out from Wesley's heavy-handed ministrations, Angel nodded.

"Chunky or creamy?" Cordelia asked.

Exasperated, the memory of Gabriel Dantz still haunting his thoughts, miring him between present and past, Angel said, "Cordelia, it doesn't matter. It's the oil in the peanut butter that will make the goo turn loose. Does the same thing for gum."

Cordelia put her hands on her hips. "Don't get all snippy with me. First it's salt for the Grobrainian demon—"

"Gorgranian demon," Wesley corrected.

Flipping goo-encrusted hair from her face with her

fingers, Cordelia said, "Whatever. Salt for the demon, peanut butter for my hair. I just have to wonder if you're getting Emeril delusions. And it's a good thing it's peanut butter and not ice cream because Baskin-Robbins has thirty-six flavors." She stopped, frowning. "Do we have any peanut butter?"

"Yeah," Gunn said from the computer. "Picked some up yesterday. It's back in the kitchen pantry. Creamy. And if you use it all, I want it replaced."

Cordelia left.

Angel gritted his teeth till Wesley finished cleaning and dressing the wound.

"There," Wesley said, stepping back.

Angel tested the wrapping around his ribs. Everything felt secure. "How did you do with *Corner of the Eye*?"

"The Gorgranian demon is dead," Wesley replied. "One of the humans helping it is dead, and I don't think the other two are going to be any problem. The authorities are going to be searching for them."

"Really?" Angel asked. He gingerly sat in the chair behind the big desk and tried to find a comfortable position.

"The top two floors of the building the tabloid was headquartered in burned down," Gunn said. "The blaze was big enough that it got covered on *Live Action News*."

Angel looked at Wesley in awe. "You burned the building down?"

Wesley hooked a finger in the collar of his shirt. "Inadvertently, of course. Such an action was certainly not planned. The authorities have discovered, after an anonymous phone call, that the building was owned by the tabloid and was currently over-insured. And the fire was obviously set by an arsonist."

"That was all the work of Plan B," Cordelia said as she passed back through the foyer with a jar of peanut butter in one hand. "Plan A didn't have anything incendiary about it."

"Merl burned the building down?" Angel asked. He couldn't believe it.

Wesley hesitated for a moment. "Yes. Yes, Merl did burn the building down, and he's very apologetic about that."

"Terrific," Angel said. "Where is he?"

"Wherever it is Merl goes when Merl's not hanging out at the places we look him up in." Wesley pushed his slimed glasses further up his nose. "Once the action was over at the building—"

"Translation," Gunn interrupted, "the damn place looked like it was going to burn down around their ears and Merl decided he needed to save his ass."

"—Merl took it upon himself to evacuate the premises before the police arrived," Wesley finished.

"The police arrived?" Angel asked.

"Only shortly before the fire department," Gunn said.

"I thought we agreed that this investigation was going to be low-key," Angel said.

"We did," Wesley agreed. "But the fire worked out for us in the end, because there was simply no way we could have carted all of those blackmail files out of the building in a short time even if we'd had a team of movers and vans on hand to do it. I hadn't anticipated so many things would be in physical form. I had expected nothing more than hard drive space. In fact, I must say that if it hadn't been for the fire, there would have been any number of things left at the site that would have been up for grabs."

Angel leaned back in his chair and tried to think. This was Wesley's case and he had no real investment in it. The Powers That Be hadn't assigned him to Nova Studios' problems, and working for a Hollywood movie studio wasn't Angel's idea of a good time. The woman he'd found at the art gallery, on the other hand, was his responsibility and meant some of the redemption he was in L.A. working toward.

"I think Nova Studios will be satisfied with our progress," Wesley said. "I'll call them in the morning and see about getting paid for our work. How did your evening with Eddie Ashford go?"

"Oh, it was yuks all the way," Angel stated sarcastically. "Ashford almost became a father tonight."

"I'm sure that wouldn't have been an earth-shattering catastrophe. Things like that—"

"He was chosen to be a host parent for a Garlock demon," Angel said.

"Oh," Wesley said.

"Host parent?" Gunn asked, unfamiliar with the term.

"Garlocks have three parents," Wesley explained. "The two who contribute biological components, and the one that actually births the young. When they're ready to be born, young Garlocks eat their way out of their host and take on some of the genetic material, which later allows them to pass as human. Females are born with that trait generally, but a young male must be born to a host parent."

"I could have lived without knowing that," Gunn said, returning his attention to the computer screen.

Wesley sat on the edge of the desk. "Cordelia mentioned she'd had a vision. About a child and a young woman. Some kind of tentacled demon."

"Yeah." Angel walked to the coat closet in the foyer and took out one of the spare shirts he kept there.

"Did you get her name?"

"No."

"She was in trouble, though?"

Angel buttoned the shirt, moving a little painfully as he resumed his seat at the desk. He remembered Gabriel Dantz's face swaddled in the shadows of the storage room. "Yes."

"What do you know about her?"

"I think she's an artist. While I was there, she was working on a painting."

Gunn looked up. "An artist?"

Angel nodded.

"Where did you find her?" Gunn asked.

"The Bronze Jade Art Gallery," Angel said.

Reaching out to the computer monitor, Gunn twisted it around to face Angel. "Is that her?" Gunn asked.

Studying the face on the screen, Angel nodded. "That's her."

"Her name's Faroe Burke," Gunn said. "I saved her from a pack of Jaakel demons earlier tonight."

"Jaakels tried to take her at the art gallery, too," Angel said. "What do you know about her?"

"I'm learning," Gunn said, tapping the keyboard and scrolling through more web pages and pictures.

Okay, so peanut butter works, Cordelia thought as she wrapped a towel around herself and tucked the ends in so it would stay up. She ran her fingers through her hair as she crossed the bathroom to stand in front of the steamy mirror above the sink.

She combed her hair out. It felt good to be clean again. After the first couple of times in the shower, she hadn't thought she would feel that way again for a long time. As she worked through her hair, trying not to remember how the demon they'd found in the tabloid offices had exploded in such a gooey mess, the mirror steamed over again.

She reached out and brushed the condensation away. Only this time she didn't find her own features beneath the layer of shower sweat.

It was the little boy she'd seen in her vision earlier.

Cordelia's breath caught in her throat as she stared at the little boy. For a moment, she thought he was looking back at her. His hand reached forward, like he was going to reach through the glass to touch her. When he pulled his hand back, though, he held one of the blocks. Patiently, he guided it onto a stack that teetered for an instant on the table before him.

Beyond the doorway to the boy's room, lay a short hallway and another room. A picture sat on an easel, and there was something familiar-looking about the blonde woman in it.

Then the tentacled monstrosity exploded around the doorframe and into the room, making straight for the little boy as the tower of blocks fell and scattered across the tabletop. He looked sad, but he didn't even know about the monster bearing down on him.

"No!" Cordelia yelled. "No!" She reached for the little boy again, but her hand slapped against the mirror. This time the mirror shattered into what seemed like a million glittering chunks that rained down into the sink basin, taking the image with it.

Tears of helpless frustration filled Cordelia's eyes as she watched the mirror bits tumbling around in the sink basin, reminding her of the boy's tower of blocks. She put a hand to her head, only then noticing that her palm was bleeding. Fear, stronger than almost anything she'd ever felt before, ran rampant through her body.

"Cordy?"

She turned at the sound of Angel's voice. "It's not fair," she said hoarsely. "He's out there somewhere, Angel, and he's not safe. He's *very* not safe. He doesn't even know that, but I do. He's just a boy, not much more than a baby. Why the hell would the Powers That Be give me the ability to see visions if I can't do anything about them?"

"It's okay," Angel said in that soft voice he had. He crossed the room from the doorway and took her into his arms.

"It's not okay," Cordelia said. She wanted to push him away, to be mad at him for daring to tell her everything was going to be okay when she knew damn well and good it wasn't going to be. But at the same time, she felt comforted. There was something very solid and reassuring about Angel when he was in Protector Guy mode.

"I'll make it okay," Angel promised. "I swear to you, Cordy, we'll find him. Whatever it takes, we'll find him."

Cordelia clung to him then, not even caring that Wesley and Gunn stood in the doorway watching.

"We found the woman in your vision," Angel said. "We know her name. After we talk to her, maybe we'll know where we can find the boy."

Chapter Eleven

"Her name is Faroe Burke," Gunn said, talking about the woman on the computer monitor.

Angel leaned against the desk and watched as Gunn worked through the files he'd brought up on the computer.

"She's an artist," Gunn went on, "but before that she was a criminal."

"A criminal?" Cordelia asked. She sat in a chair Wesley had brought up, and nursed a steaming cup of hot cocoa Phantom Dennis had whipped up for her. "I've never known a vision to send us after someone who was a criminal before."

"Faroe Burke was convicted of destroying private property on three different occasions," Gunn said, tapping a button on the keyboard.

The monitor flickered, then showed the side of a building covered in aerosol-can spray paint. The image was of a huge dinosaur eating cars.

"She did graffiti," Cordelia said.

Gunn nodded, flipping through more pictures of similar art. "Defamation of private property. Carries a hefty fine and jail sentence in the L.A. area. Buildings, railroad cars, any surface that she could find that would hold paint." He grinned. "Probably she didn't know it at the time, but she was building her portfolio."

"What's her connection to the demon world?" Wesley asked.

Shrugging, Gunn said, "You know they ain't gonna put something like that on one of these Web sites, but I can't find even a clue to point me in a direction."

"The Jaakels are mercenary," Angel said. "They work for anyone that will hire them."

"I know," Gunn replied. "And I heard them talking about the fact that they were getting paid for bringing Faroe in alive."

"By whom?" Cordelia asked.

"Don't know," Gunn said. "Things got hectic. I didn't have time to ask. But since they found her again so easily at the art gallery, I'm betting they have ways of finding her." He flicked through more pictures. "Faroe grew up on the street. Her father was a gambler, which is how she got her name. Doesn't say anything about her mother."

Angel looked at the pretty woman on the computer screen. *Why is Gabriel Dantz—if it is Gabriel Dantz—interested in her?* The obvious connection was art, but their styles were nothing alike. Gabriel Dantz had been classically trained, and Faroe Burke looked like she was anything but.

"What's she doing at the Bronze Jade Art Gallery?" Angel asked.

Gunn tapped another button and a Web site sprang up. Bronze Jade Art Gallery ran across the top of the page. "She's putting on a show," Gunn said. "According to the newspaper articles I've been reading for the last hour, there are a lot of people in the art community who think she's about to go big."

"How big?" Wesley asked.

"Some of the top art buyers in the world are going to attend this show."

Wesley stroked his chin, still festering with green goo because he hadn't yet taken time to shower. "Well, the financial end of things would certainly be of interest to some, but this doesn't sound much like something the Jaakels would undertake without being hired. Wolfram and Hart, perhaps, if they thought there was enough money to go around, but they wouldn't employ demons like the Jaakels to intercept and take Faroe Burke."

"Did Faroe serve any jail time?" Angel asked.

"She was in and out of juvenile shelters when she was a kid," Gunn replied. "But once she became an adult, she kept her nose clean."

"She stopped doing graffiti?" Wesley asked.

Grinning, obviously very much enjoying the idea of the young woman on the computer monitor, Gunn shook his head. "No. She just made sure she didn't get caught anymore. As an adult, she'd have had to make restitution, possibly for years, and there would have been time in the slammer."

"What about children?" Cordelia asked.

"She's young and single as far as I've been able to find out," Gunn said.

"Then where does the boy fit in?" Cordelia asked. "My vision had both of them. Well, the three of them if you count the evil, demony, tentacled thing. And I do. Something as horrible looking as that, I can't ignore."

"We don't know yet," Angel said. "But we'll find out. Wesley."

"Yes?"

"Why don't you start covering Faroe in the morning? You can mix in with the wine-and-cheese crowd at the gallery, see if you can dig up any dirt through gossip. If Faroe Burke is about to break out in the art world, there will be all kinds of rumors about her."

"And you know this how?" Cordelia asked.

Angel grimaced, remembering the times in the past when he'd been involved with some of the artists of the time. "Long story. Gunn, you need to see if you can talk to Faroe tomorrow as well."

"Me? Why not you?" Gunn protested.

"The gallery opens in the morning," Cordelia replied before Angel could say anything. "There's that whole morning thing and sunlight. The show's being held early. It's weird, I know, but that's life."

"The wine and cheese crowd aren't my usual mainstays," Gunn said.

"Do you have a suit?" Cordelia asked.

"Of course." Gunn only looked a little affronted.

"Cordelia and I will stay here to see if we can dig up any more on Faroe or a demonic connection to the Bronze Jade Art Gallery. She'd probably be less conspicuous at a gallery opening than you, but I want her to get some post-vision rest."

"Like maybe it was built on an old demonic burial ground?" Gunn asked.

Before Angel could reply, Wesley's cell phone chirped. He answered it and talked for a moment, obviously getting less and less happy about the whole experience. "Yes, of course. I understand completely. We'll be happy to look into it for you." He folded the phone and put it away. "That was Dale Foster. Of Nova Studios."

Cordelia smiled. "He was calling to offer a bonus because we cracked the case so quickly? Wow. Go, Dale." She pumped a fist in the air.

"I'm afraid not," Wesley said. "Apparently, the studio switchboard received a message from an unknown man saying that if money wasn't delivered tomorrow, some of the things Nova Studios would rather not have known about their stars would be front page news. The blackmail, apparently, hasn't ended." He glanced at Angel. "I told him that we'd take care of it."

"Where and when?" Angel asked.

"Dale is going to receive instructions tomorrow," Wesley said. "He'll call as soon as he knows."

Angel shifted his eyes back to the woman on the computer monitor. "Gunn, that leaves you with Faroe Burke."

"I don't think I'm the guy she's going to open up to. We met earlier. I didn't seem to be her type."

"You saved her life," Cordelia said.

"They weren't going to kill her. I think she knew that."

"Then keep her safe," Angel suggested, "till we figure out what to do next."

"Knowing who is after her would help," Gunn said.

"Then instead of being in protective mode, we could do the ass-kicking thing. I'm more geared for that than I am gallery openings."

"So am I," Angel said, glancing at his clock on the desk. It was only a few minutes short of 2 A.M. "We don't have much time before morning. Let's see if we can turn up anything else. Try the name Gabriel Dantz."

"Let me do that," Cordelia suggested, shooing Gunn out of the chair in front of the computer. "I know the information highway like the back of my hand. How do you spell that?"

Angel spelled the name for her.

"What connection does Gabriel Dantz have to Faroe Burke or the little boy in the vision?" Cordelia asked.

Angel hesitated, not wanting to go into his personal history. There had been enough problems with Darla since Wolfram & Hart had resurrected her and turned her into a vampire again. Instead, he chose to stick close to the truth. "I don't know. It's just a name I heard mentioned tonight."

"Give me a sec." Cordelia tapped the keys, slowed a little by Band-Aids on two of her fingers.

Angel retreated to the huge kitchen for a cold glass of pig's blood. Even after he drank it, he still didn't feel refreshed. He rinsed the glass out in the stainless steel sink and returned to the lobby.

"I'm not finding much on Gabriel Dantz," Cordelia told him. "He was an artist during the early nineteenth century. He did a number of family portraits, but nothing really arty that got him recognized." She leaned forward, studying the columns of script on the screen. "He was supposed to have known Lord Byron and Percy Shelley and Mary Shelley." Her brow wrinkled. "Now why does that name sound familiar?"

"You'll probably recognize her as Mary Wollstonecraft-Shelley," Wesley suggested.

"She's the woman who wrote *Frankenstein*," Gunn said.

"Exactly," Wesley said. "It was subtitled *The Modern Prometheus*. She and her husband, Percy Shelley, Lord Byron, and Dr. John Polidori were staying with Lord Byron in Geneva when Lord Byron suggested they all write ghost stories to entertain each other."

"Now that probably made for a lively evening," Cordelia said dryly.

Ignoring Cordelia, Wesley went on, "Mary Shelley wrote an eight-page short story which she later developed into the famous novel. According to legend, she got the idea about a scientist that collected body parts to create and reanimate a corpse from a nightmare she had while at Lord Byron's house."

"She wasn't Percy's wife then," Angel said. "They were just traveling together. Percy was still married to Harriet Westbrook at the time. Harriet didn't commit suicide till later that year, and Percy married Mary in December."

"He must have really worked through the grieving process," Cordelia said.

"Harriet was a madwoman," Angel said.

"You met her?"

"I heard enough stories."

"So why didn't the other people's stories become famous?" Cordelia asked.

"Lord Byron never finished the piece of vampire fiction he was working on," Wesley said. "From what I gather, Polidori, who was also Lord Byron's personal physician, wrote a rather uninspired ghost story. Shelley did the same."

"Polidori later stole Byron's idea for the vampire story and wrote it up as *The Vampyre*. Y instead of I. The story was about an aristocratic fiend that preyed on England's high society. Although there had been vampire stories throughout Europe for nearly a hundred years, none had ever been written in England. Nor had any of them featured a creature like Lord Ruthven who was at ease moving through the gentrified classes. He became the quintessential vampire in all the fiction that followed.

"Lord Ruthven was modeled on Lord Byron," Angel said, lost in the memories. "Polidori and Lord Byron had had a falling out by that time, and Polidori took the Lord Ruthven name from Caroline Lamb's book, *Glenarvon*, which was also based on Lord Byron."

"And you know all this how?" Cordelia asked.

"I was there briefly. Lord Byron extended an invitation to stay with the group in the house on Lake Leman." *And Mary's dream was no dream at all.* Angel peered at the page on the computer screen. "Are there any archived pictures of Dantz's work?" He couldn't help wondering what had become of Darla's portrait. She had gone to a lot of trouble to have it done, and the completing of it had taken more than a year by the time they'd tracked Gabriel Dantz down to Geneva.

Cordelia clicked on links provided on the Web page. "I

don't find anything here. But I can keep looking if you think it's important."

If Cordelia learned that she was looking for Darla's picture, Angel knew she wouldn't like it. "No. It's not important. Stay with Faroe Burke and let's see if you can turn up anything else we can use." But he couldn't help wondering how Gabriel Dantz had come to be in the art gallery earlier, and what he wanted with Faroe Burke.

Gunn wandered through the rooms set up in the Bronze Jade Art Gallery the next morning and felt out of place in the suit he wore. Smothering a yawn and feeling worn to the bone, he stepped around a small group of people looking at one of the large canvases Faroe Burke had on display at the gallery. All of the art was graffiti and done with aerosol spray paint.

"Simply marvelous work," a gray-haired man in a tuxedo observed. "Do you see how bravely she uses color?"

"Oh, and the shapes," a young woman in leather pants, matching jacket, and a pink-and-white frosted punk-cut said. "Man, you can really get into what she's saying in this piece. I love the attitude."

Irritated at how out of place he felt, Gunn kept moving. *Personally, I'd rather be doing the blackmail drop with Angel and Wesley.*

Nova Studios had called early that morning before Gunn had left the hotel. He glanced at his watch, finding that it was 10:13 A.M., only five minutes later than it had been the last time he'd checked the time. The blackmail drop had been scheduled for 10:30 A.M. Faroe Burke was supposed to have been at the gallery at ten, setting up for her show. The opening was scheduled for noon.

"She's going to be fashionably late," a woman said.

Startled, Gunn looked up.

An Asian woman in her early twenties smiled at him. Her thick black hair was cropped across her brow and at shoulder length. Sheathed in an elegant emerald-beaded long halter dress that showed a lot of smooth, dark skin, she caught Gunn's eye immediately.

"Sorry," the woman apologized. "I didn't mean to startle you."

"You didn't," Gunn said, then smiled at himself. "Maybe a little."

She laughed. "I'm Jennifer Wu."

"Charles Gunn."

"I work here at Bronze Jade." Jennifer extended her hand.

Gunn took it briefly.

"I know most of the people here this morning," Jennifer said, "but I don't know you."

Gunn grinned. "Now you do."

She appraised him again, looking at him from head to toe. "Do you have a card, Mr. Gunn?"

"No," Gunn replied.

"Oh?" Jennifer's brows raised and disappeared under the straight crop. "Trying to remain incognito?"

Gunn leaned in close to her conspiratorially. "I represent some investors that prefer not to be known. If I'm not known either, it helps them remain even less known." He'd found that claiming to be an investment buyer was always a good cover when dealing with heavily monied areas in L.A. Buyers represented people who didn't want their business or their interest to be known.

"So you're here to buy?" Jennifer asked.

"I'm here to look," Gunn said.

"We have some wonderful pieces Miss Burke has created," Jennifer said. "And we are taking bids on some of them."

"I've already been in contact with my clients regarding several of those pieces," Gunn said.

"Good." Jennifer smiled. "I know they'd be very happy with them. Miss Burke's talent is considerable. Very chic. Very dynamic."

A rumble of conversation started in the gallery. Heads turned toward the front of the room.

"Miss Burke has just arrived," Jennifer said.

"Fashionably late," Gunn said.

Smiling, Jennifer said, "Of course. If you'll excuse me, I've got to go help with the reception. It was nice meeting you."

"Nice meeting you, too," Gunn said, turning his attention to the front door.

Ushers opened the doors as Faroe Burke and her entourage swept into the gallery. The arriving party numbered nearly twenty people, and Gunn knew from earlier conversations that Faroe was giving interviews to the media that morning, some of whom would be accompanying her to the gallery.

The arriving party met those people already waiting, like waves beating up against a rocky shore, and in seconds Faroe Burke's forward progress stalled out. Media people brandished camcorders and reporters shoved microphones into Faroe's face.

She was beautiful, Gunn realized. And she didn't look at all like a woman who had been pursued by demons the night before. Instead, she looked relaxed and refreshed, none of which Gunn felt.

She wore a metallic black, matte jersey silhouette dress that showed off the womanly curves beneath. Pearls decorated her hair, looking iridescent in the light given off by the camcorders. Small talk came easily to her, and she seemed totally relaxed while surrounded by the crowd.

The man at her side tried to appear relaxed as he held Faroe by one elbow. Gunn recognized the man from the information he'd downloaded from the Internet last night as Lenny Thomas, Faroe's agent.

Thomas was sunlamp-tan and athletic-club fit plus ten or fifteen pounds that the expensive black suit covered well. His brown hair was going gray at the temples, giving him an immediately distinguished look. He smiled and spoke easily, but his dark eyes remained cold and distant.

Catering staff circled within the gallery attendees, moving adroitly with platters of appetizers ranging from several different cheeses to finger sandwiches. Glasses of wine followed, everything from full-bodied reds to dry whites to rose-hued zinfandels.

Gunn circled the crowd, alert for any signs of trouble. Not all demons gave their natures away by their appearance, and there were any number of humans that hired out to go places where demons couldn't.

After a few moments of basking in the fawning and adoration given up by the audience, Thomas led Faroe back through the gallery to the large room that had been set up for discussion with the artist. Faroe kept conversation going as she trailed her agent through the crowd.

Gunn snagged a glass of zinfandel and three finger sandwiches from passing trays and followed.

Before Thomas reached the podium area, a young man in a crisp Italian suit stood up from a chair in the front row. He'd been waiting there. A slimline briefcase gripped in one hand was chained to his wrist. The metal links gleamed for only an instant and Gunn doubted anyone else in the room noticed.

"Mr. Thomas, Miss Burke," the young man said, stepping in front of them and blocking the way.

Immediately, three men and one woman who had been in the pack that had arrived with Faroe Burke surged forward. Gunn assumed that the way the quartet reached under their jackets that they weren't about to ask for autographs. The four made a protective line in front of Faroe and her agent.

Bodyguards, Gunn realized. Faroe's agent might not have called off the gallery opening, but he'd taken steps to make sure she was protected. Gunn took a bite from one of the finger sandwiches and moved to the left side of the conference room so he'd have a clear view of everything that happened.

"Yes?" Thomas asked.

"I'm Stanford Gray," the young man said. "I work with Wolfram and Hart. We've talked a couple of times over the phone but we've never met." He offered his card.

"Of course," Thomas said, interest flickering in his eyes. "You represent—"

The attorney glanced around. "My client prefers his

involvement in this be kept confidential. At least at this juncture."

Thomas nodded. "We'll need to talk."

"Whenever it's convenient this morning," Gray agreed, returning to his seat, the slimline briefcase sitting neatly in his lap.

Finishing the last of his sandwiches, Gunn took a seat at the opposite end of the row from the Wolfram & Hart attorney and three rows back where he could watch the man. Any interest Wolfram & Hart showed in Faroe Burke was worth investigating.

If anything, Wolfram & Hart were a bigger threat than the Jaakel demons.

Thomas guided Faroe to the podium. Once everyone was inside the room, and it quickly became standing room only, the agent introduced Faroe and the discussion began.

"I'd like to welcome you all to the show," Faroe said, a little timidly. "I really don't know what to say past that. I know I've had weeks to prepare for this, but even when Lenny—my agent," she gestured to the man, "—told me I'd be doing this today, it still didn't seem real. Not even when I walked through those doors out there. And now, here I am."

The audience clapped enthusiastically, and polite laughter followed her words.

Gunn watched her. She had a naive charm about her, but what else was there about her that attracted demons and Wolfram & Hart? Or had inspired Cordelia's vision?

"It's amazing when you think about it," Faroe continued. "Only a few years ago, I was a criminal, and I was doing the same thing people are prepared to call art now. It's strange how things can change with a little success and recognition."

A mild buzz of conversation went through the audience.

"Oh," Faroe said, smiling, "I guess a few of you didn't know that."

Seated to Faroe's left and behind her, Thomas looked uncomfortable. He tapped his foot irritably.

I guess she wasn't supposed to bring all that up, Gunn thought.

But Faroe didn't stop talking about her past. "Part of the sales of all of my works are going into funding for art areas for inner-city kids. Kids who live on the street. Kids with absentee parents. Kids who, like me, would be lost without some means to express themselves."

Gunn's eyes met Faroe's across the room. Her eyes widened. And just for a moment, he felt that tingle of electricity that passed between them. Then her eyes moved on, and Gunn tracked movement from the Wolfram & Hart attorney as he reached inside his jacket and took out a cell phone and earpiece.

Gray spent a moment listening, then quietly got up and left the room.

Gunn gave the man a headstart, then eased out of his own chair and followed.

Chapter Twelve

Angel stood in the shadows of the alley across the street from the building that was the blackmail drop site Dale Foster at Nova Studios had told Wesley about that morning. After the call, they had traveled to the area in Angel's car, then came closer to the target building via the sewers that were L.A.'s true underground. Angel had ridden under a tarp in the backseat while Wesley had driven.

While in the sewers, they'd only had one encounter with a demon group that had brought down a victim from the streets above. The encounter hadn't lasted long, but it had taken away some of the lead time Angel and Wesley had counted on to reach and recon the drop site after receiving the call.

The building was located between downtown L.A. and Beverly Hills, in an area that was currently going through selective urban renewal. Four stories tall and made of yellow stucco brick that had gone out of style in the 1940s, the building was condemned, about to be torn down and rebuilt by a real estate developer that had contracted with a television show to explode parts of it for an upcoming episode.

Black-and-white LAPD squad cars and motorcycles remained in high-profile visibility out on the streets. Most of the officers had set up shop around the mobile food wagon at the northeast corner of the block. Red-and-white-striped sawhorses blocked traffic off the streets on three sides of the building, but a handful of vehicles—including the star's trademark silver-and-black Lamborghini—were parked at the curb.

"We're wasting time," Wesley whispered from behind Angel. "The delivery is supposed to be made at precisely ten forty-seven A.M. It's now ten forty-one. We barely have enough time to get into the building and get out of there before the blackmailer claims that we've defaulted on the delivery."

"How's the blackmailer going to know?" Angel asked.

"Know what?"

"When we make the drop?" Angel asked.

Wesley took off his glasses to clean them and think about it. "I suppose he could be watching."

Dale Foster at Nova Studios had identified the voice as being male. But it was a different voice from the one that had been threatening the studio about Eddie Ashford.

Angel glanced around the neighborhood. The alley they were in was sandwiched between a three-story building and a duplex, which were the tallest buildings around outside of the four-story structure they had under surveillance.

"Watching from where?" Angel asked.

"One of the buildings around here."

"He doesn't have a lot of choices." Angel shifted, trying to work out some pain from his wounded side. "When is the building supposed to explode?"

"From the information Dale was able to get, by ten o'clock. The television studio is only going to implode the top floor. According to Dale, the demolitions team is experiencing difficulties."

Angel glanced at Wesley. "We're supposed to deliver a blackmail payoff to a building that should have already blown up? Does that make any sense to you?"

"Dale Foster wasn't even aware the building was scheduled to be demolished until I told him this morning. And we have no way, of course, of getting in touch with the blackmailer."

Angel shook his head, trying in vain to make sense of it.

"Perhaps the blackmailer knew the building was going to be exploded and counted on it having already been done by the time he picked up the payoff," Wesley suggested. "In fact, the blackmailer might not even take possession of the pay-off today."

"Going to be a long stakeout after we make the drop, then," Angel said.

"We need to get moving."

Reluctantly, Angel agreed. Retreating back down the alley, he reached the manhole they'd come up through, removed the heavy lid again, and dropped back down into the sewer system.

Wesley paused in the alley and tied a kerchief around his mouth and nose. The kerchief had been treated with a menthol-scented liniment to block the stench of the sewage. Taking up the backpack with Nova Studios' pay-off in it, he clambered down into the dark tunnel.

"How much money is in the bag?" Angel asked.

"Fifty thousand dollars. Nothing over a twenty." Wesley dug a small flashlight out of the jacket he wore.

"Is that the same amount as the last time?"

"No. Dale Foster told me this is considerably less." Wesley switched the light on and headed down the tunnel.

Angel caught Wesley's jacket and pulled him in the other direction. "It's this way," Angel said.

"Right," Wesley replied. "I knew that." Clad in rubber galoshes, he tramped forward along the sides of the sewer waterway. His light cut through the darkness and revealed the large tunnel reeking with waste and slime.

According to the sewer tunnel maps Angel had access to, the line they followed now led under the building. There was also supposed to be a manhole located in the building's basement.

Wesley's watch flashed in the darkness and Angel knew he was checking the time.

"Does it make sense to you that the blackmailer would ask for less money this time than before?" Angel asked.

"Angel," Wesley said, "I've never been a blackmailer. And I don't know that I would agree that it's any sort of rational business."

"You burned down the tabloid's offices last night," Angel said.

"I thought we agreed that Merl had done that."

Angel ignored the statement. "There were two survivors, both known to us and any of the studios they might blackmail. Fifty thousand dollars wouldn't be enough to get out of the city and live off of for any time."

"I'm sure Cassi and Roger Cadenasso put away money while they were at the tabloid," Wesley said. "They're probably not hurting for cash."

"Which is exactly my point," Angel said. "Why bother with a fifty-thousand-dollar tap if you're going to expose yourself to an on-site drop? They could have had it wired somewhere."

"Perhaps they were concerned the police would have picked them up."

"The police are already here," Angel reminded as they followed the sewer tunnel. A long-tailed rat squeaked at them from the other side of the water channel. "For all the blackmailer knows, those police are here for him, too. That's a lot of exposure for what seems like very little payoff."

Wesley shone the flash around at the Y-shaped juncture ahead.

"To the left," Angel said. "It curves back around."

"I'm more concerned with what this blackmail does to the agency," Wesley said, trotting into the left tunnel. "This has given us a black mark. I mean, I called Dale Foster last night and gave him my word that we'd ended it last night."

"You took credit for the fire?"

"No, but perhaps I should have. And as of last night after receiving the latest blackmail demand, Nova Studios is prepared to believe the tabloid reporters had a falling out among themselves and I was prepared to take credit for that and collect our fee." He paused at the bottom of a ladder that led up to a manhole. "I'm seriously concerned that this whole debacle is going to prove injurious to our agency."

"They had the blackmail problem before they came to us," Angel said.

"Clients tend to forget that it was—and is—their problem after they've hired you, it seems," Wesley said. "From the tone in Dale Foster's voice, we're now to blame for their present situation."

"Try pointing out that we at least got him a reduction in the blackmail payoffs."

Wesley pointed the flashlight at Angel. "That was humor?"

"I was thinking maybe you might need to lighten up a little."

Wesley sighed. "Angel, I know you have your mission here, but I do care about my efforts at the agency. The work that you do is non-profit. Helping the helpless just doesn't pay."

"Money's not an issue," Angel said.

"I don't like living out of your pocket if I don't have to," Wesley replied.

"It's a deep pocket," Angel said.

"Still, there is the matter of my pride and self-respect. I want to feel that I am contributing."

"You are."

"Angel, the Watchers' Council kicked me out and I showed up on your doorstep as a rogue demon-hunter. That was not a good time for me. I've not been that dependent on anyone in years." Wesley was silent for a moment. "You exemplify autonomy. You, above anyone else, should understand the struggle that goes on within me while I'm working with you."

"You do good work, Wesley," Angel said.

"Then why don't you ask for my help more often?"

Angel nodded. "I have a hard time with that."

"Yet the help is there," Wesley pointed out. "All you need to do is ask."

"Yeah."

"It's hard for both of us," Wesley said. "Getting a contract with Nova Studios and perhaps parlaying that into continued success, that was my way of reaching for autonomy and for a sense of worth."

Uncomfortable with the conversation, Angel glanced up toward the manhole cover. "We're late."

Wesley slung the backpack over his shoulder, placed the small flashlight in his mouth, and started up the ladder. At the top, he slid the manhole cover away, shined the light up into a darkened room for a moment, then headed up.

Angel followed Wesley into the room. Rats scurried across the debris-strewn concrete floor. Wesley's flashlight beam caught their eyes briefly, turning them bright red. The stink of mildew filled the basement. Gazing around at the structure damage revealed by Wesley's beam, Angel understood why the building was coming down. Years of neglect and rot had destroyed much of the foundation.

"What are you supposed to do with the money?" Angel asked.

Wesley directed his flashlight beam toward the gaping doorframe across the room. "Leave it in the basement."

"Do that," Angel directed. "I'll be right back."

"What are you going to do?"

"Take a look upstairs." Angel crossed the room and found the stairs on the other side of the doorway.

"For what?"

"The guys working the demolitions could be involved in the blackmail payoff," Angel explained.

"You've already pointed out how little fifty thousand dollars is," Wesley said. "Now you want to start dividing it up?"

"Maybe our blackmailer is disguising himself as one of them. I want to take a look." Angel started up the stairs. He hadn't quite made it to the top when the explosion detonated above him. Freezing, knowing the blast sounded incredibly loud trapped in the building as it was, he heard the rumble start above.

Men's voices from outside yelled warnings.

Angel didn't understand what was said, but he knew things had gone badly when the ceiling suddenly dropped on him, driving him onto the collapsing stairs.

Cordy tried to ignore the headache that throbbed at her temples and was aggravated because Angel, Wesley, and Gunn hadn't bothered to check in to let her know how things were going with their respective investigations and assignments. She'd tried telling herself that no news was good news, but no news was also no news.

The phone rang and it felt like her brain was going to explode. Still, she mustered her reserves and lifted the receiver. "Hi. Angel Investigations. We help the helpless."

"Hi," an automated voice responded. "This is Joe, of Joe's Carpet and Vent Cleaning. I'm calling today to let you know about exciting discounts we're offering in your neighborhood. If you call today, we can guarantee—"

Cordelia hung up and grabbed the phone book from the desk. The automated telemarketing system chapped. The call from the carpet cleaner's had come in for the third time. *Okay, Joe, you're going to regret it today if you're in the book.*

She was flipping through the Yellow Pages when the vision hit. The pain nuked her brain, and her head thumped against the desktop, suddenly too heavy to hold up. Light coming through the foyer windows from outside seemed harsh and caused needle blasts of agony.

Trembling uncontrollably, Cordelia stared helplessly as the familiar hotel setting went away and the vision filled her mind with sight and sound.

The boy was playing at the table again. He stacked his blocks patiently, his tongue hanging out as he concentrated. The tentacled monster filled the doorway behind him, blotting out sight of the picture in the other room.

Seeming to glide across the floor, the tentacled thing closed on the unsuspecting boy. Just as the tentacles were about to close around him, Cordelia blinked. When she opened her eyes again, she was looking at a faded and dilapidated house that she knew was the boy's.

Fearful and anxious, Cordelia looked at the curb in front of the house. The yard was overgrown with weeds that towered above the waist-high white picket fence. Window boxes filled with dead flowers occupied the sills beneath one of the rooms.

Numbers, numbers, Cordelia thought. *Please let there be numbers.*

The number on the curbside looked freshly painted and read 12512. If the addresses numbered in fours as they usually did, Cordelia knew the house next door had to be 12516 or 12508.

I've got a possible house number. Work with me here, vision. I need a street.

Slowly, her perspective spun until she could see the street sign down at the end of the corner. At the distance, though, she couldn't clearly see it. A feeling of helpless frustration filled her, but then her view increased like the zoom on a camcorder.

The street sign read: CRESTVIEW STREET and CINNA-MON LANE, and the familiar mountain view in the background let her know it was in the L.A. area. Switching back to the house, Cordelia tried to go forward, wanting to know if the tentacled monster had gotten the little boy.

She jerked again as a fresh wave of pain exploded in her head. When she opened her eyes again, she saw only the foyer.

Weakly—dizzy, nauseous, and aching throughout her body—Cordelia flailed for the phone and got it. She pulled it to her ear and punched in the speed-dial for Angel's phone.

Another automated voice said, "We're sorry, but the cellular customer you've called isn't able to come to the phone at the moment."

Calling Wesley's phone netted the same result, and Gunn's answering service picked up when she tried his number.

Frustrated, Cordelia cradled the phone and grabbed her purse. Memory of the little boy stacking blocks as the demon closed in kept playing through her head. *Sitting and waiting is out of the question,* she thought.

Walking somewhat unsteadily, she headed for the door. After locking up, she walked to the curb and flagged down the first taxi she saw.

Gunn kept surveillance on Stanford Gray, the Wolfram & Hart attorney that had spoken with Faroe Burke's agent, as he walked through the Bronze Jade Art Gallery. Not everyone attended the address Faroe Burke was delivering in the conference room. Media personnel circulated the room, as did hangers-on who had seemed to come only to talk about their own work and aspirations.

Gray paced the gallery in distraction, totally committed to the telephone conversation he was having. Or rather, Gunn noted, the telephone conversation the attorney was listening to. He kept an aisle between himself and the Wolfram & Hart attorney, having no problem because Gray wasn't suspicious in the slightest and had no street skills.

A guy working the street kept a radar field around himself, always looking and checking to see who was watching. That was what Gunn did. Glass display cases provided mirrors to check the parts of the gallery he couldn't see directly.

Gray stood in front of a canvas three rooms away from the conference room. The PA pickup Faroe used to address her audience was muted with the rooms between, but Gunn still heard snatches of the attorney's conversation.

"Yes, sir," Gray said. "Yes. Yes, sir. I understand perfectly. Yes, sir. I've got my eye on her. Yes, sir. I'll be making the offer today."

Although the man's voice remained crisp and upbeat, Gunn saw the fatigue and frustration in the way he carried himself. Whatever Gray had been up against, it was almost more than he could bear.

"No, sir, I've not had an indication whether the other party is going to accept your offer," Gray said. "She's busy. Her agent is not letting me—"

Gunn stood in front of a glass display case presenting a collection of urns. Faroe Burke's collection took up most of the floor and wall space in the large gallery, but there were other art exhibits as well. The one in front of him showed a pair of killer whales, probably a mother and calf, swimming together. It had been painstakingly chipped from stone. The card at the bottom of the case announced that it was Inuit art.

Not exactly Madonna and child, Gunn thought. In the reflection of the display case, he watched a caterer approaching with a platter of coffees. The smell was definitely Starbucks. Gunn intercepted the female caterer, smiled, and took one of the coffees. When he turned back around, Gray was in motion again.

Sipping the coffee, Gunn followed.

Gray moved like a man on a mission. "Yes, sir," he said. "I'll tender the offer again today. I'm sure that— No, sir, I'm actually not sure that she'll agree. Her agent— Yes, sir, I understand that you're working on that. If you'd just tell me— No, sir, I know that you're not supposed to tell me everything you're doing. I can appreciate the position you're in, sir. I know there's the time frame we're trying to hit." He paused outside a door marked MEN. He fidgeted, one hand in his pocket jiggling keys, bouncing lightly on his toes. "Yes, sir. I'll make the offer. That's an awful lot of money. I don't know why she and her agent wouldn't go for— I don't know everything, sir. You're right. Yes. Yes. Yes. I'll call you as soon as I know. She's still speaking at the moment. Yes, sir. The moment she steps down. The very moment."

Gunn leaned against the mouth of the hallway, watching Gray's reflection in the display case in front of him and to the side. He had a perfect view of the attorney.

Gray switched the phone off and took the headset from his ear. "Son of a bitch," he whispered hoarsely. "Son of a bitch." He tucked the phone inside his jacket pocket and headed into the men's room.

Finishing his coffee, Gunn sat the mug on the empty tray carried by the next caterer that passed by, then headed into the hallway.

The men's room was small, meant for single occupancy. Gunn tried the door and found it locked. A quick look at the lock assured him that it was a cheap one, meant more for modesty than for security. Taking a laminated video rental card from his pocket, he shoved it between the doorjamb and the locking plate. He flexed the card, twisting and forcing, and succeeded in disengaging the lock.

The door rocked in the jamb as he slid the locking mechanism open.

"Hey," Gray called from inside. "It's occupied. Be out in a minute."

Gunn twisted the handle and pushed the door open, following it inside.

Gray stood at the urinal mounted beside the toilet on the wall opposite the door. A mirror on the wall above the porcelain sink on the right showed Gunn's reflection as he entered the bathroom and locked the door behind him.

"What the hell do you think you're doing?" Gray protested. He frantically tried to zip his pants and defend himself without turning around.

Chapter Thirteen

Gunn shoved the Wolfram & Hart attorney into the wall like a linebacker meeting a fullback. Gray slammed against the wall and cried out in pain. With the breath knocked out of him as it was, his voice didn't carry far and Gunn felt certain the PA overflow probably drowned it out in the hallway.

Leaning into the man, grinding him up against the wall, Gunn held him tight. "You and me are going to talk."

"My wallet's inside my jacket pocket," Gray said. "There's money. There's a corporate credit card. Please don't hurt me."

"Damn it," Gunn said, pulling the attorney back and popping him against the wall. "I'm not here to rob you."

"Okay. Okay. Whatever you say." Gray stared at their reflection in the mirror above the sink. Blood trickled from his nose and the corner of his mouth.

"I don't play games," Gunn said. "You tell me what I want to know or I'm going to leave you in a bloody heap on the floor. Do you understand me?"

"Yeah." Gray screwed his eyes up tightly and frightened tears ran down his face. "I understand you."

Gunn didn't release his hold. "You're here to speak to Faroe Burke."

Gray groaned and stared into the mirror. "You work for the vampire."

Gunn swung the attorney into the wall again. "No, I work *with* the vampire."

"He's interested in this?"

"Why do you want to talk to Faroe Burke?" Gunn asked.

"To commission a painting from her."

"What kind of painting?"

"I don't know. Just a painting."

"I need more than that," Gunn said.

"I don't know any more. I wasn't told any more."

"What about the demons that attacked Faroe at her studio last night?"

"I only heard what was in the news," Gray said. "That her studio was robbed. I didn't even know she was there."

"Who are you working for?" Gunn demanded.

"Wolfram and Hart. I've got cards in my wallet."

"Don't jerk me around. Who's the client?"

"I can't tell you that."

"Sure you can," Gunn said.

"He'll kill me."

Strengthening his resolve, remembering that it wasn't just the attack last night but also that Cordelia's vision centered on Faroe Burke and that there was a little boy out there in danger as well, Gunn slammed Gray into the wall again. "What do you think the vampire is going to do to you if you don't tell me? We're not leaving this room until I know that name. And if somebody gets nervous and calls security, you're leaving here in a body bag. Do you understand me?"

The phone in Gray's jacket pocket rang.

Gunn took the phone out and dropped it into the toilet bowl. The phone drowned out in mid-ring. "The name."

Weeping and going limp, Gray said, "Hardesty. His name is Vincent Hardesty."

"Who is he?"

"A client of Wolfram and Hart," Gray replied. "One of their special clients."

"Is he a vampire?"

"No. He's . . . something else. He's been around for a long time. Wolfram and Hart have helped him keep his business and wealth together for over two hundred years."

"He's a demon?"

"Maybe."

"What does he look like?"

"I don't know. I've never seen him. I've only talked with him over the phone."

Gunn leaned in again, listening as the person knocked on the door once more. "What does Hardesty want with Faroe Burke?"

"He wants her to do a portrait. I swear, I swear to God that's all I know. You've got to believe me." Gray went limp and cried, trembling in fear.

Gunn did believe the man. Feeling bad about what he'd done, but knowing he'd gained ground at the same time, Gunn pulled the man to his feet.

"C'mon, man, let's get you cleaned up," Gunn said.

Still trembling and overwrought, Gray got to his feet. He took the wet paper towel Gunn gave him to wash his face with. When he had a little of his composure back, he glanced at Gunn.

"What are you going to do?" Gray asked.

"Cost you your job with Wolfram and Hart to begin with," Gunn answered. "But I'm going to give you a headstart to get the hell out of town before this Vincent Hardesty finds out you've let the cat out of the bag."

"Where am I supposed to go?"

"Man, that's up to you. Stay and face the music here if you want. I'm just giving you your options."

"If Hardesty doesn't kill me, Wolfram and Hart will."

"You knew that job was risky when you took it," Gunn said. "I ain't here to discuss career options. Right now while I've got Faroe Burke in a safe place, I'm all about saving your ass. That's as far as it goes." He strode to the door and opened it. "Clock's ticking, counselor. Make the most of it."

A man stood in the hallway and stared at Gunn as he left the bathroom.

"Guy's still sick in there," Gunn said. "Give him another minute to pull himself together."

The man in the hallway nodded, then turned and walked away.

Gunn walked through the gallery with his mind racing. He took out his cell phone and punched in Cordelia's number.

Cordelia answered on the third ring. "Hello."

"It's Gunn. I got a name we need to check out." Gunn

took up a position by a wall facing the front of the conference room. Faroe Burke was taking questions from the audience.

"We?" Cordelia sounded exasperated. "By *we* I suppose you mean me?"

"I don't have a computer here with me," Gunn explained, "and I'm still watching over Faroe."

"Oh, and now you're on a first-name basis?"

Gunn listened more carefully, noting the tension in Cordelia's voice. Wind cut across the mouthpiece of her phone as well, creating a whistling noise. "Where are you?"

"I had another vision," Cordelia explained. "I think I know where the boy is."

"You realize that means the demony tentacled thing you've been seeing is there too."

"Yes. Not exactly happy about that. Thanks for the cheery thought."

"You shouldn't be there by yourself," Gunn said.

"I didn't have a choice. At the time I got the vision, Angel's and Wesley's phones were out of reach and you weren't picking up."

"Oops. Forgot I'd set the answering service to pick up. Going stealth on a surveillance gig and having your cell phone ring isn't cool." Gunn shifted, watching as the audience applauded, signaling the end of Faroe Burke's discussion. Everyone stood up and closed on her to talk further. Her exposure to the crowd also put her at risk. "Maybe you ought stay put until Angel and Wesley can shake loose from the blackmail drop."

"Too late," Cordelia said. "I'm already here. I can't ignore this. If that boy is inside the house, I've got to try to get him away." She gave him the address.

"Be careful," Gunn said. "If you get into trouble, call me."

"Why? Is your answering service armed?"

Cordelia folded the cell phone and put it back in her purse, then put the fare plus tip in the taxi driver's hand. He moved his cigar to the other side of his face, wished her a good day, and drove off, leaving her in front of the decrepit house she'd seen in the vision.

She shouldered her purse and looked at the house. It was even bigger and creepier seeing it in person. Years ago the house might have been blue, but the sun had faded it to gray. Long strips of paint curled away from the wooden sides, and several shingles were missing from the peaked roof. Dead bushes lined the front of the house and the right side. The garage door looked as though it hadn't been lifted in years.

Hopefully, Cordelia gazed at the windows, but they were dust filmed and looked like they hadn't been washed in years. She stared at the bay window to the right of the main entrance and knew that was the boy's room.

Or had been the boy's room, Cordelia amended in frustration. She felt certain that no one lived there now. Why would the vision from the Powers That Be show her a place where the child no longer lived?

Taking a deep breath, Cordelia started forward. A cold sensation soaked into her as she neared the house. Despite the fact that the day was typical warm California weather, with the breeze coming down out of the mountains and not from the ocean, a preternatural chill surrounded the house, growing stronger as she drew closer.

She tried the front door but it was locked. Peering through the front windows—even the bay windows over the window boxes filled with dead plants—proved impossible because they were covered with dark floor-to-ceiling drapes.

Cautiously, Cordelia made her way around the house. The garage was locked down tight as well. None of the windows appeared to be left unlatched either, but they were made of glass.

At the side of the house, Cordelia bent down to take a brick from the foundation. The mortar around a whole group of them had grown dry as dust and flaked away because it hadn't been cured properly. She knocked the dust from the brick, then stopped herself. The brick didn't have to be clean to heave through a window. She drew back her arm, preparing to throw.

"Hi," a voice called.

Barely able to curl her fingers around the brick and keep from throwing it, Cordelia turned to face the speaker.

The old woman she'd seen in the vision stood on the other side of the shoulder-high fence between the houses. She wore a faded sundress now, as well as a straw hat with a yellow ribbon.

"Uh, hi," Cordelia responded.

"Are you thinking about buying the place?" the old woman asked. "It would be nice to have a neighbor living there again."

Dropping the brick and hoping the old woman didn't

notice, Cordelia kept her smile in place and stepped to the fence. *Just being more neighborly,* she thought. "I'm Cordelia."

"Nice to meet you, Cordelia," the old woman said. "I'm Ginny." She extended a white-gloved hand over the fence.

Cordelia shook hands. "So, how long have your neighbors been missing?" She paused. "I mean, how long have you been without neighbors?"

"About three years now."

"Really?" Cordelia glanced at the house again. "They really let this place go. Unless you go for that whole kooky-ooky-spooky feel of the Addams Family."

Ginny smiled. "Gabe wasn't much of a hand when it came to keeping things together around a house, and he didn't let people inside much. If you didn't know him, you'd think he was antisocial."

Or a serial killer, Cordelia thought, looking at the house. "Did he live by himself?"

"Most of the years I knew him, he did," Ginny replied. "But there at the end, he had the baby. A little boy, actually."

"How old was the boy?"

The old woman shaded her eyes from the sun and looked at Cordelia. "Three or four. I don't know. I never saw him."

"Never?" Cordelia asked.

"Well, the boy had a condition, you see," Ginny said, lowering her voice sadly.

"A condition?"

Ginny waved her question away. "If you're thinking

about buying the house, you don't have to worry about disease or anything like that. I saw the boy's pictures, and the portraits Gabe painted of him, of course, but like I said, I never actually saw the boy."

"Because of his condition?" Cordelia played the images of the visions through her head again. The boy she'd seen hadn't looked sick. Then again, if she'd been seeing him before the tentacled demon had gotten hold of him, she didn't know what he looked like.

"Yes. He had one of those rare immunity disorders." Ginny shook her head and hugged herself, looking at the room with the window boxes containing dead plants. "He lived in that room in one of those plastic bubbles like you see on television."

"You're sure?" Cordelia asked.

"Quite sure," Ginny answered. "Gabe told me all about it. The whole thing was terrible. Gabe was a single father and had to handle little Alex by himself."

"Where was the mother?"

"Honey," Ginny said, "I don't know. Gabe mentioned once that the little boy's mother wasn't much of a mother, and that it was better if Alex never saw her."

"That's sad," Cordelia said. Her mind worked, trying to add up what she was learning with what she'd seen in the visions. It didn't make sense. The little boy she'd seen had been healthy, and there had been no sign of a father, only the tentacled thing that had come after the boy.

Ginny smiled. "But little Alex couldn't have asked for a better father, I'll promise you that. Whatever life the boy had, his father gave him the best. Gabe spent all his days in that house with his son. Only every now and again you'd catch him outside working on those window boxes or painting."

"Doesn't sound like a very healthy lifestyle," Cordelia said.

"Family takes care of family," Ginny replied. "That's what Gabe always said. You should have seen the paintings he did of young Alex. He was a very talented man."

"Gabe did paintings?"

"Oh, yes. He was an artist. Didn't I mention that? I suppose I should have. You must have been wondering how Gabe supported himself and little Alex."

Cordelia hadn't been, but now she was. Faroe Burke was also a painter. Was that their connection?

"Gabe did all kinds of paintings," Ginny said. "Magazine covers and layouts. And paperback covers. My goodness, he did a lot of paperback covers in the 1950s. Detective novels, science fiction novels, romance novels. Even some of those soft porn books. Just everything you could imagine." She grinned and even blushed a little. "They were what my mother used to call *hot* and my father used to call trash. You can find some of them on eBay now, only they list them as Good Girl Art."

"In the 1950s?" Cordelia repeated. "And he had a baby? How old was this guy?"

"Why, honey, to be doing that kind of work back then, Gabe would have had to have been in his seventies."

"And he had a baby?"

Ginny smiled and lowered her voice. "Gabe always acted younger than he looked. And he was a good listener. Women admire that in a man. I have to admit, I found him quite attractive myself." She patted her hair and her cheeks colored just a little.

Okay, Cordelia thought, *TMI. Too much information.* "So where is Gabe these days?"

"In Seattle. At least, that's where he was three years ago after he moved out. I didn't even see him leave. One day he was there, and the next he and little Alex were gone."

Or the demony thing got them.

"Are you sure he was in Seattle?" Cordelia asked.

"I got a postcard from him a week after he'd gone," Ginny said. "Truth to tell, I hadn't even noticed he was gone till I got the card. Then slowly, the flowers in those window boxes started to wilt and die. I watered them for a few days. There wasn't any sense in it, of course, but I hated the thought of them just wasting away. Just took them a little longer to die, is all."

"You never saw anyone taking any furniture from the house?"

"No. But that week, my husband and I were out of town on vacation. Probably why I didn't see him go."

"Would anyone else around here know anything about him?"

"Honey, this is an older neighborhood. A lot of people that were here three years ago are gone now."

"I'm sorry to hear that," Cordelia said.

Ginny laughed and waved the thought away. "Oh, it's not like that. It's just that most of the people who lived here bought their houses when they were young. By the time they got to retirement age, like my mister and I were, why those houses were worth small fortunes. As I'm sure you'll find out when you talk to the real estate company you're dealing with."

A phone rang.

At first Cordelia thought it was hers, thinking maybe Wesley or Angel had noticed they'd missed her call. Then Ginny pulled a cordless phone from the pocket of her sundress.

Ginny talked for a moment, then glanced up at Cordelia. "I've got to take this, honey," the old woman said, covering the mouthpiece with one hand. "It's my baby sister in Vegas. She just got married again and wants to lie to me about the honeymoon. It was nice meeting you." She cackled with glee, then turned and walked back toward her house.

"I'm just going to look around a bit," Cordelia said.

Ginny waved good-bye without looking around, thoroughly engrossed in her conversation.

Stooping, Cordelia picked up her brick again and went around to the back of the house. A small sunroom faced the western sky. Greenhouse glass made up half the roof and three of the walls. The fourth wall was the back of the house. Shelves inside held more dead plants, and baskets hung from ceiling mounts.

For someone who had moved out, the mysterious Gabe sure hadn't taken much with him. And if he'd left, why hadn't he sold the house? For an instant, dread filled Cordelia when she considered that what she might find inside the house were skeletons of a father and son, left by a flesh-eating demon clever enough to have mailed a postcard from Seattle to the only neighbor Gabe had that would have missed him.

Cordelia took off her jacket, wrapped the brick in it,

then whacked one of the lower sections of greenhouse glass. For one frozen moment she waited for something—probably something with huge fangs, lizard skin, and breath that would blister metal—to come charging out of the house.

She breathed hard, holding onto the jacket-wrapped brick, prepared to use it as a bludgeon if she had to. After a few minutes when nothing at all happened—including Ginny the neighbor lady coming over to see what had been broken—she dropped the brick, pulled her jacket back on, and crawled into the house.

The mold and mildew built up in the place over the years gave her a sneezing fit for a moment. Then she got control of herself and approached the back door.

It was locked as well, but the top half of the door held a dozen glass panes.

Cordelia turned and brought her elbow crashing into one of the panes. She removed the broken shards that remained, then reached through and unlocked the door. *Definitely been hanging around Angel way too long.* But the thought of the little boy drew her on, overcoming her fears of all things demony as well as police.

The back door opened onto a kitchen with a small breakfast nook and a refrigerator. Opening the refrigerator was a big mistake. It smelled like dead things in there, but there were no identifiable body parts. Cordelia chose to take that as a good sign.

Canned food and boxes of dry food—primarily cereals, and macaroni and cheese—stood in neat ranks on shelves in the pantry. All of them were covered with layers of dust. *Gabe and baby didn't move out,* Cordelia thought.

They jumped ship. And she thought she knew what had scared them off.

She left the kitchen and made her way through the formal dining room. More dust covered the table and chairs there. Continuing through the house, she found it filled with dust and furniture. Evidently Gabe had taken nothing but his son when he'd left.

The living room was sparsely furnished with a sofa and recliner. There was no television set, no entertainment system, and no video game setup. Lamps hung from the ceiling and from walls, well out of reach for a three- or four-year-old. A Victrola sat on a small antique table. Below it was a collection of records. A quick inspection of the records revealed that they were all classical music: Bach, Mozart, and Wagner.

Okay, definitely not a top-forty guy here. Cordelia stood and brushed the dust from her hands off on her jeans.

The child's bedroom was across the narrow hallway/ foyer outside the living room. The door was closed but unlocked.

Heart racing, afraid of what she would find on the other side of the door, Cordelia gripped the knob and pushed the door in. The door opened on rusty hinges that shrilled and creaked.

"Wow," Cordelia whispered, unable to keep her surprise to herself, "déjà vu all over again."

Chapter Fourteen

As the door swung open to the child's bedroom, Cordelia saw the table where the little boy had played in her visions. A short stack of blocks stood in the middle of the table while others lay scattered around it and across the hardwood floor. A child's bed occupied one corner of the room, all handmade elegance with images of forest creatures carved into it. Books filled the small shelf over the bed, stories about Peter Pan, Robin Hood, King Arthur, Winnie the Pooh, Greek mythology, the Books of Fairies, and Laura Ingalls stood in neat organization. Comic books featuring Mickey Mouse, Donald Duck, and other Disney favorites occupied a wicker basket beside the bed. Wooden cars, trucks, and animals filled a handmade toy box.

Cold dread ran through the pit of Cordelia's stomach. She'd come too late; the boy was gone. Hot tears burned at her eyes, but she refused to shed them.

No, you just get a grip, she commanded herself. *The Powers That Be—no,* Doyle—*did not give me these vi-*

sions just so I could see what I might have done, who I might have saved. There's another answer. I just have to find it.

She glanced above the desk and saw a dozen simple crayon and pencil drawings decorating the wall. All of them were held in place by Scotch tape that had yellowed with age. Seeing the child-engineered art reminded her of the painting she'd seen in her vision; the one that had seemed to strike a familiar chord.

Turning, getting herself positioned in the room, she gazed at the wall to the left of the table and saw the door there. She crossed to the door and opened it, amazed at the number of canvas paintings stacked on the floor and leaning against the walls.

The painting on the easel didn't match the one she'd seen in her vision. Time had passed since that window of whatever past the vision had tuned her in to. The painting on the easel looked like the cover to a romance novel, a woman in an elegant dress throwing herself against the bare chest of a Viking holding a battle-axe in one hand. But other paintings showed cowboys, aliens, and detectives.

The ceiling above Cordelia creaked. She froze as a tingle sped up her spine, letting her know she was no longer alone. Someone had entered the house, but they hadn't used a door to do so.

The creaking continued, moving in a straight line across the upper floor. From the direction the sounds took, Cordelia knew whoever it was had headed for the stairs.

Following the blind terror that threatened to consume

her and tightened her breath in her lungs, Cordelia glanced around the room filled with paintings. Spotting a closet door, she moved over to it, silently shifted the paintings leaning against it, and squeezed inside.

She closed the door, leaving only a small gap that she could peek through as the footsteps descended the stairs. The steps sounded heavy, too heavy to be anything human outside the NFL or WWF.

The steps kept coming down the stairs, then turned and headed for the boy's bedroom.

As Cordelia watched, a snake bobbed into view. At least, she thought it was a snake at first glance. When a second snake-like appendage joined the first, then a third, and finally a dozen, Cordelia knew she was looking at the demon that had appeared in the visions.

The thing stepped into view, its tentacles lifted, weaving patterns in the air. It stood at least seven feet tall, with the segmented body of an earthworm beneath the dozens of tentacles that sprouted from it like spines from a thistle. The reptilian skin was indigo, though flashes of light caught it and showed that it might have been a deep metallic blue. The tentacles moved restlessly, in constant motion as if caught in a current or riding on a breeze.

The head twisted and looked around, but Cordelia thought that was more a mannerism than necessary. Inhuman features—a multitude of ink-black eyes like those on a spider and a wide lipless mouth that had undulating mandibles like those of a lobster—spread across a skull that resembled an arrowhead. The head had width and height, but seemingly next to nothing in depth. Shaped like an ace of spades, the head fluttered in slow motion like a ribbon tied to a fan.

Tentacles waving, stretching out from the hideous body till they reached eight feet and more to touch the walls and the ceiling, the demon opened its mouth and spoke. "Baby."

"Baby," the creature crooned again, twisting her two-dimensional head. "Where are you, baby? Is your father hiding you again? He's hidden you for so very long."

Shaking with nausea while trapped in the closet, Cordelia watched as the demon moved forward. The tentacles roved over the scattered blocks, slithering over the child's toys with a gentleness that Cordelia wouldn't have counted on.

"Baby," the demon called again. "Where are you? Mommy's home. Don't you want to see Mommy?"

Mommy? Thinking of the innocent face she'd seen, blond hair and blue eyes, chubby cheeks still showing the promise of babyhood barely left, Cordelia had to put her hand over her mouth to keep from screaming out or throwing up. Then, when the demon's flat head turned in her direction, Cordelia held her breath.

Angel woke under a pile of debris that had filled the stairwell. Pain throbbed at his temples. He blinked against the swirl of dust that still sifted down from above.

"Damn it!" a man outside the building swore. "What the hell happened up there?"

"Don't know," another man called out. "We packed those charges according to specs. There should only have been an implosion, not an explosion."

"The building's foundation and infrastructure was damaged more than we predicted. Did you get the shot you needed? From the looks of things we're not going to be able to blow it again."

Angel reached through the debris, trying to slide out from under the crushing weight and gain the leverage he needed to get free. If he'd been human, he would have died. Boards and Sheetrock cracked and shifted over him.

Wesley! The thought filled Angel's mind as he fought to free himself. Pale yellow light gleamed from inside the basement, proving that Wesley's flashlight had survived, but there was no guarantee that Wesley had.

Unable to get out from under the weight of the debris on his own, Angel morphed, drawing on the demon's strength that filled him. He felt the added strength flow through his body, but he also felt the demon's hunger. He scented the fresh blood in the air. If Wesley hadn't been killed in the explosion, he'd been injured.

Surging up, Angel stood. The debris sloughed off him with shattering cracks, sliding around his body as he fought his way to the top of the heap. Luckily, there was enough crawlspace for him to reach the basement doorway.

The deluge of broken building materials falling from above had torn the basement door off and widened the doorway. The flashlight beam revealed the cracks running across the basement ceiling. Thick chunks of poured concrete hung down, ready to fall at any moment. For the most part, the carnage that had dropped from the building hadn't invaded the basement yet.

Angel crawled down the debris, struggling to stay on

his feet. Nails and sharp rocks tore at his flesh. He went for the flashlight first, picking it up from the floor, then searching for Wesley.

Wesley lay only a few feet away. Concrete dust coated him, making him resemble a rough marble statue in progress. Broken boards and chunks of Sheetrock covered him. A dark stain spread out from his forehead and led to a pool on the cracked floor.

Groggy and disoriented, Wesley opened his eyes. "Angel?"

"Yeah, buddy."

"What happened?"

"They blew up the building."

"Oh. Okay. That's what I thought happened." Wesley closed his eyes.

Angel tapped Wesley's face again.

"What?" Wesley asked.

"We need to get going. The building may still try to come down on top of us."

Angel helped him to his feet.

"What about the blackmail money?" Wesley asked.

"I thought you had it."

"I did until the building blew up." Wesley glanced around.

Angel shone the flashlight on the basement floor. He didn't see the backpack containing Nova Studios' fifty thousand dollars, but he spotted something else. "The money's gone."

"What are you talking about?"

"Look." Angel pointed the flashlight at the open manhole.

The area around the manhole was covered with concrete dust and plaster chunks, but one side of the manhole had been disturbed. A short distance from the manhole, the disturbed area ended but footprints showed.

"Were you over there before you woke me?" Wesley asked.

"No." Angel approached the manhole and examined the footprints. "Someone came in after we did. After the building blew."

"The blackmailer?"

"That would stand to reason. He'd be the only person that knew we were down here. Unless one of the rats we saw has a backpack fetish that we don't know about."

"Let's get after him, then," Wesley said. "He might have only just left."

Keeping the flashlight, Angel led the way down into the sewer. Once there, they stopped and waited, hoping to hear footsteps or anything else that would point them in the right direction.

"He's gone," Wesley said a few minutes later.

Angel nodded in agreement. "He was waiting for us outside. When the building blew, he followed us inside and took the bag." He played the flashlight over the sludge coating the sewer tunnel. The muck and the mud there was too thin to hold footprints.

Wesley took a handkerchief from his pocket and pressed it to the cut on his forehead. "We're a fine pair of detectives, aren't we? I shouldn't wonder if Dale Foster and Nova Studios summarily fires us once the results of this fiasco are known."

Angel started back along the sewer tunnel the way they had come. "Take it easy. This isn't over."

"You think you can find the man who did this?"

"I think the man who did this will be making another call to Nova Studios. Fifty thousand dollars isn't going to last as long as he thinks it is."

A few minutes later, they were once more in the alley, then in the Plymouth Belvedere GTX. Angel lay in the backseat and covered up with the protective tarp. His mind worried at the situation that had been put before them. Wesley's blackmailer didn't make a lot of sense to him, and then there was the problem of Cordelia's visions.

His cell phone rang.

Angel fumbled for the phone, being careful to keep the tarp pulled over him. Wesley had the car out in the traffic now, in full view of the sun. "Hello," he answered.

"It's me," Gunn said. "Where the hell have you guys been? I've been calling and calling, but kept getting told you guys were out of the service area."

"Probably had something to do with the explosion," Angel said.

"Explosion?"

"I'm in the car," Angel said, "trying not to work on my tan. Maybe I'm wrong, but I'm really kind of hoping that you didn't call just to chit-chat."

"No. I've got a couple irons in the fire here. We'll talk when we get together. The main reason I called is because of Cordy."

"What's wrong with Cordy?"

"Nothing that I know of. She called a little while ago and told me she had another vision. She thinks she knows where the house is that the little boy is in. She's probably there now."

"Where?"

"Crestview and Cinnamon. I didn't know if you guys could shake loose. If you think I should leave Faroe—"

"No," Angel said. "Faroe was in the vision. I don't want her left on her own."

"I agree. I ran into a Wolfram and Hart attorney brokering a business proposition for a client with Faroe. The way those guys are, I figure they're tied up in Cordelia's vision too."

"Stay with her. Don't let her out of your sight. Wesley and I will find Cordelia."

"If you need me," Gunn said, "you know where I'll be."

Angel punched the END button, then speed-dialed Cordelia's cell phone number. The address wasn't too far from where he and Wesley were.

The phone rang once, then there was the distinct sound of the connection being broken. Angel tried the number again. This time it was answered.

Watching the indigo demon's spade-shaped head whirl in her direction as the phone rang again, Cordelia lifted the cell phone to her face, and whispered, "One of these days, I'm going to call you when you're in a closet trying to hide from a demon."

Tentacles fluttering before her, the demon started toward Cordelia's hiding place. The tentacles pushed her along, so smooth it seemed like she was gliding.

"What?" Angel asked.

Cordelia exploded from the closet, shoving the door

toward the approaching demon, then bringing her arms and knees up high as she sprinted toward the other door in the room.

A horrendous crash sounded behind Cordelia. Glancing over her shoulder, she saw the tentacled demon wrenching the shattered door from its hinges. The demon threw the door away, smashing it up against a pile of paintings, and resumed the chase.

"Cordelia," Angel called, his voice sounding tinny and distant because Cordelia had the phone in her fist and not to her ear.

"Demon!" Cordelia panted.

"What kind of demon?" Angel's voice shifted away from the phone. "Wesley, floor it!" At the other end of the connection, rubber shrilled.

"Big," Cordelia gasped, catching the doorframe ahead of her with one hand and yanking herself around into the narrow hallway. The large living room lay at the other end of the hallway. "Tentacles. Bunch of eyes. Oh, and gross. You wouldn't believe the stink. Did I mention big?"

"Get out of there," Angel said.

"Ya think?" Cordelia asked. She skidded to a halt in the living room at the door. When she tried it, the door was locked. She pulled at the plywood covering the windows and found screws held them in place. It would take time or a crowbar to get them off.

Turning, Cordelia glanced back into the hallway. She didn't see the demon anywhere, but she was certain the creature had followed her out of the art room. The hallway was to the right of the stairs leading up to the second floor. To the left of the stairs was the doorway leading to the formal dining room.

Does the door on the other side of the hallway opposite the painting room lead to the dining room? Is that where the demon has gone? Or has she ducked back into the painting room thinking I'm going to think she's in the dining room and she's going to reach out and grab me?

Making her decision, Cordelia ran for the dining room. She'd almost reached the threshold when she saw questing tentacles slithering across the floor like a group of snakes getting ready to strike.

Cordelia grabbed the doorway and backpedaled. She ducked as a trio of tentacles slapped against the doorjamb at the height her head had been only moments ago. Each tentacle split into a mouth filled with vicious greenslimed fangs.

The fangs were no surprise. If demons didn't want to possess their victims, rend them into pieces, or make them over in their image, they wanted to eat them. Cordelia was betting this was an eating demon.

Getting traction, one foot on the hardwood floor in the dining room and one still on the carpet of the living room, Cordelia threw herself back toward the stairs. *Are the windows covered on the second floor?* She couldn't remember, but even if they were, maybe the coverings weren't screwed into the wall. *Or maybe it doesn't like stairs.*

Cordelia caught the corner of the staircase and started up. Tentacles shot through the openings between the stairway railing. One of the vicious little mouths caught the toe of her right foot but couldn't bite through. *Italian leather,* she thought. *You gotta love it.*

She tried to kick the tentacle loose but it wouldn't

budge. Other tentacles shot through the railing, snapping at her. She batted two of them away with the cell phone, then lost it from the force of the blow and watched it shatter against the stair step.

I didn't give Angel the address. Closer to panic now, Cordelia shook her foot again, slipping her foot from her shoe. She turned and lunged up the stairs, following the ninety-degree turn up to the second-floor landing.

A figure in a shapeless black cloak stepped from the shadows. A wan, feverish face peered out at Cordelia from beneath a peaked, wide-brim hat that put her in the mind of a Puritan witch-hunter. Cancerous boils showed on his face, dragging one corner of his mouth in a leering rictus that looked obscene. The bloodshot, yellowed eyes held a stirring of insanity.

"What are you doing here?" the man snarled.

Before Cordelia could reply, the tentacled demon with the flat head appeared below. Pausing only for a moment, the demon rushed up the stairs, gliding as the tentacles slammed into place beneath her with meaty *thwocks!* Even at the speed she was traveling and the force that she used to move, the demon made almost no noise.

The demon or the madman, Cordelia thought, and glanced over the side of the staircase for good measure. *When things are looking dark, it pays to see all the darkness.*

The madman grabbed her wrist and pulled her forward. His strength surprised Cordelia. With his slender build and poster-child-for-plague appearance, she didn't see how he got himself around. Before she could move to defend herself, he stepped in front of her in a swirl of material.

"Watch out for those tentacles," Cordelia said. "They've got mouths."

"I know," the madman said. He pulled a gleaming rod less than two feet long from his side. As the tentacles reached for him, he slapped them away with the rod.

The demon stopped at the first landing in the elbow of the staircase. The thin-lipped, wide mouth parted in a harsh growl.

"Well, it's official," Cordelia said. "She doesn't like that."

"No," the madman agreed, slapping the tentacles away in flourishing strokes.

"Magic wand?"

"Copper. It hurts her. She knows if she comes any closer, I'll hurt her more."

The demon bellowed in anger.

Cordelia glanced at the rooms on the second floor. All of the doors were open, and all of the rooms she could see into had plywood screwed over the windows. "Is there a way out of here?"

"The way you came in," the madman answered.

"Oops," Cordelia said. "That would be downstairs."

"Then perhaps you can get one of the coverings off a window."

"Okay. You don't mind doing the whole rescue thing by yourself? Because the people I hang with, they kind of get into that the-whole-group's-a-hero-or-nobody's-a-hero mentality. Those-who-slay-together-stay-together. That kind of thing. And then Angel gets this major broody thing going on that just—"

"Get out of here, girl," the madman snarled as he continued to bat the fanged tentacles away in an amazing display of martial arts skills.

Cordelia turned to go.

"Where is the child?" the demon demanded.

Child? Unable to leave, Cordelia turned to the madman.

"Leave, girl," the madman ordered.

"Sorry," Cordelia said. "No can do. I need to know about the kid." She tried to sound hard and offhand about it, but the image of the smiling little boy wouldn't leave her mind.

The madman redoubled his efforts to defend them against the demon. The tentacles whipped through the air thick as a bee swarm. Incredibly, the madman fended off every attack by the monstrous apparition. But he couldn't hold his position. He stepped back.

"Fall back, girl," the madman ordered. "Go toward that yonder bedroom and be quick about it, else she'll snatch us up and there won't be naught we can do for it."

"Yonder bedroom?" Cordelia repeated.

"Hurry, damn it!" the madman yelled. "She's a thing of darkness. She'll fear the light if we can get to it."

"You don't have to be rude about it," Cordelia objected. She ran for the farthest bedroom and yanked at the plywood covering the window. Screws held the plywood there as well. "I can't get it."

Glancing back, she watched as the madman kept slapping the questing tentacles out of his way, using the copper rod and his cloak to keep the demon at bay. He gave ground faster now as the demon glided up the steps.

Thinking quickly, Cordelia shoved the mattress and

box spring from the bed. Metal slats crossed the frame. She yanked one of them free and shoved it behind the plywood covering the window to use as a pry bar as the madman fought the demon. Bracing one foot against the wall, Cordelia pulled with all her strength. *Leverage, got to have leverage,* she told herself, pulling again. Metal shrilled through wood as the screws started to turn loose.

One corner of the plywood turned loose with a shriek.

Cordelia moved the slat up higher and pulled again. The second corner tore loose with only one pull. Dropping the slat and grabbing the edge of the plywood, Cordelia pulled it open, then folded it back against the wall.

Only a little daylight fell into the room. The reverse shadow of the window fell onto the dust-covered hardwood floor.

Cordelia backed against the window as the madman entered the room with the demon hot on his heels. Eyes focused on the demon, Cordelia fumbled for the window latch and shoved it over. Her fingers found the bottom of the window and she shoved up.

The window remained locked down tight.

"Where is the baby?" the demon demanded as she entered the room after the madman.

"Safe," the madman gasped. He brandished the copper rod before him, letting it catch the light.

"How long have you kept him hidden?" the demon asked.

"Not nearly long enough," the madman replied. He stepped into place beside Cordelia, but she noticed that he kept his face and arms shielded under the shade of his hat and cloak.

"Did you think you could hide him from me forever?"

"You would never have known."

Cordelia turned and used both hands on the window. Then she noticed the screws holding the window closed. Someone had wanted all the windows locked down tight. The house was like a prison.

Chapter Fifteen

The little boy, Cordelia realized as she gave up trying to force her way through the window. Screwing the windows shut wasn't to keep anyone trapped in the house; it was to keep the little boy safe. She drew her elbow back, preparing to drive it through the glass and take her chances with getting cut.

But she couldn't leave until she knew that the little boy wasn't on the premises. She looked at the madman. "Is he here?"

The madman didn't look at her, keeping his attention on the demon. "Who?"

"The boy," Cordelia said.

The demon waved her tentacles, filling the air with twitching ink-black appendages shining with a metallic blue luster. A pair of the tentacles got too close to the sunlight. When the light touched them, they turned to ash and blew away.

A painful squall erupted from the demon's too-wide gash of a mouth as the other tentacles jerked back.

"I don't know what you're talking about," the madman told Cordelia.

"Yes you do," Cordelia said. "You told her you knew about the boy."

The madman's face hardened. He gave more attention to Cordelia, but he remained wary. "This is none of your concern."

"Trust me," Cordelia said, thinking of the little boy's face, "I'm making this my concern. I didn't have those stupid headaches from those visions the Powers That Be gave me for nothing. I don't know what you people want with that little boy, but you're not getting him."

The madman reached inside his cloak and brought out a small silver case. He held it out into the sunlight, catching the light and reflecting it toward the demon.

The demon jerked away, raising its tentacles like an elderly woman yanking up a granny skirt to let a mouse go by, then jerked to one side like a limbo dancer.

"During the night, she's a queen of all she surveys," the madman said, "but she has to fear the light of day." He moved the case again, reflecting a beam of light that smacked squarely into the creature's mass.

Powdery, white-gray ash spots showed on the demon's hide like blemishes. She lifted her voice in a hideous cry of pain and rage.

Cordelia smelled the stink of burning demon. She knew from years of experience there was nothing like it. Then she noticed that the tentacled demon wasn't the only one burning. The madman's hand holding the silver case shook as blisters started to form on his pale, waxy flesh. Capillaries broke beneath the skin and caused instant bruising. He wasn't as susceptible to the sun's rays, but they were harmful to him.

"Give me the case," Cordelia said.

"She must be driven away," the madman said.

"I'll do it," Cordelia said. "You're getting hurt."

The madman gazed at her through pain-filled eyes. His hand smoked and the blisters writhed. Reluctantly, he handed the case to Cordelia and snatched his hand from the light.

Turning her attention to the sunlight and the demon, Cordelia made the creature retreat by burning her again and again with the reflected sunlight. The demon left the room, tried only for a moment to hang outside the doorway till Cordelia proved too quick and too accurate with the case, then went back down the stairs.

Cordelia breathed hard, listening intently for any sign of the demon's return. Then she adjusted the reflection from the silver case, letting the madman know she was prepared to use it.

"You know where he is," Cordelia accused.

The madman said nothing.

Cordelia took a step closer to him, using the reflection from the silver case as a threat. "I want the boy."

"Why?"

"Because I'm supposed to help him."

Doubtful curiosity filled the madman's wax face. Perspiration dripped down his slack cheeks. "You don't even know him."

Cordelia hesitated. "No. But I'm sure I'd like him once I saw him. I help lots of people I don't even know. Like helping you get away from that demon."

"Your presence here drew her to this place. She hadn't known about it until you arrived."

"I didn't do anything."

"You came here.

"Yes."

"Because you're supposed to help the boy?"

"Good. You were listening. Because I hate having to explain all this stuff over and over."

The madman's good hand flicked out, snatching the silver case from Cordelia's hand. Disarmed, Cordelia stepped back. Leaning in, keeping his wrecked face sheltered from the sun with his broad-brimmed hat, the madman locked eyes with Cordelia.

"Stay away from this, girl," the madman threatened in a hoarse voice thick with emotion. "You've already interfered too much."

"Me?" Cordelia couldn't believe it. "Hey, mister, if I hadn't taken the case and done the Jedi knight–laser beam thing on the demon, she would have killed you. I could have broken through that window and stood out on the rooftop in full sunlight. She couldn't have come after me."

"She didn't come after me," the madman said, pocketing the silver case. "She wanted you. She wanted your flesh to use as her own."

Okay, and that sounds positively icky, Cordelia thought. A brief image of the demon ripping the flesh from her body filled her head. *Now that I did not need.*

The madman turned away from Cordelia and walked toward the hallway.

"Where do you think you're going?" Cordelia demanded.

"Away from this place. There's nothing more I can salvage here."

"You can't just leave."

"Stop me."

Frustrated, not wanting to leave the safety of the sunlight, Cordelia stood her ground. "I can help you. Have you ever heard of the Powers That Be?"

The madman halted then at the top of the stairs. He stared back at Cordelia.

Gathering her courage, remembering that the small boy was still out there somewhere needing their help, Cordelia reached into her purse and brought out a business card. Fearfully, expecting the tentacled demon to drop down on her from the ceiling, she walked toward the madman with the card.

Suspicion in his bloodshot and yellowed eyes, the madman looked at the card but made no move to take it.

"I work at a detective agency," Cordelia said. "We specialize in helping the helpless."

"I'm not helpless."

Cordelia wanted to argue the point, but she didn't. "Take the card. Please. For the boy. In case you find out you do need help."

The madman hesitated for a moment, then he plucked the card from Cordelia's fingers and started down the stairs.

"If you can't expose yourself to the sun," Cordelia shouted after his retreating back, "how do you think you're getting out of here?"

The madman didn't answer.

"And where's the demon? Did you think about that?

She may be down there waiting to pounce on you. Demons do that, you know."

"She's gone." The madman quit the stairs and headed for the dining room.

Cordelia peered over the staircase, looking in all directions. "Demons are good at hiding. And if sunlight kills her, how did she get out of the house? In fact, how did she get into the house?"

"If you are truly here to help, then you and those you work for have my welcome. But I suggest that you leave," the madman advised without breaking stride or turning around. "You don't know what you're dealing with here. You're going to get yourself killed." His cloak whirled as he stepped into the dining room and out of sight.

"Hey," Cordelia called after him. "Hey, you come back here. I haven't finished convincing you yet." Drawn by the need to help the little boy and certain the madman knew where he was, she continued down the stairs. "Hey, are you listening to me?"

She reached the bottom of the stairs and listened. There was no sound of the madman or the demon. Of course, people couldn't always hear demons. That was part of their pouncing ability.

Someone moved at the front door.

Cordelia screamed, took a step back up onto the stairs, tripped, and fell. Something slammed against the door, then she heard Wesley's voice yell out in pain.

"Wesley," Cordelia called.

"Cordelia?" Wesley replied. "Are you all right?"

"Yes." Cordelia got up and crossed to the door. She unlocked it, then swung it open.

Wesley stood on the stoop rubbing his shoulder. "I was coming to your rescue," he explained. "But that door is much more stout than it looked."

"Good thing I didn't really need help," Cordelia said.

"There was always the window."

Cordelia rapped the plywood covering with her knuckles. "Boarded over."

Wesley pushed his glasses up his nose. "Well, you didn't need our help anyway."

"Not now," Cordelia said. "If you'd have been a few minutes earlier, maybe you could have helped kill the demon."

Wesley blinked at her. "You've already killed the demon?"

"No," Cordelia said. "I had to settle for chasing it off. It's got this whole aversion to sunlight thing—"

"Speaking of aversions to sunlight," Angel said, "I'm getting a little nervous here."

Peering past Wesley, Cordelia saw Angel standing at the side of the house and using his trench coat as a protective shade from the sun. "Those I work with are welcome here. Come on in," she said.

Wesley stepped into the house. Angel followed him.

For the first time Cordelia noticed that Wesley and Angel were covered with grime and plaster dust. Wesley also had a bump and a deep scratch on his head.

"Did something go wrong with the blackmail drop?" Cordelia asked.

"We were blown up," Wesley replied.

"Did you catch the guy who did it?"

"A Hollywood special-effects team blew up the building."

"I knew that," Cordelia said. "I was talking about the guy doing the blackmailing."

Angel led the hunt for the demon and the madman, going back through the dining room and into the kitchen. The sunroom Cordelia had broken into didn't leave much leeway for anyone susceptible to the sun's rays to get out of the house without being exposed, and presumably none at all for the demon if it had been as big as Cordelia had said. Judging from the damage inside the house, Angel didn't doubt the size.

He located a door in the kitchen by a pantry still stocked with canned goods. Opening the door, he gazed down into the darkness, seeing only the start of the stairs. He felt for a light switch on the wall.

"What is that?" Cordelia asked, standing slightly behind him.

"Basement," Angel said. "If the demon and the guy you saw didn't go out into the backyard, they had to have had another way out."

Cordelia frowned. "This helping-the-helpless thing gets complicated."

"That's what makes it worth doing," Wesley said. He peered over Angel's shoulder. "Maybe the light switch is farther down."

"In the dark?" Angel asked. Going down into the dark didn't sit too well with him. If the demon had gone down into the basement to hide, she wouldn't like being invaded.

"Could be," Wesley said.

Something clicked on the wall beside Angel and the

basement was filled with light. He glanced over at Cordelia.

"Two light switches," she said, pointing. Then she pointed at the light in the middle of the kitchen ceiling. "One light. Ergo, the other switch does something else. I'm thinking, dark basement, maybe someone would want to turn the light on before they went down into it."

Angel nodded.

Cordelia folded her arms. "Since I found the switch, I'll stay up here and keep a lookout."

"Sure," Angel said, starting down the stairs.

"And remember: The demon doesn't like sunlight," Cordelia called after him.

"There's going to be a rather short supply of that down here," Wesley said.

Moving slow and balanced, keeping his body centered for instant movement if it became necessary, Angel went down into the basement. The area was at least twenty feet square, framed by poured concrete walls and filled with wooden shelves of canned goods and other living supplies.

"If you didn't know better," Wesley commented, "you'd swear that this was the home of a survivalist."

Angel walked through the rows of shelves. Nothing hid in the shadows, and nothing leaped out at him. It was kind of disappointing in a way, because action of any sort would have brought them some form of answers. He stared at the rows of canned food and bags of dry goods. Why would anyone hide here?

"Angel," Wesley called. "I've found something."

Crossing the room, Angel found Wesley peering at one of the walls behind a shelf that held baby clothing.

Wesley took the flashlight he'd carried into the sewer from his pocket and shone it onto the wall. "You don't see it until the light hits it just right," Wesley said.

He played the beam over the wall.

Angel saw the hairline separation on the wall that formed a rectangular shape. "That was good work. I missed it."

"Try this," Wesley suggested, handing him a big flat-edge screwdriver.

"You're bringing tools now?" Angel asked.

"There's a toolbox back here," Wesley said. "It appears our mysterious resident was something of a handyman."

"Makes sense." Angel slipped the end of the screwdriver into the crack. "If he didn't manage the upkeep on the house, repairmen would have to come inside."

"And they would have been a threat?"

"This guy would have thought they were." Angel pushed on the screwdriver handle. The screwdriver snapped.

"Hey," Cordelia yelled from upstairs. "Is everything all right down there?"

"It's fine," Wesley said. He turned his attention back to Angel. "You think he was just a demon in seclusion?"

"Cordelia said he lived here for over twenty years," Angel said, tossing the broken screwdriver aside. "I'd say that was pretty secluded."

"Do you think he kidnapped the child?" Wesley asked.

"Don't know." Angel stepped back from the crack. He drew his leg back and reached inside himself. The demon came, rampant and ready to be unleashed. Feeling his face change, feeling the extra burst of strength filling him, Angel drove his foot into the rectangle on the wall.

Concrete shattered. The sound echoed down the hidden tunnel behind the secret door as pieces of concrete thudded against the basement floor.

"Now that doesn't sound all right," Cordelia said.

"We found a secret door," Wesley explained.

Angel reached back for the flashlight, pointed it down the tunnel dug out of the earth and floored in plywood that had warped and shredded from years spent in dampness. Less than twenty feet ahead, he reached a large metal pipe.

"Sewer tunnel," Wesley said.

Angel played the flashlight beam over the section of pipe that lay on the plywood. Someone had used a cutting torch and gotten into the sewer a long time ago. The metal surfaces that had been cut were pitted and rusty.

"He had an escape route," Wesley said.

"It's probably how the demon got here and left," Angel agreed. He leaned into the sewer tunnel and played the flashlight beam around.

"Well," Wesley said, "we could attempt to follow the man and the demon."

"There's only two directions here," Angel said. "This tunnel leads to other tunnels. Not far away, it becomes a maze. We won't find them here."

"Then what do we do about the boy?"

"We keep looking. We haven't seen the rest of the house." Angel turned back and followed Wesley back into the basement.

Cordelia stood halfway down the rickety wooden stairs. "Demon?"

"Gone," Angel said. "He built an escape route into the sewer system."

"Everybody gets around in this town through sewers," she said. "But building your own access tunnel? That's preparation. Maybe before he got really ugly and creepy looking, he was a Boy Scout. Did you find his body?"

"No body," Wesley said.

"Maybe the demon ate him," Cordelia said. "Though, from the way he looked, I can predict indigestion."

"How did he look?" Angel asked, joining her on the stairs and heading up. His wounded side protested the climb and he tried to ease the pain, but it didn't work.

"Black hat," Cordelia said, drawing up one hand above her head and closing the fingers. "Really pointed. Like a witch's hat. Black cloak. Pretty much dressed all in black, actually."

A vague stirring of unease filled Angel. "What about his face?"

"Thin. Sallow. Mostly dead-looking." Cordelia frowned and gestured to her own face, mimicking growths on her neck and cheeks. "And he had these boil thingies. Like acne on steroids. He was a poster child for 'Give Me A Dream Makeover, Ricki.'"

"Did he give you a name?" Angel asked as they stepped into the kitchen.

"We didn't exactly get around to swapping four-one-one. There was that whole pursued-by-a-demon thing going on at the time. But I did give him one of our cards."

Angel walked back into the living room. "The boy's room is this way?"

"Yes." Cordelia pointed.

Chapter Sixteen

Stepping into the boy's bedroom, Angel took in the furniture and toys. It hurt to think that the boy was out there somewhere, alone and unprotected, waiting for him to come rescue him. *If that happens.* Angel knew that he didn't always get to save the people the Powers That Be sent him after. He tried to put the idea of failure out of his mind.

"You said there was something else important that happened in your visions," Angel said. "Something that you saw."

"Something that I almost saw," Cordelia replied. "In here." She walked into the adjoining room.

Angel followed her, staring around at all the canvases scattered around the room and the broken closet door hanging at a rakish angle from the top hinge.

"These are paintings," Wesley said as he joined them.

"Wow, you really nailed that one," Cordelia said.

Drawn by the style of the paintings, Angel knelt down, taking care with his injured side. He knew the style and the use of color, even though the images of detectives, frightened women, and spaceships weren't like anything he'd ever seen the artist do.

"You said the neighbor talked to you about the man that lived here," Angel said. "Did she give you his name?"

"She called him Gabe."

"Gabriel Dantz?" Angel asked. He started going through the paintings, keeping them organized as he searched for one that had to be among the ones in the room.

"She didn't give me a last name," Cordelia responded. "What are you doing?"

"Looking for a picture," Angel answered.

"What picture?"

Angel ignored her. If the picture wasn't among the others he didn't intend to tell Cordelia or Wesley any more than he had to.

They continued searching. Every now and again, Wesley would talk excitedly about a cover he'd found that he remembered. Then Cordelia found the stack of portraits of the boy from her vision.

"Oh, my God," Cordelia exclaimed. "This is him. This is the little boy from my visions."

Abandoning his own quest for a moment, Angel walked over to her. He looked at the paintings, studying the child's face. Gabriel had painted the child in glowing detail. The blond hair and blue eyes looked angelic.

This is some of Gabriel's best work, Angel thought as he touched the painting. Then he noticed the signature in the lower right corner. "Are you sure this is the boy?" he asked.

"Yes," Cordelia said. "This is him, Angel."

"Something's wrong," Angel told her.

"What do you mean?"

Angel tapped the signature. The painting had been signed Gabriel Dantz '82. "If this was the baby you saw, he's grown up by now."

A frown filled Cordelia's face. She shook her head. "This is him, Angel. This is the boy I saw in both visions. How can that be?"

"Maybe we're trying to rescue the grown-up version of the boy," Wesley suggested.

"Then why not show me him as a grown-up?" Cordelia asked.

"I'm sure I don't know," Wesley said.

Angel shook his head in frustration. "How many paintings are there of the boy?"

Cordelia counted the stack she'd found, moving each picture to verify that it was of the boy. Angel counted with her, noting that the pose the boy was in was always a seated one that showed him from the waist up. In some pictures the boy held stuffed animals and balls and toys.

"Twenty-six," Cordelia said. "That's a little obsessive, wouldn't you say? The guy must have been painting one a month."

"No," Angel said. "It was longer than that."

"The boy can't be over three or four in these pictures," Cordelia said. "The earliest ones are of him as a baby. That means they had to be painted in three years, four years tops."

Going back through the stack, Angel pulled out a portrait and handed it to Cordelia. "Look at the signature," he suggested.

Cordelia read the signature out loud. "Gabriel Dantz, 1973." She looked up at Angel. "That can't be right. The picture we found earlier was from 1982."

Angel slid another portrait free and handed it over. "And this one is signed in 1998."

Wesley joined them. "Let's spread the pictures out and put them in chronological order."

The work only took a few minutes for the three of them. Angel suggested they use the living room where they had more space.

"He did a painting a year," Cordelia said as they stared at the line of pictures.

Angel looked at the images of the child. In twenty-five years' worth of portraits, the boy aged only three or four years.

"And they're all in chronological order," Wesley said. "Notice how the boy only seems a little older in each picture."

"Yeah," Cordelia said. "Got that. But why?"

"Perhaps Gabriel Dantz was obsessive about this child," Wesley suggested.

Angel left the living room and returned to his search through the paintings. Cordelia and Wesley followed him.

"Those portraits weren't what you were looking for?" Cordelia asked.

"I didn't know about those portraits," Angel said, sifting canvases. The strong smell of paint assaulted his nostrils.

"Then what portrait are you looking for?" Cordelia asked.

As Angel shifted the last painting, a picture of a cowboy fighting with a knife against an Indian brave armed with a tomahawk while a voluptuous redhead with her dress nearly ripped away looked on, Angel stopped. He stared at the painting lying revealed on the pile, recognizing the woman there and still not expecting the amount of emotion that would slam into him when he saw it.

"Hey," Cordelia said, "that's Darla. I mean, it looks enough like her to be her. Is it?"

Angel took the portrait from the pile. "Yeah. It's Darla."

"Gabriel Dantz painted her?" Cordelia asked.

"Yeah."

"And you knew that?"

Angel nodded. He stared at Darla, remembering so many things that he did and did not want to. His whole life was like that. As a vampire, he'd gone all over the world, seen all kinds of things, and had experiences most people only dreamed of. If he'd been human, maybe he could have relished more of those memories. But in most of those days, he'd had the demon for company and those memories came tainted in blood, pain, and misery—hardly any of it his own. After that, guilt had been his constant companion, and he'd had immeasurable pain to carry with him in his travels.

In the picture, Darla stood in the shadows of a bridge over a canal. She held her hands behind her, looking young and innocent.

"Where is this?" Cordelia asked.

"Venice," Angel answered.

"I didn't know you'd been there."

"A long time ago."

Cordelia looked at him. "How long ago?"

"This painting," Angel said, "was done in 1815."

Wesley approached. "That's a museum piece. Even the frame is Old World craftsmanship."

"I know," Angel said.

"You're saying Gabriel Dantz painted this?" Cordelia asked.

"Gabriel did paint it," Angel said. "The bridge Darla is standing in front of is the *Ponte Dei Sospiri.*"

"*Ponte Dei Sospiri,*" Wesley said. "Wasn't that the bridge that condemned men were forced to walk from the Doge's Palace to the prison where they were executed?"

"Yes," Angel said. "*Ponte Dei Sospiri* translates to the Bridge of Sighs. It was named that because that was supposed to be the last sound made by condemned men crossing the bridge to meet their executioner."

"Lovely place for a portrait," Cordelia said.

"Darla thought it was a joke," Angel said.

"But if Gabriel painted this, that would make him over two hundred years old," Cordelia pointed out.

"He is," Angel said.

"He's a vampire?"

"He wasn't when I knew him," Angel said. *But there were other problems.* And now that he thought of the tentacled demon Cordelia described, there was even more ties between then and now than he'd at first believed.

"I thought Darla was a vampire then," Cordelia said. "She killed and raised you back in the 1740s."

"It was the 1750s," Angel said.

"Like another ten years tacked onto two hundred and fifty is going to matter," Cordelia said.

Angel ignored Cordelia's sarcasm, knowing she was worried about the mysterious boy in her visions. "Darla was a vampire then."

"But this portrait shows her standing out in broad daylight."

"Darla had Gabriel paint that in."

"Oh," Cordelia said. "Early CG work."

Angel studied the portrait, feeling the pull of memory.

"So you knew this portrait would be here?" Cordelia asked.

Shaking his head, Angel said, "No. Not until I recognized some of the artistic style in the paintings. Even then, I thought this painting had been lost. I was looking for another painting."

"Why did Gabriel Dantz paint Darla's portrait?"

"Because Darla told him she'd kill him if he didn't."

Cordelia nodded. "Oh. Well, you gotta love the incentive plan."

"Even then, it took Gabriel over a year to complete the portrait," Angel said.

"Why?"

"He got busy." Angel wasn't ready to tell them the other part of the story yet. He still hadn't quite believed it himself all those years ago, and didn't know if he was ready to embrace it now. If what he remembered was true, it threw the mystery of the boy into even stranger circumstances.

"You're calling him Gabriel," Cordelia said. "Did you guys get chummy?"

Angel shrugged. "I almost killed him. Darla kept me from doing it after she found out he was a painter. Even made me save him from guys who were going to kill him and cut his hand off. I got to know his name. Back in those days, there were a lot of people—" He stopped, conscious again of all the carnage he had wrought. "There were a lot of people whose name I never got."

"If Gabriel was painting the covers of paperback novels in the 1960s and 1970s," Wesley said, "then there's a chance he's still alive."

"He is," Angel said, standing and holding onto the picture of Darla. "You met him today. Gabriel Dantz was the man dressed in black."

"Then who is the boy?" Cordelia asked.

Angel shook his head. "I don't know. But we're going to find out."

Wesley stopped sorting through paintings and turned to Angel. "I think you need to have a look at this." He carefully extracted a painting and turned it toward Angel.

The portrait featured a tentacled demon in a birdcage roasting over the flaming pits of Hell. The pits of Hell were made more recognizable by the horned demons with tridents and spiked tails.

"That's her," Cordelia said. "That's the demon that was here earlier."

"Evidently Gabriel Dantz was on intimate terms with the demon," Wesley said.

More intimate than you know, Angel thought. "Do you recognize what kind of demon it is?"

Wesley studied the picture. "No."

"We need to find out," Angel said, "because I saw that demon in Switzerland nearly two hundred years ago."

Seventeen

Venice, 1815

"I say we kill him and be done with it," Angelus growled as he walked along the canal.

"I don't want him killed," Darla argued. "At least, not yet. He hasn't finished the painting."

"And I'm telling you he's not going to finish the damned painting," Angelus roared. Several passersby looked at him, then gave him a wide berth.

"Gabriel will finish the painting," Darla said. "He knows I'll break both his hands and crush his finger bones so he'll never paint again if he gets me angry."

"You aren't already angry?" Angelus asked. "Then why did you tear up that tavern only last week when you found out Gabriel still hadn't finished the damned painting?"

Darla smoothed her hair. "I was only disappointed."

Angelus looked around the darkened two- and three-story houses on both sides of the narrow canal. Even at this late hour there were a few people still up arguing in their homes or on their boats, moored on either side of the canal as well. Only a few lanterns aboard the boats or in the houses lit the night. Reflections of windows branded the dank canal water.

"You don't understand the importance of this portrait," Darla continued stubbornly. "I believe Gabriel is going to be a great artist. He's immensely talented."

"You and Hardesty are the only ones who seem to believe that," Angelus said sullenly. "Nobody else in this city is beating a path to Gabriel's door to have their likenesses painted. We're having to pay for his studio and everything he eats. An' have you seen how much that man eats? He's likely to eat us out of house an' home before long, he is."

"Hardesty seems convinced that Gabriel is a great artist," Darla said.

"So?" Angelus turned, his attention momentarily caught by a gondolier poling his craft almost silently down the canal.

"What do you know about Hardesty?" Darla asked.

"He's a rich man," Angelus said.

"What else?"

He growled and shook his head. "What else is there worth knowing?"

"He's a collector of art," Darla said. "An educated man and a man of breeding."

"Give me enough money," Angelus taunted, "an' I could say the same for myself." Ever since Vincent Hardesty had come to Venice four or five weeks ago, he'd been adamant about hiring Gabriel and taking him back to his estates in London. Angelus had been willing to let Gabriel go, after pocketing some of the gold Hardesty was willing to part with to secure a contract with the artist, but Darla had refused. As a result, Angelus had been stuck in Venice with her while she waited on the portrait that seemed would never be finished.

"They say that Hardesty is also quite versed in the black arts and demonic powers," Darla said. "A man who knows much about such things."

"Makes no difference to me," Angelus said, grinning. "For all his knowledge, then, he doesn't know we're vampires. An' we've been around him quite often these last few weeks. What with the way he's given to bumping into us at all times."

Darla was quiet for a moment. "I think Gabriel would have went with him."

"You should have let him," Angelus said.

"I told Gabriel if he did I'd track him down and take his hand myself. Both of them, in fact."

Angelus sighed. "You should have let him go. Then we could have quit this town and gone abroad again. I want to travel."

"And I want my portrait done by someone who is going to be an artist of standing," Darla said. "Because then I will be a work of art. Immortal."

"Keep away from stakes an' your pretty head on your shoulders," Angelus advised, "an' you're already immortal."

"This would be different."

Angelus cursed. "Give me old-fashioned immortality. Let me live forever and drink the blood of those I wish. I'll live happily."

"You," Darla said, "have limited vision." And she increased her stride so that she left him behind.

Men's voices shouting at each other captured Angelus's attention. He glanced up at the building ahead, realizing that it was his building and that the noise was coming from there.

A lantern arced out one of the windows and landed on the sidewalk in front of the building almost at Angelus's feet. The glass reservoir shattered, spilling oil all over the cobblestones. The flaming wick caught the oil on fire, igniting the pool of oil.

"Angelus!" Darla called, starting up the stairs to the room they kept.

Drawing the sword he wore at his hip, Angelus started up the stairs after Darla, cursing the fact that he'd been vexed enough at her to end up with part of a winehead. Still, he'd been in much worse shape before and survived battles.

He was a step behind Darla as she reached the rooms they rented. The windows were small and rectangular, not allowing much sunlight in during the day, but also not letting in much cooling breeze at night.

Gabriel Dantz's studio supplies—canvases, easel, and paints—took up most of the room in the living area. The bedrooms were in the back. Due to the fact that Angelus and Darla always moved quickly, they had no load of baggage that followed them around. The rooms were spartan, which suited Angelus fine.

Vincent Hardesty stood inside the doorway in the room. Five men fought with Gabriel.

"Stop!" Gabriel yelled. "Stop it, I say!" He punched

and kicked with all his strength and speed, causing the five men who grappled with him to curse vehemently.

"Be careful of his hands," Vincent Hardest ordered in a stern voice. "If any of you men break his hands, I'll have your heads broken in return."

Hardesty stood over six feet tall and was broad shouldered. Clad in an elegant burgundy suit with a ruffled white shirt, he was a striking figure. He wore a Vandyke beard, dark brown with only a few gray strands that matched the ponytail he wore.

"What the hell do you think you're doing?" Darla shouted as she entered the room. She grabbed one of the men struggling with Gabriel and threw him toward a shuttered window.

Screaming, the man burst through the closed shutters and sailed into the canal only a few feet from the sidewalk. Angelus knew that only because the man's scream cut off abruptly at the same time as a splash instead of a splat.

Angelus engaged one of the men with his sword. Hesitating, he didn't see his opponent lift a knife from a boot in time to stop it from plunging through his chest. Hurting, Angelus glanced down at the blade embedded in his chest. Smiling despite the fiery pain that filled him, he freed the demon inside himself, feeling his face change, then he yanked the knife from his chest. With a move too quick for the human eye to follow, Angelus slammed the knife into his opponent's thigh.

Screaming, grievously wounded but not mortally so, the man collapsed and grabbed his leg.

"Damned vampires," Hardesty said. He twisted the

cane he held and drew forth the cunning blade hidden inside.

Darla hit another man, knocking him off his feet and into the wall behind him. His skull hit the wall hard and he was unconscious by the time he hit the floor.

The other two men backed away from Darla and Angelus. Fear twitched on their faces. As soon as they felt safe enough, they turned and ran from the flat.

"Cowards!" Hardesty roared after them. "Come back and fight, you curs!"

Still holding his sword and wearing his demon's face, Angelus approached Hardesty. The man swiped at Angelus's midsection, but Angelus easily turned the blade.

"What are you doing here?" Angelus demanded.

"They were after Gabriel," Darla said.

Hardesty attacked Angelus with the sword cane.

Parrying and riposting with the lightning speed allowed him while the demon was free within him, Angelus beat down Hardesty's offense, then his defense, and finally succeeded in knocking the sword cane from the man's grip.

Laying the tip of his sword blade against the man's Adam's apple, Angelus leaned forward and stared into Hardesty's eyes. "Tell me the truth, Hardesty, or I'll gut you right here and just disappear come morning to let the magistrate's lackeys deal with your murder." He pricked the man's neck with the sharp blade. Hunger flared within Angelus as he watched the lone drop of blood skate down the man's neck.

For a moment, it looked as though Hardesty was going to put up more resistance. Then Angelus watched the fight and bravado drain out of the man's eyes.

"Because Gabriel Dantz has the power," Hardesty said.

"What power?"

"It's an old power. One that came about when the demons first started getting forced from this world. In the old texts I've found, it's called *Weid Deus*, which translates loosely into 'Idea of God,' or 'Godlike Idea.'"

"What can it do?"

"With it, he can paint reality," Hardesty whispered hoarsely. Insane lights danced in his pale green eyes. "Only a few artists are blessed with such a gift. But only once, and only when a burning fever comes over them. Most never even know what it is. They have to be carefully supervised so they don't waste the powers. The last known such occurrence of a painter having this ability was nearly two hundred years ago. It was a Russian monk who painted a field of flowers in the harshest winter Siberia ever knew. They didn't last an hour, and hardly anyone believes the story." He paused. "Don't you see? Without proper guidance, without knowing that the power is upon him or her, an artist can introduce anything to this world. But if they knew, if the power could be better controlled, can you imagine the kind of wealth and power you can control? Nations—no, the whole world—can be made to do what you want."

"I've never heard of such a thing," Darla said. "And what the hell would you do with the whole world anyway? Sounds like too much work to me."

"He's a madman," Gabriel accused.

"Listen to me," Hardesty said. "He has the power. You've got to believe that. I know what I'm talking about.

I don't have to be greedy, and you don't have to be stupid."

Angelus pressed the sword more firmly against the man's throat.

"Killing me," Hardesty whispered, not risking speaking in a full voice in case it would serve to get him cut, "would be the stupidest thing you could do." He swallowed gently. "You're not a stupid man, Angelus. You just don't know what you have."

"I'm going to check my painting," Darla announced.

"Please," Hardesty implored. "Please listen to me, Angelus. The diviners I hired, demons I bound to my service a long time ago, have sought out the information I've looked for all my life. They tracked the omens to Gabriel Dantz."

"He's nothing," Angelus said. "He's an artist that can't even deliver a painting in a short time." He snorted with derision. "How the hell do you expect him to paint reality?"

"Because he is destined," Hardesty said. "The power falls to individuals who have the potential to do good or evil in the world. It's one of the chaotic moments brought about by the forced exile of many of the demon races mankind chased from this world. Mankind was cursed with this power, not given it gladly out of the hearts. The Powers That Be stood against such a thing because it can affect the balance between good and evil that is loose in this world. But it was given to mankind as a cruel joke. Artists are given the power to alter reality, or to create new ones, or any number of other things that they can think of."

Gabriel leaned against the wall and dabbed at his head wound with a handkerchief. His gray eyes held Angelus's gaze for only an instant, then turned away so quickly that Angelus knew Gabriel was hiding something.

For a moment, Angelus almost wavered in his certainty. Could Gabriel have power like Hardesty described? Since becoming a vampire and stepping into the world of demons and seeing all the things that were out there to be seen, Angelus had come to realize that there was much he didn't know. *Hadn't known,* he corrected himself, because he'd learned a lot since leaving his native Galway, Ireland.

But every now and then he still bumped into arcane things and demons he'd never met before. It was enough to keep him the least bit humbled.

If Gabriel hadn't acted so guilty, perhaps Angelus would have believed it was all a madman's folly.

Without warning, Darla screamed and cursed. She came back into the room, livid with rage. "He painted another woman." She faced Gabriel, who cringed against the wall, shielding his face with his arms.

"I'm sorry," Gabriel said. "The need came upon me tonight. I couldn't stop myself."

"I want my portrait finished," Darla threatened.

"I'm working on it," Gabriel promised.

Desperation tightened the artist's voice, but something else was in there as well. Angelus heard it, but he didn't know what it was. Hardesty shifted in Angelus's grip, drawing his attention again.

"I must see the painting," Hardesty said. "Please. If he has already squandered his power, then there is nothing we can do." He paused. "You must see it, too."

Angelus kept Hardesty pinned against the wall. Glancing over his shoulder, Angelus told Gabriel, "Go get the painting."

Reluctantly and with some hesitation, Gabriel went into the other room and returned carrying a canvas. He handled it gently, and the wet gleam of the paints showed that the picture had not yet dried.

The picture was of a woman sitting on a fallen tree in a shadowed swampland. She had thick black hair and a generously curved figure barely hidden by the scrap of cloth wound over her loins. Her breasts were bare, but her arms folded in front of her hid them from view. She looked savage, feral, and had an intensity about her that was undeniable.

The work didn't seem to be as polished as Gabriel's other work, or as polished as the job he was doing on Darla's portrait. Angelus saw nothing special about it except for the titillation it provided. And, possibly, the arrogance of the woman. Breaking the arrogance of such a creature was a joy, Angelus had learned over his years.

"No," Hardesty gasped as he stared at the picture. He sagged against the wall, no longer fighting Angelus's grip on him. He turned his attention to Gabriel. "All that power at your hands, the power to change the world in your grasp, and all you could think of was your own carnal lusts?"

Angelus was starting to get a headache from too much wine and too much stress. He wanted everything over with, and an end to the insanity he was dealing with now. Gabriel's nearly naked jungle savage was almost laughable—if he'd been in any mood to be entertained.

"I've had enough," Angelus said. He glared at Hardesty. "How do you know if he's already used up this special ability you say he was supposed to receive?"

"Because I can see the magic in that painting," Hardesty answered. "When I summoned the demons to give me more information about the power, I also had them change my eyes. I can see the magic in that painting."

Angelus glanced at Darla, who was still frowning angrily at the nearly nude woman in the swampland.

"Get him out of here," Darla ordered.

"Alive or dead?" Angelus asked.

"Alive," Darla said. "Someone might come looking for him."

"Fine." Angelus pulled Hardesty toward the window Darla had thrown the first attacker through.

"You're a fool," Hardesty accused Gabriel. "You had so much in your hands, and you squandered it because you wouldn't listen to me."

Angelus held the man by the window. "Did you tell him he was going to have all that power?" In a way, even though he didn't believe any of what Hardesty had told him, it was still entertaining to taunt the man because he did believe it.

"No," Gabriel said. "He only told me he wanted to hire me to paint something for him."

"What?" Angelus asked.

"A portrait of himself," Gabriel said, "as emperor of the world. As I told you, he's a madman."

Angelus pulled Hardesty close again, almost nose to nose with the man. "Don't come around me again. Next time, I won't be afraid to make a mess of you. I've got a trail of bodies littered after me all through Europe." He studied the man. "Do you understand me?"

Hardesty nodded, all of the fight gone out of him now. He gazed past Angel at the canvas with the nearly naked woman on it.

Without another word, Angelus tossed the man through the window. Hardesty yelled as he arced through the night, no longer as ambivalent about things as he'd been. His yell was cut off in mid-scream as he struck the canal water and sank like a stone.

Leaning out the window, Angelus watched as Hardesty surfaced. Then Angelus heaved the wounded man and the unconscious one through the window as well. They ended up in the canal too, and the one Darla had knocked out never resurfaced.

Later that night, while lying in bed in Darla's embrace, Angelus woke. He still felt the effects of all the wine he'd consumed in the rented apartments trying to calm Darla down. Gabriel had sat in the front room listening to Darla rant and rave while he covertly mooned over his new portrait. Angelus had felt certain that if Darla had caught Gabriel rolling a calf-eye at the painting she'd have killed him on the spot. He was certain the artist was convinced of it too.

Angelus had spent the time trying to persuade Darla it was time to kill the artist. Perhaps, had Gabriel gotten nothing done on her portrait that day while they were gone, she might have killed him and drank his blood and raised him later, then staked him through the heart to make things final. She'd done that before to others.

But the little bit of work Gabriel had done on her portrait had somehow been enough to satisfy her, and Angel resigned himself to a longer stay in Venice.

Rising from the bed, gently disentangling himself from Darla, Angelus padded naked through the apartments.

He still didn't know what had awoken him. Lantern light in the living room area let him know Gabriel was still up, and the gray dawn starting to form outside the heavily draped windows well out of reach of the bed, let him know it was early morning. Angelus figured the artist was working on Darla's picture, wanting desperately to get back into her good graces.

But Angelus heard Gabriel talking, urging someone to join him.

"Please," Gabriel said. "It's only a short distance. You'll like it here. It's nothing like what you're used to. We can be together."

Easing the door open, Angelus peered into the living room. He saw Gabriel standing in front of his new portrait of the feral woman. He looked shy and expectant, and he talked as though the picture listened, pleading with the woman in it to join him.

Just as Angelus was about to interrupt the artist and jeer at him, the woman on the canvas moved and the picture looked even more three-dimensional. Her arms came away from her breasts, leaving no doubt that she was nude and nubile.

In the next minute, she stretched an arm out from the canvas.

Watching in stunned disbelief, Angelus saw Gabriel take the woman's hand and pull her from the canvas. As she left the painting, she grew into a full-sized woman. She stood before Gabriel and threw her arms around him. The wispy white cloth around her bronzed loins looked at though it was going to fall off at any moment, but somehow stayed in place.

Gabriel held her tightly and kissed her. She kissed him back and they laughed together. Then the woman looked over at Angelus as if she'd known all along that he was there. She walked toward him, her hips rolling with the movement, and stopped in front of him.

Over her shoulder, Gabriel looked terrified. "Stay away from him," the artist said.

"It will be all right," the woman said. "I can handle myself."

"You don't know him. You don't know the evil he's capable of."

"You're holding Gabriel captive, aren't you?" the woman asked Angelus.

Angelus didn't say anything. He was beginning to believe he was dreaming, was still in fact asleep in Darla's arms but just didn't know it.

The woman cocked her head and looked at him.

The hard look in her eyes threw fear into Angelus, something that he hadn't truly felt in a very long time. He started to move.

"And you're not human either, are you?" The woman smiled. "Too bad. You're a pretty one. You would have made a good addition."

Before Angelus could get it through his wine-soaked head to ask the woman what he would make a good addition to, she lifted her hand like she was blowing him a kiss. Instead, sapphire powder gusted from her hand. The powder covered his face, burned into his eyes and his nose and lips. Then the world swirled and turned black.

Chapter Eighteen

"What happened to Gabriel and the woman?" Cordelia asked when Angel stopped speaking. "I mean, after she blew that powder into your face?"

"I woke up the next morning on the floor," Angel replied, looking at the portrait he'd uncovered. "Gabriel, the woman, and Darla's portrait were gone. He left a note for Darla that he would finish the portrait soon and get it back to her. He knew we wouldn't stay in Venice, so he named an art gallery in France he'd done business with where she could pick the portrait up when he was finished."

Cordelia stared at all the portraits and paintings in the room. "If Gabriel had Darla's picture here, then she must have never gotten it."

"She got it," Angel said. He searched the room and found a protective casing for the portrait. "We caught up to Gabriel in Geneva.

"It was in June of 1816," Angel said. "Not quite two hundred years ago. Darla and I didn't just go looking for Gabriel. In fact, I didn't look at all. I didn't care."

"But weren't you curious about Hardesty's claim that Gabriel could paint reality?" Wesley asked.

"Yeah," Angel said. "I checked into that. Turns out Hardesty was right about that. And it is called *Weid Deus*, one of the oldest magicks learned by mankind. Demons can't work something like *Weid Deus*. It's too formless and abstract, too chaotic. At least, that's what I was told."

"But Angel," Cordelia said, "having the ability to paint a new reality, that's just so . . . so . . . so *big*."

"It was a blessing and a curse," Angel said. "And that just how the Old Powers wanted it to be. In those days, mankind was becoming too powerful too quickly, rewriting reality on a daily basis. They were shoving the demons out of this world, exterminating them and banishing them to other worlds. The Old Powers wanted some kind of checks and balances system. There are other things they allowed mankind to have; things that could empower mankind, or destroy it. Like the practice of science and witchcraft. In some people, those powers manifest very strongly. Learning power like that, it's like taking a demon into yourself." He paused. "Like becoming a vampire. There are parts of the becoming that are just too much to resist if you take away compassion and responsibility."

"What happened in Geneva?" Wesley asked.

"While we were in France checking in at the art gallery for Darla's portrait—"

"Still wasn't finished?" Cordelia asked.

Angel shook his head. "While we were there, Darla spoke with the gallery owner and asked him about Gabriel."

"I can imagine how that conversation went," Cordelia said.

Angel shrugged. "He lived. The gallery owner told us Gabriel was spending time with George Gordon Noel Byron in Geneva."

Wesley's eyebrows shot up. "You told us that in the office earlier. When you suggested we investigate Gabriel Dantz. I still can't believe you knew Lord Byron and you've never mentioned it."

Angel shrugged. "We met a few times."

"He was the most famous of the English Romantic Poets," Wesley said. "And as a satirist and journal keeper, Lord Byron was legendary."

"He was a womanizer and a party guy," Angel said. "Good for a few drinks and a few laughs."

Wesley looked crestfallen.

Angel ignored that. In his experience of the last two hundred fifty years, famous people weren't often much more than regular people who had made more of the opportunities that came their way or had a chance to explore more avenues. "George rented a place called Villa Diodati by Lake Leman to spend the summer. He invited his doctor, John Polidori, and Mary Wollstonecraft and Percy Shelley. Darla and I crashed the party looking for Gabriel, but we arrived before Gabriel did. George asked us to stay."

Sudden understanding showed on Wesley's face. "Gabriel was at Villa Diodati that infamous summer."

"What infamous summer?" Cordelia asked.

"The weekend when Lord Byron suggested all of the guests write ghost stories to entertain each other."

"All of the writing guests," Angel corrected. "George didn't ask Darla or me to write anything, although we told some stories that Polidori later used in *The Vampyre*. George thought they were great fun." He looked at Wesley and Cordelia, who gazed at him in disbelief. "Maybe you had to be there."

"This was the weekend that Mary Shelley wrote *Frankenstein*?" Cordelia asked.

"Conceptualized it, actually," Wesley said. "She wrote the book later."

"Okay," Cordelia said. "Done with *Jeopardy!* Did Darla get her painting while she was there?"

"Yes," Angel replied. There were complications, though, and he didn't feel like going into them at the moment. "Gabriel arrived in two days and had the painting with him. He had just finished it. That's probably the only thing that kept Darla from killing him. That, and the fact that George wouldn't have liked it much. Darla took the painting and later stashed it in some of the places we used to keep things we wanted. I guess she never made it back there and at some point Gabriel found the portrait again."

"Then the painting you were actually looking for is the one that contained the woman Gabriel drew under the influence of the *Weid Deus* power?" Wesley asked.

Angel nodded.

"After he'd taken the woman—his apparent lover— from the painting," Wesley asked, "why would he keep it?"

"Because she lived in the painting," Angel replied. "In the world that the painting featured. And here. As it turned out, she couldn't stay here long because exposure here was harmful to her."

"So she commuted?" Cordelia asked.

Angel considered the comparison. "Yeah."

"Through the painting?"

"Right."

"So what Gabriel actually painted was a gateway to a demon dimension," Wesley said.

"Yes." Angel hadn't discovered that until the night in Geneva. "But it could only be used by her. Gabriel couldn't go there to meet her, and she couldn't bring anyone from there."

"She only came here to visit."

"And to kill and to maim and to torture," Angel added. "She also had this whole flesh-absorption routine she had to go through to manifest in this world."

"Somehow," Cordelia said, "I knew we'd be getting to that part."

"Gabriel loved her," Angel said.

"Well, he did create her," Cordelia reminded. "I knew a lot of guys back in high school, and a lot of them in L.A. that could so totally get into that whole idea. Kind of like Internet relationships only you can pull someone through a screen every now and again."

"But he didn't create her," Wesley said. "He only thought he did."

"I don't know if he ever reached a point where he didn't think he'd created her," Angel said.

"But he knew that she hurt people?" Wesley asked.

"Gabriel knew that she hurt people and killed them," Angel answered. "He excused her from it, and he thought he could save her from that flaw. He blamed himself for her feral side, thinking he'd made mistakes in the painting."

"How did he choose her?" Wesley asked.

Angel shook his head. "Back then I never thought to ask. I didn't care. And I haven't much thought about Gabriel and his demon, or even Darla's portrait, since then."

A cell phone shrilled, sounding out of place in the silence of the house.

Wesley reached into his pocket and answered, "Angel Investigations. Wyndham-Pryce speaking. Hello, Dale. Yes, Angel and I did deliver the blackmail money. Well . . . no, actually. No. No. We didn't see the blackmailer." He paused, straightening his spine. "No, Mr. Foster, I most emphatically assure you that litigation is not an avenue I wish to explore in our involvement with you. I understand that Nova Studios does have a well-staffed legal team and doesn't mind trotting them out. Results within forty-eight hours? Under the circumstances, I couldn't guarantee anything in less than a week.

"No," Wesley assured the man. "I wouldn't want our agency's reputation tarnished. Yes, I understand there is a lot of work that can be done in this city by a reputable investigations and security firm. Of course I'd like to see Angel Investigations be that firm. Results in twenty-four hours?"

"We're supposed to have something done for them in twenty-four hours?" Cordelia asked.

Wesley waved her off. "No, twenty-four hours will be fine. You have my word on it."

The cell phone clicked dead.

Wesley glanced at Angel. "I'm sorry. I thought solving Nova Studios' problems with *Corner of the Eye* would necessitate some work on our end, but I did not foresee the repercussions possible out of this. Dale—Mr. Foster—tells me that the board he reports to believes that *we* may be engineering the blackmail."

"All the dirty secrets they have," Cordelia exploded, "and they think all we'd ask for is a lousy fifty thousand dollars?"

"There is the matter of the newest attempt to collect blackmail from Nova Studios," Wesley said.

"What new attempt?" Cordelia asked.

"Apparently, another male voice called Mr. Foster and threatened to go to the media with the same information we paid off for on the first delivery."

"Another male voice?" Angel repeated.

"Yes. Very similar to the first, according to Mr. Foster."

"What did he want?"

"Another fifty thousand dollars. Mr. Foster is giving us twenty-four hours to come up with answers for him or he's going to swear out a complaint to the LAPD against Angel Investigations. The studio will also be seeking to assess liability damages and sue us in civil court."

"Ewwww," Cordelia said. "Not good."

"No." Wesley sighed. "Even if we are eventually proven innocent of blackmail, the court costs and lawyers' fees spent fighting such legal action could be staggering."

"Okay."

Wesley blinked at him. "Okay?"

"I'll go get the blackmailer and make him turn over the documents he's using to blackmail Nova Studios with," Angel said.

"You'll get the blackmailer?"

"Yeah," Angel said. "Seems the easiest way."

"You know who it is?" Cordelia asked.

"I think so," Angel said, trying to lay out the best course of action on all fronts. "While I'm doing that, I need you guys to find out what kind of demon that is." He pointed at the painting of the demon in a birdcage. "You've got the keys to the car. Use it. I'll stick with the sewers."

"Won't you need backup?" Wesley asked.

Angel briefly considered it. "No. It may take me a while to run him down and I'd rather have you guys finding out whatever you can about that demon. I think that Gabriel tried to paint reality again and put the demon into a cage."

"If Gabriel's human," Cordelia asked, "how is it he's lived over two hundred years? Not that he's really looking all that healthy because of it."

"I don't know," Angel said. "When we find him, we'll ask him."

"You think he's the blackmailer," Cordelia said. "That's why you're going after him."

Angel shook his head. "No. I'm going to catch the blackmailer while you guys work on catching Gabriel and his demon." He turned and left them there, walking through the living room past the organized rows of the young boy featured in the portraits. All the players were in motion, but it remained to be seen how the pieces fit together.

"You look bored."

Turning, somewhat startled by the sound of Faroe Burke's voice so close to him, Gunn gazed down at the artist. Despite the hours that had passed, she still looked energized and ready to go. After spending the last night fleeing from demons, then having the meeting at the hotel, Gunn felt like toast. He'd wanted Cordy to go to the opening—it was more her scene—but as Vision Girl, her presence was required alongside Angel and Wes.

"No," Gunn told her. "I'm fine."

Crossing her arms, Faroe gave him a disbelieving glance. "I should call the police," she said.

"Is it against the law to come to an art gallery opening?" Gunn countered.

"There are laws against stalking."

"I'm not stalking you."

"You've been here all day," Faroe said.

"The opening has gone on all day," Gunn said.

Faroe turned back to the crowd. "You're telling me. When my agent told me they wanted to do the opening in a two-tier media event, I didn't know it would go on this long."

"He didn't give you an itinerary?"

"Yes." Faroe frowned. "But those time frames didn't look this long on paper."

"Maybe it's the crowd," Gunn suggested. The caterers cycled through the new opening attendees. Faroe had given her second speech of the day nearly an hour ago, then been consumed by the media personnel in a second wave.

"Maybe," she said.

"At least the crowd is giving you a breather at the moment."

"They're dealing with Lenny," Faroe said. "He's in his element."

Gunn followed her gaze and spotted the agent at the center of a large crowd. "Busy guy."

"I know. I don't see how he does it."

"Does he know about the demons from last night?" Gunn asked. He watched as the confidence on her face cracked a little.

"Lenny doesn't believe in demons."

"But you do," Gunn said.

Faroe turned to him and her eyes glistened with hardness. "Maybe it was a mistake coming to talk to you." She turned to walk away.

"If you'd thought it was a mistake," Gunn told her in a quiet voice that didn't carry, "you wouldn't have come over here in the first place."

Turning to him, Faroe regarded him silently for a time. "You think you know me?"

Gunn held the eye contact for a moment. "No, I don't know you. But I know what you're about."

"You think so?"

"I think," Gunn said, "that you're about as comfortable in this place as I am."

"You don't look comfortable," Faroe challenged. "I do."

"That's one difference between us," Gunn admitted.

"And there are a lot of other people here who weren't exactly born with a silver spoon in his or her mouth."

"Probably ," Gunn agreed. "But how many of them do you think grew up on the streets with a part-time gambler for a father?"

Faroe walked back to Gunn so quickly he thought she was going to hit him. He regretted his words somewhat, but the hours of sitting and waiting, of watching over her and wondering if there was going to be a visit from the Wolfram & Hart people or Vincent Hardesty, were beginning to tell on him.

"You got a hard way about you, Gunn," she said. Her nostrils flared in anger.

"It gets me by," Gunn replied. "You see, I play my cards face-up on the table. I know you're in danger from someone, and you know it too. You just won't admit it."

"Those demons last night," Faroe said, "that was just a fluke. They were just hitting places to rob. Looking for quick cash."

"Yeah," Gunn said. "Wally's Gym is well known for all the quick cash that walks into and out of that place."

Faroe hesitated for a moment, her eye contact not quite so certain. "They read about me in the paper."

"The paper and television interviews didn't mention where you lived. I know. I read them and I watched them last night."

"Wally knew who I was."

A flicker of anger passed through Gunn. "Wally's as honest as the day is long. He wouldn't tell anybody like those demons where you were."

"Then how did they get there?"

Gunn looked pointedly at her agent. "One guy I know has your number and your address."

Shaking her head, Faroe said, "Lenny wouldn't do something like that."

"What did the Wolfram and Hart guy want earlier?"

"I don't know. Lenny just told me there was some kind of deal working. This second opening we're doing tonight? Everything auctioned off during this time has a percentage that goes into the programs the city has to keep kids off drugs and off the streets. Lenny told me Wolfram and Hart has agreed to rep me and find a producer who will help me get more attention for that."

"You do that for the kids or for the publicity?" Gunn asked.

Faroe did slap at him then.

Gunn never flinched, just reached up and caught her hand. The movements were so quick that no one around them even noticed.

"No," Gunn said calmly. "I didn't think so." He locked eyes with her. "See? That's what I'm saying. You and me, we've walked the same streets of this city. We've been scared of the same shadows. Only now I fight some of those shadows and you're working to help kids come out of them."

"I don't trust guys off the street," Faroe told him. "They lie. They cheat. They steal."

"I never have," Gunn said. "I never will."

Faroe's dark brown eyes searched his. "Do you know how hard today has been? How scared I've been? Not just from waiting for more of last night to happen again today, but from all these people—" Her voice broke. "—from all these people finding out what a fake I am?"

Gunn felt the trembling in her hand then. "Faroe

Burke," he said in a low voice, "you're no fake. I get the impression you're one of the realest women I've met."

"I'm a street kid," she told him, "doing television interviews and potentially making thousands of dollars for the same thing that used to get me arrested. How weird is that?"

"I'm going to give that an eight," Gunn said. "It has a good beat and I can dance to it."

For a moment she just stared at him, then she started laughing and wiping the tears from her eyes. Her voice was a hoarse whisper when she spoke again. "Tell me. What would you have done if a demon had broken in here today? Would you have tried to save me?"

Gunn answered without hesitation. "Yes."

"Why?"

"It's what I do."

Glancing over her shoulder, Faroe checked on her agent. The man was still deep in the middle of a crowd, talking animatedly.

"He's going to be there for awhile," Gunn said. "After all, he's in his element."

She smiled at him.

"In the meantime, I was thinking we could slip away for a few minutes," Gunn said. "I followed you back to the reception room at lunch. With all the talking, you hardly touched your salad. I figure you're probably hungry by now. Did I mention that I'm a detective? Well, I detected a greasy spoon up the block where you can get a thick cheeseburger and a mountain of fries. Probably serve diet soda there so you don't have to come back all full and guilt-ridden. And since you're still waiting for your first million to roll in, I'll spring for it."

"I don't know. Lenny might—"

"Lenny," Gunn said, "might let you starve."

"You're right. I think everybody here is done with me for awhile. Lenny's working out appearance dates and details like that. He'll probably be so busy he won't even know I'm gone."

"Okay then." Gunn kept hold of her hand, then guided her arm under his like he'd been doing it forever. Together, they ducked out of the gallery and headed for the restaurant.

Chapter Nineteen

"Who knew there were so many flesh-eating demons?" Cordelia asked as she flipped through the latest musty tome of the stack piled on the desk where she and Wesley worked.

"At one point," Wesley said, removing his glasses and rubbing his eyes tiredly, "I did. At least, I knew all the ones that the Watchers' Council knew about. Then more demons started showing up with the same gruesome predilection, and others changed their dietary habits after they got among humans."

Seated at the desk in the cavernous hotel, their voices sounded loud even when they spoke softly.

Fatigue pulled at Cordelia's eyelids, threatening to close them. She shook herself back to wakefulness, then reached for the Starbucks cup in front of her. When she picked it up, she noticed that it was empty.

"I've got a fresh pot of tea in the back," Wesley offered.

"No thanks."

"Maybe you should consider getting some sleep."

"We never sleep," Cordelia said. "It kind of gets in the way of us helping the helpless. Hey, that actually sounds kind of good to add to our mission statement."

Wesley smiled, but it wasn't one of the genuine smiles that Cordelia was used to seeing out of him these days. At least, on days when it didn't seem like the whole world might end if Angel didn't come up with another miracle.

"Don't worry," Cordelia said.

"I'm not worried," Wesley replied.

"Yes you are. I can see those little worry lines across your forehead."

Wesley flipped more pages in the book he searched through. "If you must know, I'm concerned for the welfare of this agency. Not for myself."

"Oh, really?" Cordelia asked. "Planning on taking up the old rogue demon-hunter riding leathers again if things don't work out?"

Wesley frowned. "Actually, I would detest that."

"You've gotten addicted to the whole three-square-meals-a-day thing, haven't you?"

"The rogue demon-hunter business didn't pay that well, I have to admit," Wesley said. "But I worry more that I might have inadvertently harmed Angel's chances for earning his own redemption by taking this task on."

"Wesley, look. Angel's not here," Cordelia said. "Ergo, he's out solving the case. You see, Angel's not going to let you screw up things so badly that he can't fix them."

"That's supposed to make me feel better?"

"Yes."

Wesley hesitated for a moment, then nodded. "Okay, I can see that."

"Besides, what's a little legal trouble when potentially the fate of the whole world might be at stake? And no one can claim any of that is your responsibility."

"That's true." Wesley looked at her and smiled a little. "You know, you have an amazing way of putting things into perspective."

"It's my mutant ability," Cordelia said. "However, I also have to point out that Angel hasn't yet made his return or called in, which means that the case has not yet been solved. But that only translates to: We just have to wait a little longer." She turned her attention back to the book, tried the empty Starbucks cup again, then stood up. "I've got to get more coffee or I'm not going to make it. Do you want anything?"

"No, thank you."

Cordelia got a light jacket and started to head for the door when the phone rang. She smiled at Wesley and pointed to the phone. "That's probably Angel now, calling to let us know that the case is solved and he has the blackmailer." She scooped up the handset. "Angel Investigations. We never sleep and we help the helpless."

"Cordy," Gunn said, "I've only got a minute."

"Art show keeping you busy?" Cordelia asked.

"No. My cheeseburger's on its way to the table and I want to eat it while it's hot."

"They serve cheeseburgers at art galleries now?" Cordelia thought that food with her Starbucks coffee would complement each other. She hadn't eaten since morning with all the running around they'd been doing. And the demon researching that had been going on.

"No," Gunn said. "They've still got those cheese things and

the finger sandwiches. You'd have to eat your weight in them to fill up. Believe me, I've tried. Listen, this is the first chance I had to make a private call. While I was at the gallery today, I ran into a Wolfram and Hart attorney. He's repping a guy who wants to set up a deal with Faroe Burke and her agent.

"This lawyer I talked to gave me the name of the guy who wanted to meet with Faroe's agent," Gunn continued. "I figured maybe you could check him out on the Internet."

Cordelia grabbed a pad and pencil. "What's the name?"

"Vincent Hardesty. I don't know what he does."

Cordelia stared at the name she'd written. "FYI? Vincent Hardesty is very bad news. He's been around a couple hundred years. Angel faced him back in Venice in 1815. I'm telling you now from experience, anybody that's been around that long: Really Bad News. He's associated with the whole *Weid Deus* legend."

"And that is?"

"Painters who can paint new realities. Only they don't know they have that ability until they do it." Cordelia underlined Vincent Hardesty's name. *Why didn't he change it?* Then she wrote *egotistical* under Hardesty's name and underlined that as well. "Don't worry. We'll brief you on the whole *Weid Deus* thing when we see you."

"Cheeseburgers?" Wesley said when she hung up the phone. "You know, that actually sounds good."

"I can bring something back," Cordelia said.

"Actually," Wesley said, "why don't I bring them back? You can poke around on the Internet and find out information on Vincent Hardesty."

"You're busy looking for the demon. I think that's a number one priority here."

Wesley laid the book he was holding down on the desktop and pushed it toward her. "I found the demon."

Cordelia looked at the page, seeing a double of the one that was on the portrait and that she had seen in Gabriel Dantz's house. "A Tharrolf demon?"

"Yes, and I should have thought of it," Wesley admitted. "They're not very common, but the Watchers' Council and slayers in the past have encountered them. It's thought that H. P. Lovecraft must have learned of them at some point, because many of his mythos were based on creatures similar to the Tharrolves."

"Good," Cordelia said. "Now we know how to kill it."

Wesley cleaned his glasses and gazed at the demon. "Unfortunately, no. You see, the Tharrolf demon is almost indestructible while on this plane of existence. Their natures only allow them to be killed in their home plane."

Cordelia considered that. "So it's probably not a good idea to let one loose in our world."

"No," Wesley agreed. "Tharrolves have the ability to look human, usually female, but they can't exist in our world long. Something about the rays from a yellow sun."

"Ah, reverse Superman. I suppose they live on a planet with a red sun."

"According to legend, they live on a plane that has a blue sun."

Cordelia read the entry. "They have to consume human flesh to maintain corporeal existence." She looked at the next picture. The drawing showed the squid-looking, tentacled demon with human arms and legs sticking out of it, obviously in the middle of digesting them.

"The demons absorb their victims," Wesley said. "They give off an acid that breaks down human flesh and allows them to suck what's left through the membrane of their skin. However, they have to do this often to stay here because even at night the reflected yellow sunlight from the moon breaks their bodies down."

Reducing them to human stew? Ewww, Cordelia thought. She closed the book. "I still want that cheeseburger."

"With fries?" Wesley asked.

Cordelia hesitated. "No."

Wesley looked at her, then said, "I'll bet that the restaurant serves a big order with their cheeseburgers to go. If you want, you can have a few of mine."

"Thanks," Cordelia said, and turned her attention to the computer. She typed in Vincent Hardesty's name and started searching.

Standing in the shadows at the back bar in Caritas, the karaoke bar run by the Host, Angel watched the crowd and listened to Lorne finish off a B. J. Thomas medley, ending with "(Hey Won't You Play) Another Somebody Done Somebody Wrong Song." Angel joined in the applause as Lorne took a bow.

"Thank you, ladies and gentlemen," Lorne said, standing in the baby spotlight in his silver glittering jacket and matching pants. His green face clashed with the suit, but it went well with the horns that jutted up from his forehead.

The Host introduced the next singer and summoned a round of applause, then he stepped out of the baby spotlight and joined Angel at the bar.

"Ah, you're a man on a mission, I see," Lorne said, taking a barstool next to Angel. "You didn't come here for the ambience or for companionship."

"I've got a lot of irons in the fire, and I'm kind of on a deadline," Angel admitted, looking around the crowd again. "Have you seen Merl around tonight?"

"Speak of the devil." Lorne aimed his green, pointed chin at the doorway.

Glancing back at the doorway, Angel saw Merl walk into the club. The demon had upgraded his wardrobe, now wearing new chinos, a blazer, and a shirt left open at the throat to show the gold chains around his neck.

"Now there's a lad that looks as if he's come into a windfall," Lorne said, accepting a drink from the female bartender.

"Yeah, well he's about to lose it, too," Angel said.

"That's the way it always is with ill-gotten gain," Lorne said. "Easy come, easy go. And that reminds me of a song. Haven't covered any of the king's stuff in a long time. Maybe I can pep things up just a little while tonight."

"Catch you later, Lorne," Angel said, sliding off the stool and heading in Merl's direction.

"You'll see me sooner than that," the Anagogic demon predicted. "Be sure and listen to the singers that come up while you're here."

Angel waved to the Host. His attention was locked solely on Merl.

The demon usually stood at the bar and nursed a beer all night while he plied his trade as a snitch. Caritas was only one of the places Merl hung out, but it was the first one of those places Angel had cornered his quarry in.

Tonight, though, Merl took a table out on the floor. He flirted with the cocktail waitress, folding a twenty-dollar bill in his hand and smiling at her.

The waitress took the twenty and her hand back. She held the bill up to the light.

"Don't be like that," Merl whined. "It's good."

"And I've never known you to be a tipper," the waitress said, "much less a big one."

As she moved away, Merl stared after her swaying hips with slack-jawed interest. "There's more where that came from. Just treat me nice and we'll see how friendly I—" He stopped talking as the waitress passed Angel.

As his eyes locked with Merl's, Angel saw the fear in them.

Cursing, Merl vaulted up from his chair, knocking over the table, and racing for the door.

Using only part of the incredible speed he was capable of, Angel caught Merl and kept him moving, one hand tight in the demon's new jacket. He dragged Merl into the bathroom and threw him up against the wall beside the sink. The mirror on the wall held Merl's reflection, but it didn't hold Angel's.

"I don't have a lot of time here," Angel said, "so we're going to talk and you're going to tell me what I want to know."

"I don't know anything," Merl protested.

"Then I'll find a rope and we're going down into the

sewers." Angel had discovered Merl was a lot more forthcoming with information while being dunked in the sewers.

"Man, I hate you guys." Merl brushed at his jacket, checking for tears and trying to smooth the wrinkles out.

"Where'd you get the money for the jacket, Merl?"

"I've been working. Did some work for Wesley last night. Or didn't he tell you about the whole *Corner of the Eye* case? I thought you guys talked to each other."

"I know how much he paid you," Angel said.

Merl acted mad, stepping from the wall and thrusting a forefinger out at Angel. "Yeah? Well I've been wanting to talk to you about that. Throwing me up against that Gorgranian demon, that was worth way more than Wesley paid me."

"I know how you got the money," Angel said.

"The striptease thing?" Merl nodded. "Man, I wasn't into that scene at all, I have to tell you, but when that woman started dropping money on the desk, it was just no problem at all." He grinned. "I may have found a new line of work."

"You can do it instead of the blackmail business you've gotten yourself into."

Merl hesitated, then shook his head. "Don't know what you're talking about."

"You found the Nova Studios' blackmail files while you were at the tabloid offices," Angel said. "It had to be you. Cordelia reminded me of how everybody seemed familiar with the sewers as a way to get around the city, but that's not true. There aren't that many of us—"

"More than you think," Merl said defensively. "I mean,

sometimes it's like rush hour traffic down there."

"You took those files while Wesley was fighting the demon," Angel said, "and you set up the drop at the condemned building because there was sewer access. I want the money you took, and I want those files."

Merl stared at him for a moment.

Angel knew the demon was thinking, struggling to figure out some way to hang onto the money and his blackmail revenue. "Merl," Angel said softly, "Wesley's neck is on the block because of what you did, and before I see him go under, I'll take you apart. You've got my word on that."

"Damn it," Merl sighed. "You know, I can just never get ahead. I've got the money hidden back at my place. I've spent some of it."

"We'll work out a payment plan," Angel said.

Merl stared at him, looking like a whipped puppy. "Man, you guys are harsh."

"Where are the blackmail files?" Angel asked.

"They're at my place, too."

"Good. Then we only have to make one trip."

Merl pointed to the waitress placing a coaster and his drink at the table. "Hey, can't I have my drink first? It'll be the first one I've ever had at the table."

"No," Angel said.

An eight-foot-tall Valdariath demon built like a diesel truck and sporting foot-long tusks and the sloping forehead of a lowlands gorilla started by the table and saw the drink sitting unattended. He swept it up in one massive paw and kept going.

"Hey, that was my drink," Merl said.

"You want to go tell him that?" Angel asked.

Merl watched the huge demon walk toward the bar. "Not particularly."

"And now," the Host called as he stepped into the baby spotlight's glow carrying the wireless microphone, "I bring you a performer new to this stage with a special dedication going out to someone he loves. Let's bring him up with a big welcome." Lorne applauded as a lone figure hesitantly walked up onto the stage.

Angel recognized Gabriel Dantz at once, still dressed in the peaked hat and the black cloak. He joined the Host, looking uneasily out into the crowd. In the glare of the baby spotlight, his waxy flesh looked even more inhuman and diseased.

"Here he is," the Host said, "to sing Rod Stewart's 'Forever Young.'" He extended the microphone to Gabriel.

Chapter Twenty

Gabriel Dantz held the microphone with a shaky hand. Silence hung over the crowd, and for a moment Angel thought the man was going to throw the microphone down and walk away. His breathing rasped over the loudspeaker. "This is for my son," he said. "We're apart now." His voice broke. "And the time apart is hard on me and I don't know what to do about it. For over twenty years, it's been just him and me. Some people might say that's a small world, but it's been big enough for him and me. I learned a long time ago not to expect much from the world, and I know my son can't expect much either." He paused. "I came here tonight because someone told me that you can get help here. I hope that's true."

The honest emotion rolled over the audience, and Angel felt the weight of it.

"My life . . . my life has taken some twists and turns that I hadn't counted on," Gabriel said. "Like a lot of you, I got mixed up with the wrong people for the wrong reasons. But I never thought it would take my son from me.

We belong together." Making an effort to regain control over himself, he waved and the music started. He sang, giving himself over to the words. Surprisingly, his voice was strong, a clear baritone with whiskey-throated dryness that put an edge on the pain he unleashed in the song.

Angel heard the pain in the words, formed by the song but given voice by the artist.

"You got a special interest in this song?" Merl asked.

Angel ignored him.

"The reason I asked," Merl said, "is because you gave me the impression of a guy in a real hurry. We're standing here and I could order another drink. Maybe we could even get a table. There's one over—"

"Shut up," Angel said.

Merl shut up.

Gabriel Dantz finished the song to thunderous applause. Several people gave him a standing ovation.

The Host rejoined him on the stage and tried to take the microphone.

Gabriel didn't release the microphone. His body jumped and jerked and a dozen tentacles exploded from his chest. Long and stringy, the tentacles leaped out at the Host for a moment, then disappeared back within Gabriel's cloak. He staggered, pulling the microphone back.

"I was told there would be help," Gabriel said.

"There is," Lorne said.

"People on the street told me you could come here and get help." Sweat poured across Gabriel's waxy face, making his eyes look even more feverish.

Angel stared into the man's face, trying to match Gabriel Dantz's young and handsome features with the monstrous visage before him. Like before and after maps of a region that had been hit by horrendous volcanic activity, there were a few points of reference but everything else had been changed, been resculpted.

"Help is here," the Host said, looking into Gabriel's eyes.

Drawn to the man's pain, knowing that he was doing the right thing, Angel made his way through the karaoke club audience and stood at the foot of the stage. "Gabriel," he called.

Gabriel swiveled his misshapen head. The growths on his face showed more predominantly. "Angelus." His eyes narrowed in recognition and fear.

"Yes," Angel said.

"You're involved in this."

"I'm trying to protect Faroe Burke," Angel said. "She's the next artist who's going to have the *Weid Deus* power, isn't she?"

"I can't trust you," Gabriel said.

Lorne smiled at the audience and leaned into the microphone. "We don't just offer a home for singers who haven't gotten their big break, folks. We also give time up for actors working on their improv."

Angel didn't know if the audience was buying the excuse or not, and he didn't care. Caritas had a reputation for weird events. Tonight was mild by comparison.

"A lot of things have changed since we last saw each other," Angel said.

Gabriel looked through the crowd as Lorne made another attempt to pull the microphone away. The tentacles snapped free of Gabriel's chest and chased him back.

"Where's Darla?" Gabriel asked.

"Gone."

"I've got her portrait."

"I know." Angel held out his hand. "Let me help you."

Gabriel stared at the hand before him.

"Let him help you," Lorne urged, leaning in and speaking quietly. "You came here for help. Now you've got it. This is what Angel does."

"Angel? Not Angelus?" Gabriel asked.

"Not for a long time," Angel said.

Gabriel fumbled in his cloak, handing the microphone over to the Host. Lorne backed away quickly with the microphone. Showing Angel the card he held, Gabriel said, "Angel Investigations?"

"That's me," Angel said.

Gabriel looked frightened and exhausted. "Vincent Hardesty is back. He has my son. He made me help find the woman."

"Faroe?"

Nodding, Gabriel said, "Those of us who have experienced *Weid Deus*, we recognize it in other people. Hardesty learned that, and he used me to get to her. And he's using my son as bait for his mother. Hardesty's controlling her by offering my son to her once she helps him get what he wants from the young artist."

"We'll fix it," Angel said. "I swear to you, Gabriel. We'll fix it and we'll find your son."

Tears brimmed in Gabriel's eyes. "He's innocent, Angelus. Like nothing you've ever seen before."

"I've seen his pictures," Angel said, remembering the portraits of the boy in the house. "I believe you."

Hand shaking, Gabriel reached out and took Angel's hand. "I ask myself how I can trust you, Angelus, after knowing everything about you that I do."

"You don't know everything about me," Angel said. Merl tried to slip from his grip, but he tightened his other hand, holding the jacket and the flesh beneath.

"Then I pray that I am right," Gabriel said, "because if you lie to me, if you cause harm to come to my son, I swear that I will kill you."

"They've got pie on the menu," Gunn said, looking over the laminated sheet the waitress had given him. "Cheese-cake. Ice cream. They've even got Italian ice."

"No thank you." Faroe Burke sat across the narrow booth from him. "That sandwich was enough."

They sat at one of the booths at the front of the small diner two blocks up the street from the Bronze Jade Art Gallery. Red vinyl upholstery coordinated with cream-colored linoleum. Light fixtures in the shape of kettles hung over the tables and booths. The diner occupied the street corner, and two of the walls were filled with win-dows that looked out onto the streets. Night filled the city, bringing out the shadows in a rush that was only in-terrupted now and again by casual traffic. The main es-cape from the work areas of L.A. were removed from the corner.

"I appreciate you being there last night," Faroe said.

Gunn smiled. "Sure couldn't have told it from the way you left me in the parking garage."

Embarrassment filled Faroe's face, drawing Gunn's attention again to how beautiful she was. "Comes from living on the street too long. I don't trust many people."

"Me neither," Gunn admitted. "The guy I'm working with now—"

"Angel."

"When the chips are down, I'll bet on Angel."

Faroe met his gaze with hers. "That's what you're asking me to do, isn't it?"

Gunn put the menu away, knowing they'd moved down to brass tacks. "Yeah. I guess I am. Unless there's somebody else you have who can watch your back."

Sighing, Faroe leaned back in the booth. "You don't know what kind of trouble I'm in. I don't even know what kind of trouble I'm in."

"There's demons," Gunn said. He hadn't gotten into the whole vision thing with Cordelia. "Angel's really big on helping people sort out their problems when it involves demons."

Her dark eyes held his. "This is going to get worse, isn't it?"

Gunn didn't hold anything back. "Probably. But Angel's not the kind of guy to quit on something." He paused. "Neither am I."

"I didn't figure you for that." Faroe glanced at the laminated menu. "I think you should order key lime pie."

"You do?" Gunn smiled.

"I've been told it's good here."

Gunn flagged down the waitress and ordered, requesting two forks. "In case I drop one," he told Faroe. "It happens sometimes."

"I see." Faroe leaned forward again. "Tell me, Charles Gunn, has anyone ever painted you before?"

"No."

"I want to at some point. So you can't just vanish after buying me a cheeseburger."

"Okay," Gunn said.

Angel leaned against the doorway in Merl's hideout down in the darkened sewers. From the haphazard way the demon kept everything in the small room, a rat's nest would have been a living quarters upgrade.

Merl took loose cinder blocks from the back wall and placed them at his feet. "You know, it doesn't have to be like this."

"Yes, it does," Angel replied. He checked his watch. It was after eight and night had returned to the city; his best active work shift because all of the city was open to him. Unfortunately, more demons roamed L.A. then, and a lot of them were stronger than they were during the day.

Gabriel Dantz stood only a little farther down the tunnel from Angel. Several times during the last few minutes of the trip to Merl's crash site, Angel had seen or felt Gabriel watching him with suspicion, but he'd been guilty of the same. Gabriel had known Angelus, and Angel knew that Gabriel was no longer human. The trust was necessary but not a natural thing.

Merl reached into the opening he'd made in the wall. "I mean, there could be, like, a finder's fee involved in the recovery of the money. Big companies do that, you know. Twenty percent, something like that. We don't have to be greedy about it."

"*We*," Angel said, "didn't blackmail the studio in the first place. You did."

"Ten percent?" Merl took the backpack from the hiding place and looked hopeful.

"Your reward," Angel said, stepping into the room and taking the backpack, "is going to be me not telling the studio who blackmailed them. The only reason I'm doing that is to protect Wesley."

"Some reward," Merl grumped.

"And I'm throwing in a free pass on the butt-kicking you deserve for betraying Wesley." Angel opened the backpack and saw the bundles of money inside.

"Boy, that makes me feel so much better." Merl stood in the center of the room and looked crestfallen.

"Is this all the money?" Angel asked.

"Yeah. Except for about two thousand that I already spent."

"Empty your pockets," Angel commanded.

"What?"

"Do it, and hand over the cash."

Merl emptied his pockets. He had four hundred and three dollars in cash.

"Put it in the bag," Angel said.

"This is my money," Merl protested.

"It's been contaminated by the blackmail money," Angel said. "It goes in the bag."

"You're *asking* him for the money?" Gabriel asked from his position farther down the sewer tunnel. "Money that he stole from someone you were hired to protect?"

"Yeah," Angel said.

Surprise littered Gabriel's fever-ravaged features beneath

his peaked hat. "I knew a time when you would have killed him for money that was entirely his."

"I do too," Angel said. "Occasionally, I miss those days." He stared at Merl. "The blackmail files. Now."

Scowling, Merl reached inside the thin mattress in the far corner of the room and took out a bundle of manila file folders. He shoved them into the backpack.

"Make no mistakes about this, Merl," Angel said, "if this isn't everything, if another studio gets a call about materials you took from *Corner of the Eye,* I will kill you. Understand?"

"Sure, sure. But that's everything." Morose and sullen, Merl flopped down on his bed and stared up at the stained ceiling. "You're leaving me broke, you know. Just to take back what's really pocket change to a multimillion-dollar movie studio."

Angel zipped the backpack closed. "Yeah, I know."

"They're not going to thank you or even respect you for it."

"I'll do that for myself," Angel said. He settled the backpack over his shoulder and walked toward Gabriel Dantz.

They walked in silence for awhile. Angel heard voices in the sewers, as well as other footsteps as they walked the route he'd learned would take them back to the hotel.

After a time, Angel glanced at Gabriel, finding the man sweating profusely and looking more sickly than ever. "You doing all right?"

Gabriel looked at him and laughed. The effort caused his chest to ripple again, exposing the tentacles that whipped the air in front of him.

"What's so funny?" Angel asked.

"You," Gabriel said. "After knowing you and Darla in Venice and in Geneva, it's strange hearing you ask about someone."

Angel nodded. "Yeah. I can see that. But you've changed too."

"This?" Gabriel brushed at the curious tentacles sprouting from his chest, smoothing them back into the shadows of his cloak.

"Yes."

Gabriel broke eye contact, but Angel saw the flicker of sadness in his gaze. "Cara caused that. She changed me." He paused to kick out at a rat that had crept too close. "She changed a lot of things. My whole life has been affected by her. You'd met her before, right?"

"Yes," Angel said. "We weren't introduced in Venice before she put me to sleep, but I met her at George's rented place in Geneva."

"Ah yes. It has been so long I'd almost forgotten that. Poor Mary Wollstonecraft. She got the scare of her life, didn't she?"

"What she saw that night caused her to write *Frankenstein*."

Gabriel laughed, but the sound was hoarse and as jarring as shaking a tin can filled with glass. "If Cara still cared about things like that I'm sure she'd find that amusing."

"That was Cara back at your house, right?"

"Yes," Gabriel answered. "She seldom puts on a human appearance these days." Thin tendrils shot from his face and twisted around like snakes' tongues sipping the air. "After discovering how much work it actually takes to keep even a semblance of a human body together, I don't blame her. And she already has her gateway into this world where she can hunt at her leisure."

"You're no longer together?"

"No." Gabriel shook his head and the tendrils standing out from his face sank back under the skin. "She left me over a hundred years ago. I never got used to her killing people. And she killed a lot of people."

"I remember," Angel said.

Chapter Twenty-one

Geneva, 1816

"Shhhhh, shhhhh," Angelus whispered, helping Darla up through the second-story window to the cottage Lord Byron had rented for the summer by Lake Leman. "We're guests here, Darla. It won't do to wake up the house, now will it?"

Dressed in a shimmering blue gown under a calf-length coat against the night chill that hung over the area from the lake, Darla grinned at him. "It's night, love. They should be up reveling in the moonlight."

"But they aren't," Angelus said, guiding her toward the bed in the small room Lord Byron had lent them for their stay. He and Darla had ventured out to the nearby town to feed. "They're abed and getting prepared to greet the morning and once more go out and enjoy bountiful nature so they can get that much closer to it."

Darla flopped back onto the bed, making it squeak. She frowned and gave an exasperated sigh that usually signaled death for someone. "Damn it, Angelus, if I have to listen to one more sonnet about the beauties and wonders of nature and simple things, I'm going to tear someone's throat out. I swear it."

"We won't be here that much longer. Don't forget: George is a friend and we are guests here."

"Being someone's guest only means that we generally don't kill them right off."

Angelus crossed the room to the chest at the foot of the bed. He picked up the portrait and held it so the moonlight streaming through the window could illuminate the image. "You have to admit now, some of this art they practice has its rewards. Such as this fine portrait Gabriel painted for you. Everybody here has admired it."

Darla played with her hair, smiling. "Yes, they have, haven't they? The portrait brings me pleasure. That's the only thing that's kept me from killing Gabriel for deserting us last year in Venice. And for making me wait so long to get the portrait."

Angelus replaced the painting at the foot of the bed, not daring to take a chance on damaging it. "It was worth the wait if you ask me." He joined her on the bed. "Besides, if you want, we can kill Gabriel before we leave Geneva."

Darla leaned over him, her body cool from the night they'd just walked through, but warmed by the blood she'd consumed. Tracing the line of his chin with a forefinger, she said, "Maybe. The idea appeals to me."

"Aye. I knew that it would." Angelus smiled up at her, loving the feel of her body pressed against his so soon after they'd killed and fed together.

"I think he has changed," Darla said. "Do you think he has changed?"

"No."

"You wouldn't notice it. You're much too full of yourself. But I've noticed it. He isn't as friendly and as outgoing as he always was before."

"When you were threatening his life every day?"

"Yes. Now he's pensive. He's not really very much fun at George's parties. His girlfriend is much more entertaining. At least, George, Percy, and Dr. John seem to think so."

"They're easily distracted. And if Gabriel has changed for the worse, I'd say it was because of her. Her flirting with the other men bothers him."

"What do you think of his girlfriend?" Darla asked.

Angelus took a moment to think about that. He'd never told Darla about the night he'd seen Gabriel Dantz pull the woman he'd painted from the canvas.

"Do you think she's beautiful?" Darla prompted.

Oh, and that was the way of it, Angelus thought. *Now we're in some dangerous currents.* "She has a certain charm about her."

"For pity's sake, Angelus," Darla said, "you lie so badly. Would you like me better if I were a redhead like Cara?"

Bringing his forefinger to his lips, Angelus quieted her, listening to the furtive noise he'd heard outside the door to their room. Silently, Darla rose from the bed with him.

A loose board creaked out in the hallway.

Moving into place beside the door, Angelus had his sword naked in his fist as he eased the door open and peered out.

Clad only in breeches and a nightshirt, Gabriel Dantz crept through the hallway and down the stairs leading to the first floor. He carried a single candle in a hurricane glass to light his way. In the darkness that filled the house, the light wrapped a golden bubble around him.

Darla jabbed Angelus with an impatient forefinger, letting him know she was as curious as he was. Stealthily as two shadows drifting through a graveyard, Angelus and Darla followed.

Gabriel showed no hesitation about finding his way through the house. As quickly as he went, Angelus was willing to wager that he'd made the journey a number of times. Only a little farther on, the artist reached the kitchen area and pulled up the cellar door cut out of the floor. He descended the ladder, gradually disappearing from sight but leaving the cellar hatch open.

When the candlelight dimmed, Angelus hurried to the cellar door, followed by Darla. He kept his sword in his hand as he lowered himself down the ladder. Without looking at Darla, he knew she was as curious as he was. Granted long lives by their vampirism, curiosity became their grandest adventures.

The cellar was large and stank of potatoes and dank earth. It also, as Angelus discovered, had an escape route that led out from the cellar. Wine racks, most of them full because George had insisted they be well-stocked, filled the cellar's main area.

"Cara!" Gabriel said in a hoarse whisper. "Oh god! What have you done?"

"Be at ease, Gabriel," the woman said, "no one will notice these missing. And if they are noticed overmuch, the townsfolk will blame it on the vampires that struck in their midst tonight."

Although Angelus recognized the woman's voice, it sounded very different from when they'd had dinner and when they'd met earlier in the day. He kept moving forward, his feet not making a sound on the earthen floor as he stayed behind the wine racks.

Gabriel's candle only lit up a small part of the cellar. "Cara, you can't do this."

"No," the woman replied, "I can't not do this. I've told you before, sweet Gabriel, if you want me here in this world, you have to suffer me these moments to replenish myself."

Angelus listened to the liquid gurgling noises that echoed within the cellar as he sidled behind the last row of wine racks. With Darla at his side, he peered through the space between the shelves. Even after nearly seventy years of living as a demon himself, Angelus was caught unprepared for the scene lit by Gabriel's candle.

Gabriel hunkered down on the floor in front of a quivering glob of indigo flesh with iridescent blue highlights as large as an elephant. Arms and legs and heads of three men and two women jutted out of the flesh glob. All of the people trapped within the demon's body were dead, but only recently so.

Angelus smelled the fresh blood that clung to the corpses.

"Cara, this is unnatural. It's horrible. God will punish you. He'll punish us both." Gabriel rocked back and forth, in shock.

"You only fear for your soul, Gabriel," Cara replied.

One end of the demonic glob quivered suddenly, then stretched up and became the head and shoulders of Gabriel's lover. By some miracle, her red hair was dry. Her body continued shooting up till her head, shoulders, naked breasts, and half of her stomach were visible and looked human. Her skin still held an eerie bluish cast like that of an asphyxiated corpse.

The corpses within the rest of her body gurgled and shuffled positions. As the dead rolled within the grasp of Cara's flesh like they were being tossed on a restless sea, Angelus saw the glistening sheen on them. He guessed that the demon was basting her prey with some kind of corrosive acid and dissolving them.

"You shouldn't bring those here, Cara. Not in this house."

"You insisted we come here. I captured these people in town, but it takes time to digest them, and when I do, I'm at my most vulnerable. You know that. You've seen me feed before."

"Cara, please," Gabriel pleaded, "this can't go on."

"It has to," Cara responded. "Would you have me torn from you, Gabriel? Shoved back into those swamplands that you took me from? Never be able again to leave that painting that you made of me even for these short times we have together?"

"No," Gabriel said. "No. You know that isn't what I'd want. I want you, to love and to cherish."

"Then you'll have to put up with these things from me." Cara reached out and smoothed the artist's brow. "You're human, Gabriel. My time in this world, *our* time, is going to be unnaturally short compared to what I'm used to because humans die so quickly, and because they are so fragile."

Without warning, a shrill scream filled the cellar.

Whipping his head back, throwing one arm out to capture Darla behind him and catch her up in his embrace, Angelus spotted young Mary Wollstonecraft standing beside the wine racks in a housecoat and gown.

Mary had her hands up to her mouth, still screaming, but now no sound was coming out. She shook her head. Even traveling with Percy Shelley, who was a volatile poet and had a madwoman for a wife, hadn't prepared Mary for the sight of the jumble of half-eaten arms and legs visible in the morass of Cara's demonic body. In the next instant, Mary passed out, slumping to the floor.

Gabriel ran to Mary, pressing a hand up against her neck. "Thank God, she's still alive," he told Cara.

"She's seen me," Cara said in a harsh voice that wasn't quite human. "I want her dead."

"No," Gabriel replied. "If she turns up dead or mysteriously disappears, Percy will never give up the search for her until he finds out what happened to her." He gathered Mary Wollstonecraft in his arms.

"They don't have to find the body," Cara said. "I could take her as well as these I've already caught." Small tentacles shot from her lovely face for just a moment, then retreated and left only unblemished skin behind.

"No." Gabriel remained adamant. "Percy told me Mary sometimes sleepwalks and often has vivid dreams. I'm going to leave her in the study. Perhaps she'll think she walked in there while still asleep, and that all of this was a bad dream."

Hiding in the shadows, Angelus watched the artist carry the unconscious woman back toward the ladder. A few minutes later, Cara finished her grotesque feast. Silently, holding Darla against him, one hand over her mouth in warning, Angelus watched as Cara resumed her human shape. When she stood again on two legs that were trim and shapely, she was naked and there was no sign of the bodies she'd dragged into the cellar to feast on.

Still unashamedly naked, Cara walked to the ladder and crawled up. "Sweet Gabriel," she called in a seductive voice. "Come see me, my love. I am made whole again. You know how you love to love me when I am again of fresh flesh."

Even after the demon had disappeared, Angelus sat in the darkness and held Darla for long, silent moments. She finally took his hand from her mouth.

"Would you still be wanting your vengeance against Gabriel Dantz?" Angelus asked as they stood on the earthen floor.

"What is she?" Darla asked.

"I don't know." Angelus crossed the cellar to the section of the floor where Cara had fed on the victims she had captured. He touched the hard-packed earth and stone, but found it dry, not slimy as he'd expected.

Not even a drop of blood remained to mark the deaths of those Cara had feasted on.

The cellar hatch opened abruptly and Gabriel dropped down, still holding onto the candle. He stared at Angelus, who held the sword and the shoe.

"You saw what happened?" Gabriel asked.

"Aye," Angelus agreed. "Every bloody bit of it, we did.

What is that thing you're keeping company with these days, Gabriel?"

The artist's face hardened. "No worse company than that which I was keeping in Venice."

"So says you."

"Give me the shoe, Angelus," Gabriel said. "I have to have it if I want to make sure Mary believes she was only dreaming."

"And to protect that monstrous thing," Angelus taunted.

"She's no thing," Gabriel said. "She's a woman. I love her. God help me, but I love her more than honesty and decency." His eyes shone bright with unshed tears. "Give me the shoe, Angelus, otherwise Cara will come down here and get it herself. You wouldn't want that."

Angelus brandished the sword. "Why, if she came at me, *sweet* Gabriel, I'd carve the life from her, I would."

Gabriel shook his head. "Men and demons have tried before, Angelus. They died in the same gruesome fashion you witnessed this night." He took a step forward, reaching for the shoe. "And if you harm me, she'll kill you."

With reluctance, Angelus handed over the shoe. He offered Gabriel a grim smile. "It appears the scales between us have shifted tonight."

"Yes," Gabriel said. "You and Darla will never again make me live in fear as you have."

"And you're saying that you don't live in greater fear now?" Darla asked. "*Sweet* Gabriel?"

Without another word, Gabriel snatched the shoe from Angelus's hand and fled back up the ladder. He and Cara were gone before morning.

Chapter Twenty-two

"What happened to you?" Angel asked as he and Gabriel continued through the sewer tunnel.

"You mean, how did I become something more or less than human?" Gabriel smiled, but there was no humor, only a rictus of the wreckage of the expression that he'd once had. "It was Cara's doing. Over the years, I grew older, and she began to see that I was going to die like every other mortal. She took me into her embrace—at all times unwilling on my part, I assure you—and she replaced my failing flesh with tissue from her own demonic body."

The tendrils burst free of Gabriel's face again, testing the air and flexing.

"Why did she do that?"

"At first I believed it was because she was lonely. She told me that, and I wanted it to be true. Then, when I realized the truth, that she needed me here to keep the gateway open, it was too late."

"Too late?" Angel asked.

"During years of drinking to forget the evil that I had unleashed into this world, I lost the painting I'd made of her," Gabriel explained. "Only I have the power to destroy the painting and seal her back into the world that she came from." He paused. "Or if I die, she'll be trapped in this world or her own." He gazed at Angel. "You can destroy her by destroying me."

Angel looked at him. "That would leave your son without a father."

A hesitant smile twisted Gabriel's lips. "My God, how you have changed."

A small twinge of guilt filled Angel, but he pushed it away. All the things he'd done in the past were gone. He was working on his redemption now. He couldn't do anything about those past events, but he could alter the things in the present. "Where is the painting?"

"Vincent Hardesty has it. He came to me in Venice, remember?"

"I remember," Angel said.

"Hardesty is even older than we thought he was in Venice," Gabriel said. "He found out about the *Weid Deus* talent hundreds of years ago. He had an artist that he found back then paint a portrait of him that would keep him young forever."

"Dorian Gray," Angel said.

Gabriel nodded. "The myth about Vincent Hardesty was one of the legends Oscar Wilde based his work on."

"Can Hardesty be killed?"

"Yes. I tried, but I never got close enough to him. By the time I recovered from my attempt, he'd discovered I was staying in the house on Cinnamon Street. We fled, just left everything in that house years ago, and I found a new place to stay. But Hardesty found us again. Hardesty's demons broke in and kidnapped Jacob only weeks ago."

"Jacob is your son."

"Yes."

"And Hardesty's threatening to give your son to his mother?"

"She'll kill him, Angelus, as sure as I'm here talking to you."

"Why?"

"Because Cara's a creature of hate, and because she's gotten so full of herself. I think, if she didn't depend on me, that she would kill me as well."

"And Hardesty forced you to find the next person with the *Weid Deus*."

"Once Hardesty had Jacob, I had no choice but to do as he commanded. He has an affinity for the manifestation of the *Weid Deus* talent, but he needed me to track down the exact person in L.A. With the increase in population density, it's harder for him to use his means. But those of us who have experienced *Weid Deus* stay connected with each other."

"And Faroe Burke is going to be the next artist?"

"Yes."

"You could have told Hardesty you didn't know," Angel pointed out.

"I tried," Gabriel said, "but I also wanted to find Faroe first and talk to her on my own."

"Why?"

"For my son. For Jacob." Gabriel's face exploded into a

mass of writhing tentacles again. He smoothed them absently with a hand. "I thought maybe she could help him."

Before Angel could ask Gabriel how Faroe Burke was supposed to help, his cell phone rang. He took it from his pocket and answered it.

"Angel?" Cordelia asked.

"Yes," Angel said.

"Bad news. This guy, Vincent Hardesty? Turns out he's probably the same guy you ran into in Venice."

"He is," Angel replied.

"Oh. You knew that. Well, what you might not have known is that Gunn just now called and Hardesty has arrived at the gallery. You see, Gunn chased off a Wolfram and Hart lawyer earlier today who was trying to set up this deal for Hardesty earlier. I thought maybe Hardesty was figuring he'd close the deal himself."

"You and Wesley need to get there as quick as you can," Angel said.

"We're already on our way. I haven't been able to reach your cell phone."

"I'm in the sewers."

"It's dark. You could have taken a cab."

Angel glanced at Gabriel, who was still having trouble keeping his body together. "That wasn't an option. Hurry. We'll meet you guys there. We're only minutes away."

"We?" Cordelia asked.

"Yeah," Angel said. "I'm bringing a friend."

"Look, Faroe, this could be a big break for you," Lenny Thomas said. The agent smiled and glanced back at the group of men waiting in the conference room.

"What do you know about Vincent Hardesty?" Faroe demanded.

Gunn stood behind her and gazed at the group of men within the conference room. He picked out Vincent Hardesty at once as the guy with the best suit and the most attitude.

Hardesty wore a neatly trimmed Vandyke beard and his hair clipped close to his head. Jeweled rings glittered on his fingers, and a thick gold-and-platinum bracelet shone on his right wrist. He took a thick gold pocket watch from his vest, flipped it open to check the time, then impatiently put it back. He didn't look more than fifty years old, a lot less than the two hundred Wesley and Cordelia were clocking him at according to the information they'd gotten.

"I know that he's a powerhouse in the art circles, Faroe," Thomas said. "A guy like Vincent Hardesty makes and breaks the careers of artists, and we're fortunate that he's taken an interest in you. What more do I need to know?"

"What does he want with me?" Faroe asked.

"He wants to commission you to do a painting for him," Lenny said. "That's all."

"What kind of painting?"

"I don't know." Lenny shrugged. "It's obviously something he thinks you could do or he wouldn't be asking you."

"Why doesn't he buy one of these we've got on display here?"

"He wants to commission one. A special one."

Faroe looked at the agent. "He's going to tell me what to paint, Lenny?"

The pained expression on Lenny's face told Gunn that the agent knew he'd stepped off into a bad area.

Faroe folded her arms. "I don't paint commissioned artwork. You knew that when you took me on. I paint what I feel."

"Look," Lenny said, "Hardesty is willing to pay you a million dollars for the painting he wants, and will put you up any place around the world that you want while you do it. With that kind of money you could take a lot of financial pressure off yourself. You could paint more. Now that's a hell of a deal if you ask me."

Yeah, Gunn thought sourly, *but wouldn't you want to know why somebody like Hardesty would be willing to shell out so much jack for an artist who is just getting known?*

"Your percentage of that wouldn't be small change, would it, Lenny?" Faroe asked.

"Faroe, I'm your agent. I swear I'm trying to do what's best for you," Lenny promised.

"I don't do commissioned pieces," Faroe insisted.

"Faroe," Lenny pleaded, "at least listen to the guy. Hear him out. Give him a little ego stroke, without committing, and at least sleep on it. We're talking about serious exposure here."

Gunn scanned the dwindling crowd that remained in the gallery. Most of the media people had gone home, but there were still some late-evening arrivals that drew the appreciative attention of the gallery staff working to close deals on any unsold pieces of Faroe Burke's artwork or to direct buyers in the direction of other pieces.

Cordelia and Wesley rounded a display area, stopped for a moment to look around, and spotted Gunn.

Gunn waved, letting them know it was okay to join him. He'd been expecting them since the phone call only moments ago let him know they were on their way.

"Where's Angel?" Gunn asked.

"On his way here," Wesley said. "Is that Miss Burke?"

"Yeah."

"What about Vincent Hardesty?" Cordelia asked.

Gunn nodded in Hardesty's direction in the conference room. "There. Faroe's agent is trying to persuade her to do a commissioned painting for Hardesty."

"She can't do that," Cordelia said. "Hardesty knows she's about to enter her *Weid Deus* phase."

Concern filled Gunn. "Okay, now *that* we're going to have to talk about. You haven't mentioned *Weid Deus* to me." Anytime something weird turned up in one of Angel's cases, it usually wasn't good news.

"That's what this is all about," Cordelia said. "*Weid Deus* is old magic."

"Wild magic," Wesley chimed in. "A chaotic and totally unstructured force containing great power."

"What does it do?" Gunn asked.

"Anything," Cordelia said. "While in his or her *Weid Deus* phase, an artist can paint in new things into this world. Or change things in this world."

Gunn looked at Faroe, who was still arguing quietly with her agent. "And she doesn't know?"

"No," Wesley said. "That's part of the chaos of *Weid Deus*. While researching the magic, we discovered that

Atlantis sunk because of it. At least, that may have been part of the reason."

"Hardesty plans on using that power," Cordelia said. "And he doesn't strike me as being a charitable person."

"No," Gunn agreed, "he doesn't."

"Or a patient one either, apparently," Wesley said.

Glancing back at the conference room, Gunn saw Hardesty march from it, aiming straight at Faroe with his entourage in tow. Gunn stepped forward, closing on Faroe.

"Well," Hardesty said in cultured tones as he glanced from Lenny Thomas to Faroe, "I see there appears to be some dissention in the ranks."

"Give us just a few more minutes, Mr. Hardesty," the agent requested. "I'm sure that I—"

"No," Hardesty said. "We've spent more than enough time here, and it appears the barbarians are gathering at the gate." He glared at Cordelia, Wesley, and Gunn.

"Mr. Hardesty," Faroe said, "I don't know what Lenny has led you to believe, but I don't do commissioned works."

Hardesty regarded her with a cold smile. "You will, child. You will." He snapped his fingers.

Immediately, two of his men surged forward and captured Faroe by the arms. She fought against them but couldn't break their grip.

Gunn crossed the room, going straight for Hardesty. If he controlled Hardesty, Gunn figured he would control the situation. With superhuman speed, Hardesty backhanded Gunn, hitting him so hard that he left his feet and flew backward into a display. The impact knocked

Gunn's breath from him, but he struggled to get back to his feet, falling forward to his hands and knees.

"You'd better let her go," Cordelia said. "If you don't, Angel's going to find you and kick your butt the way he did back in Venice."

"Take her as well," Hardesty commanded, glaring at Cordelia. "She works for the vampire. It might be useful to have a bargaining chip."

Two more men rushed forward. Cordelia put up a fight, but it didn't last long. Wesley stepped to her aid, but Hardesty unsheathed a sword cane and slashed the air in front of Wesley's face, narrowly missing him. Having no choice, Wesley stepped back.

"Tell Angelus," Hardesty said, backing away with his men, "that if he wants to see these young ladies alive again, he should stay out of my affairs. When my painting is done, I'll gladly return them." He saluted with the sword, then turned and walked toward the rear of the gallery. His men covered his retreat, holding pistols in their fists.

Having no choice, Gunn shoved himself to his feet and watched in helpless frustration as Hardesty took his two prisoners out the back of the gallery. Following only a short distance behind, Gunn and Wesley stood back as Cordelia and Faroe were loaded into one of the two long, black limousines that filled the alley.

"We've got Angel's car," Wesley said in an undertone. "We can tail them."

"Where is it?" Gunn asked.

"Farther back in the alley."

Looking over his shoulder as he stepped outside,

Gunn spotted the Plymouth Belvedere sitting in the shadows by the Dumpster behind the gallery.

"Okay," Gunn said. Together, he and Wesley looked on while the two limousines took off, roaring out the other end of the alley, their brake lights flaring crimson only for a moment before they pulled out and cut off oncoming traffic.

Immediately, Wesley bolted for the convertible, taking keys from his pocket as he slid behind the steering wheel.

Gunn vaulted into the passenger seat. "You got weapons in the back?"

Wesley pulled the transmission into gear and floored the accelerator. "All the usual stuff, yes."

"Just the two of us won't be enough to pull this off," Gunn said.

The tires shrieked as the car took off. "Yes, well, we'll call Angel once we know where we're going." Wesley gripped the steering wheel with both hands, looking like a defiant madman.

Gunn belted up as Wesley reached the end of the alley, briefly checked the oncoming traffic, then pulled out into it. Horns blared but the sound was lost in the automatic-weapons fire that crescendoed through the night.

Noting the muzzle flashes ahead of them, Gunn reached across the seat and grabbed Wesley's jacket, pulling him to safety as bullets ripped through the windshield and scattered glass over them.

Then the front end of the convertible dropped and the car pulled into the curb and lurched to a stop.

Aware that he might have his head blown off by the

next barrage of gunfire, Gunn looked over the dash. Gaping holes showed in the windshield and there were tears in the metal of the hood.

One of the limousines occupied the street in front of them. Two men stood on the sidewalk with assault rifles. Satisfied with the carnage they'd rendered, they loaded back into the limousine and it sped away, disappearing in seconds.

"Damn," Gunn said, hating the helpless feeling that filled him.

"Are you guys all right?"

Surprised to hear Angel's voice, Gunn looked up and saw him standing there.

"Hardesty," Gunn said. "He took Cordelia and Faroe. They're gone."

"No they're not," Angel said, moving to the front of the car. "There are a couple of spares in the back of the car. Get them." He popped the bullet-riddled hood.

"You have two spares?" Wesley asked as he peered into the trunk.

"It's a big trunk," Angel replied.

"You're kidding," Gunn said.

"No," Angel said, taking the bumper jack Wesley handed him. He slid the jack into place and started raising the car on the driver's side while Wesley fumbled with the tire iron.

"Let me," Gunn offered, holding a hand out for the tire iron. "I can take care of this in a second. We don't have much time."

Wesley handed it over without complaint.

Gunn started removing the wheel nuts. "You know where to find Hardesty?"

"No," Angel said. "But Gabriel does."

Looking up, Gunn saw the man in the peaked black hat standing over him. About that time, the man's face came apart in a bunch of writhing tendrils. He smoothed them back into place.

"Hardesty has my son," Gabriel said in a hoarse voice. "I can find him. The bond between us is too strong for Hardesty to disguise. Alone, I was too weak to try to take Jacob back. But together—" He hesitated. "Together we at least have a better chance."

"Good to know," Gunn said as he reached out and removed the bullet-shredded tire.

Cordelia woke in darkness. Her head throbbed painfully from the chloroform Hardesty's goons had used on her in the limousine. She lay on her back and glanced around the room, recognizing it as a small bedroom. Must pervaded the room, letting her know it had been unused for a long time.

"Hi," a tiny voice said.

Squinting her eyes against the darkness, Cordelia tracked the voice to a small boy standing beside the small single bed she'd woken on. She recognized him as the boy from her visions, all wispy blond hair and innocent blue eyes.

"Hey you," Cordelia said, still reeling in the stupor that was part of the after-effects of the chloroform. "I've been looking for you."

The little boy's eyebrows rose. He looked all of five years old. "You have?"

"Yes." Cordelia tried to sit up but regretted it instantly when the room started to spin. She groaned.

"Are you going to die?" the little boy asked.

Despite the fact that she was captured and wasn't feeling well at all, Cordelia laughed. "No. I'm not going to die." *Angel will find us*, she told herself.

"Okay," the little boy said. "I'm glad you're not going to die."

"Me too," Cordelia said. "What's your name?"

"Jacob," the little boy said. "My dad's name is Gabriel. Have you seen him? He losted me."

Remembering how gruesome Gabriel Dantz looked, Cordelia couldn't believe he was Jacob's father. There was no family resemblance. She smoothed the boy's blond curls instinctively. "I've seen him."

"Why hasn't he come back for me?" Jacob asked. "I haven't been bad." Tears welled up in the blue eyes. "I promise I haven't been bad. And if I was, I'd stop."

Cordelia's heart felt close to breaking. "I'm sure you weren't bad, Jacob. When I saw your dad, he was worried about you. But he has things he has to do before he can pick you up."

"It's been a long time."

"I'm sure it seems like it has. But it's almost finished now." *One way or another*, Cordelia thought, and she hated the negative way that came out. *Come on, Angel*.

The little boy laid his head on the bed. "I've been scared for a long time. I don't like being scared."

"Me neither," Cordelia admitted.

"When I was with my dad," Jacob said, "I was never scared."

"That's good," Cordelia said, though she didn't know how it was possible. "Do you know where we are, Jacob?"

"At Mr. Hardesty's house," Jacob said. He looked up at Cordelia and whispered. "I don't like Mr. Hardesty. My dad told me to do whatever Mr. Hardesty said, but I think he's mean."

Cordelia lowered her voice and whispered. "Me too." She checked her pockets for her cell phone, then remembered she'd broken hers and used Wesley's to call Angel earlier. She glanced at the window to her left. Security bars covered it. *Now that doesn't look very promising.*

"What's your name?" the little boy asked.

"Cordelia," she told him. "But my friends call me Cordy."

"Can I call you Cordy?"

Cordelia smiled at him. "Of course you can. You're my friend, right?"

Jacob thought about it for a moment. "Sure. I'm your friend. I've never had a friend before."

"You haven't?"

"No. Just my dad."

Poor kid, Cordelia thought. *After Gabriel Dantz kidnapped you, he kept you locked away from everyone. He must have been afraid someone would recognize you.*

"But I always wanted a friend," the little boy said. "I'm glad you're my first friend."

"Me too," Cordelia said. "But we've got to see about getting out of here."

Jacob's face brightened. "You can take me to my dad?"

"Sure."

"Good. Because nobody makes cheese toast the way he makes cheese toast. And they don't let me watch cartoons here."

"That is mean," Cordelia said. Gingerly, she dragged her feet over the bed's edge and tried to sit up.

"Let me help," Jacob volunteered. He scrambled around the bed.

When Jacob came around the end of the bed, Cordelia saw that he didn't have two legs. Instead, he had six. All six of the boy's legs were stumpy tentacles attached to his lower body. A pair of Batman shorts, carefully sewn to fit all six of his legs, covered him. The contrast between the blond-haired, blue-eyed upper half of the boy with the demonic lower half was brutally shocking and unexpected.

Before Cordelia could stop herself, she screamed.

Chapter Twenty-three

"My son isn't human," Gabriel Dantz said from the Belvedere's passenger seat. "He doesn't even age like a human. He's almost thirty years old, but to look at him you'd think he was no more than five."

"That's why you've kept Jacob hidden away?" Angel asked as he drove through the downtown area. He wove in and out of traffic, keeping an eye out for police cars. So far, their luck was holding.

"Yes," Gabriel answered. Sadness resonated in his hoarse voice. "I can pass as human most of the time when I'm not stressed and I can control the demon flesh that has replaced so much of my own body. But Jacob can't. His lower body is all demon."

"Your son took on his mother's demonic attributes?" Wesley asked from the backseat.

Gabriel turned to face Wesley, tentacles stretching out from his features and hands. "We both did."

"But you aren't a demon?" Gunn asked.

"No," Gabriel replied. "I was as human as you almost

two hundred years ago. Cara—that is Jacob's mother—"

"The woman from the painting?" Gunn interrupted.

"Yes. She kept replacing my failing human flesh with flesh she'd altered. She killed and ate people here in this world, then used their flesh to keep her body here."

"So what you're actually made of is reprocessed dead human flesh and demon flesh?" Gunn asked.

Gabriel hesitated. "Yes. I wish there was a gentler way to express it."

Glancing at Gabriel, Angel saw that the man was uncomfortable with the discussion. "Maybe we should stick with Jacob," Angel suggested. They were tracking Hardesty through the link between Gabriel and Jacob as well as the link between Gabriel and Faroe Burke.

"And you have this link with your child because you're actually the one who gave birth to him?" Wesley said.

"I didn't give birth to Jacob in the way that you think," Gabriel said.

"In 1971," Gabriel said, "I was in Paris trying to find the painting I'd done of Cara. I'd been tracing it for years, but I wasn't a well-known artist and hadn't done as much work as I'd wanted to. I'd managed to track down the portrait I'd done of Darla, but I couldn't find the painting I'd done of Cara. Then, one of the dealers I was using let me know that it turned up in Paris around 1965."

"You think your girl, Cara, had something to do with that?" Gunn asked.

"I don't know," Gabriel said. "Before I left Paris, she found me again. It had been years since she had found me, and I'd aged a lot. I was a stooped old man by that time, and my body had begun to fail. I'd started having hopes that I would die, but I wanted to destroy the portrait to make sure Cara had no time left in this world."

"But she found you and did that flesh-swapping thing with you?" Gunn asked.

"Yes. Only this time as I began to heal, I found a growth on my back that had never happened before. At first I thought it was some kind of parasitic growth, but I was afraid to touch it. I consulted a doctor who dealt with demons and sought to have the growth removed. That was when he told me the growth was my son."

"You grew your son out of your back?" Wesley asked.

Gabriel nodded. "Stories about such births are rife throughout legends and mythologies." He turned to Angel. "We just passed them."

Angel whipped the convertible around in a tire-eating U-turn and floored the accelerator. Every moment counted.

"Faroe Burke is close to achieving *Weid Deus*," Gabriel said. "This close to her, I can feel it. The fever burns within her to paint."

"Jacob's mother," Wesley said, "never knew about her son?"

Anger flamed in Gabriel's fevered eyes. "Jacob is not her son. He is mine. And no, she doesn't. I have kept him hidden from her because she would kill him to further hurt me. But when Hardesty found me again—through my search for Cara's painting—and forced me to locate Faroe Burke, I got the idea for Jacob's salvation from his mother—and from his . . . condition. I wanted to petition her to paint a world for Jacob. A place where he could know other children and be free to run in daylight and play. He's never had that."

"He's thirty years old," Gunn said.

"He's thirty years old, but he's still a child," Gabriel said as Angel drove through an intersection. He pointed. "There."

Angel pulled the wheel hard. "Wesley, check that list Cordelia printed out regarding the properties Vincent Hardesty owns in this area."

Wesley unrolled the printout sheets in the backseat. "We're in luck. There's only one. An import/export warehouse near the docks. The upper floors are private residence areas, but they haven't been used in years."

"What about the warehouse?"

"It's a modestly thriving business," Wesley replied, then gave the address.

Angel glanced at Gabriel.

"Faroe Burke is in this direction," Gabriel said, "and so is my son. If they're there, Hardesty won't be far from her. I'm willing to wager that your friend won't be either."

Angel nodded and put his foot down harder on the accelerator.

When Cordelia screamed, Jacob slapped his small hands over his ears and screeched too. Fear filled his face and tears spilled from his blue eyes. His six tentacle-legs curled up beneath him as he hunkered down, then exploded into motion and took him away from her.

"I'm sorry!" the little boy yelled. "I'm sorry, I'm sorry, I'm sorry!"

Cordelia forced herself to stop screaming, realizing that she had hurt Jacob's feelings and scared him. *Get a grip,* she told herself. *Six tentacles or not, that is a little boy over there.*

Jacob continued screaming.

"Hey," Cordelia called softly. "Hey. I didn't mean to scare you. It's just that I have this headache."

Pressing up tight in the corner on the other side of the room from the bed, Jacob peered at her doubtfully. He stopped screaming, but he still sobbed and hiccupped pitifully.

"Really?" he asked. "You're not mad at me?"

"No." Cordelia made herself smile. Crossing the room, she dropped to her knees and held Jacob. She had to fight not to cringe when his tentacle brushed up against her, but when he threw his little arms around her and held her tight, all the cringing feeling went away. There was, she discovered, not another feeling like that in the world. She hugged him, surprised at the lump that formed in her throat.

"Don't worry, Jacob," she whispered. "Your dad will be here soon."

"Do you swear?"

"I swear."

"How do you know?"

"Because he's with a friend of mine named Angel," Cordelia said. "And Angel never lets anyone down."

"Will you share?" Jacob asked.

"Share?"

"Your friend?" Jacob asked. "Can I be Angel's friend too?"

Cordelia wiped a tear away and held the little boy. "Sure you can."

The door opened and a demon with an assault rifle stepped into the room. He was tall and thin, with a trio of horns jutting from the top of his narrow, lizard's face. "Hey," the guard said. "Mr. Hardesty says to knock it off in here or I'm gonna have to chloroform you both. The artist is starting to paint."

Cordelia glared at the demon till he stepped back out of the room. Then she looked back at Jacob. "Are you all right?"

"Yeah." The little boy sniffled. "Those guys get mad all the time when I cry. Sometimes I cry a lot."

"I bet," Cordelia said. "I don't blame you. I'd cry a lot too if I was here." She searched the darkened room, spotting a closet door. "I need to go look for something."

"Okay." Jacob released her, but scuttled along on his six tentacles after her as she walked over to the closet door.

Cordelia opened the closet door and smiled when she saw the three-foot metal pipe running the length of the small enclosure. The pipe sat in notched two-by-fours at either end of the closet and wasn't secured.

"Yay, us," Cordelia said, taking the pipe down with ease.

Jacob clapped, stopped, then said, "What?"

Cordelia held the metal pipe. "I think we can get out of here now. Can you scream and cry again?"

"Sure. I'm good at it. Sometimes, when those guys forget to feed me, I scream and cry and they bring me pizza."

"Good," Cordelia said. "Let's go with that. Stay here. Wait until I get ready." She went over by the door and raised the pipe. "Now scream."

Jacob screamed, and the ululating wail seemed like it was going to blow out Cordelia's eardrums. The guard opened the door again, stepped into the room, and never saw Cordelia.

"Damn it," the demon snarled. "I told you—"

Cordelia brought the pipe down against the back of the guard's head with a dull, metallic thud. The demon collapsed at once, sprawling across the floor.

"Boy," Jacob said in a small voice, "I bet that hurt."

"Me too," Cordelia said. She led him out into the hallway.

The hallway dead-ended to the right of the door Cordelia stepped through, but it went to a flight of stairs at the other end. Only shadows filled the hallway, except for the soft glow of a television from the room nearest the stairs. An announcer's practiced voice gave details about a basketball game.

Heart thumping, Cordelia looked at Jacob and put a forefinger to her lips.

Jacob put a forefinger to his own lips and nodded.

Together, they crept by the door where another demon guard watched a basketball game on a small color television and ate popcorn from a bag. A barred window near the top of the stairs showed a view of the street outside. Tires shrilled in the street, drawing Cordelia's attention.

There in the moonlight, Angel's convertible slid sideways in the street and came to a halt.

"Hey," a deep voice said. "What are you doing out?"

Turning instantly, Cordelia whipped the metal pipe around, releasing Jacob's hand long enough to take a two-handed grip. The pipe crashed into the demon's knee. When he bent over, Cordelia hit him in the head.

The blow didn't knock the demon unconscious, but it dropped him to the carpet in a ball of agony. Unfortunately, the ball of agony was also capable of screaming for help.

"Wow," Jacob said quietly, staring down at the writhing guard. "Remind me to never get you mad at me."

"Okay," Cordelia said, "how fast can you run?"

"Really fast," Jacob said. "And I've got more legs than you do."

"You're going to need them," Cordelia said as she sprinted down the stairs. She glanced over her shoulder to make sure Jacob could keep up. Instead, with his longer stride, the boy paced her with ease.

"I told you I could run," Jacob said proudly.

They ran.

Controlling the convertible's skid, Angel brought the Belvedere around to face the warehouse's metal doors. The building was three stories tall, the warehouse taking up the bottom two floors and the private apartments the third. It had been built back in the 1940s when Hollywood was in its heyday of transforming the city.

"Those doors don't look thick, do they?" Angel asked. "I mean, the car's already shot up and will be in the shop anyway. And Hardesty's people probably already know we're in the neighborhood." Before any of his stunned passengers could react, he floored the accelerator.

The Plymouth Belvedere shot forward.

Angel held onto the wheel and said, "Duck."

Gabriel, Wesley, and Gunn all scrunched down as the car bore down on the doors. When the convertible hit the doors it tore them from their moorings, blasting them open. Continuing through the warehouse, the car became a dreadnought of destruction. Crates broke open, spilling pottery and paintings and statuary in all directions. A lot of broken debris that had once been collectible antiquity crunched under the tires.

Senses keyed and knowing he would need his private demon's strength and speed for the coming combat, Angel morphed. His dark nature, ever ready, stole over him before the Belvedere lurched to a halt. Grabbing the top of the windshield, he vaulted up from his seat, tucking himself into a flying flip that left him standing in front of the convertible.

One of the car's headlights had gotten smashed during the assault, but the other played on the macabre scene at the far end of the warehouse.

A dozen or more demons guarded the periphery of the space that had been left in front of the office against the wall. Rows of crates made battlements at the top for other demons with assault rifles.

Faroe Burke stood at the center of the warehouse clearing with a can of spray paint in one hand. Before her, a canvas ten feet long and eight feet high awaited her skill. Broad lines in neon colors had already been laid in. She turned, staring at the car, and recognized Gunn.

"Gunn," she said.

"I brought some friends," Gunn said as he walked up to join Angel. "Don't worry, Faroe, this is something we're good at."

Mocking laughter roared from Vincent Hardesty as he stepped in front of Faroe Burke. His eyes sought out Angel's.

"So, Angelus, it is you," Hardesty said. "When I heard stories from my attorney at Wolfram and Hart of a vampire who had involved himself in my affairs, somehow I knew it had to be you."

"That's me," Angel said, glancing at the demons at the top of the crates with assault rifles. "I had a busy week going, but I decided to pencil you in."

"And save the world while you're at it?" Hardesty asked.

Angel shrugged, filled with the demon's bravado although he struggled to hang onto his human perspective. "A guy's gotta prioritize. I should have killed you back in Venice."

"They told me you had changed, Angelus," Hardesty said, smiling mirthlessly. "And I see Gabriel is with you. Hale and whole, it seems. At least, as hale and whole as he can be these days. I assume you met Cara, his lover, his creation from his time with the *Weid Deus*."

"We met," Angel said. "I wasn't impressed."

"I have her under my control." Hardesty waved to a jumble of shadows behind a line of crates at the back of the clearing.

The squid-demon rose up to ten feet. Her tentacles twitched and quivered at her sides. Her eyes, on either side of her spade-shaped head, glowered hatred.

"It seems she has some unfinished business with Gabriel. He had a son by her, one that he never told her about."

"And she wants to kill the boy," Angel said. "Yeah. Got that. But you only retain control over her as long as Gabriel is alive." He reached back, knowing from his vampire's senses exactly where Gabriel was. He closed his fist in Gabriel's clothing and yanked him forward.

The Tharrolf demon came forward immediately.

Angel stomped his foot on a broken shard of board, catching it easily in the air, then holding it ready to shove through Gabriel's chest. "I wouldn't do that," Angel advised.

The Tharrolf demon quivered all over, but she stopped.

"Stand-off," Angel declared. "Pack your things and get out of town and you get to live a little longer. But keep a look over your shoulder, Hardesty, because one day I'll be there to finish what we're not finishing here today."

"Idle threats," Hardesty said. "I'm going to have Miss Burke paint me into my new reality. And this time I'm not going to settle for something chintzy like immortality. No, this time I'm going to be ruler of the world. What do you think?"

"I think you're insane," Angel said.

"Even if you alter reality," Wesley added, "it's going to be a long time in coming. I've read over the materials regarding the *Weid Deus*. The power will make the artist's image real, but as with Gabriel's attempt to capture the perfect woman, it may fail or bring dire consequences as a result."

"No," Hardesty said. "It was the dreamer that was weak, not the dream. The spray cans that Miss Burke is using have been loaded with my blood mixed in. I will succeed where he failed."

"You don't know that," Wesley said. "You may doom the world. Atlantis sank because of a *Weid Deus*-influenced painter."

"Atlantis was rife with demons," Hardesty said. "That's what sank it." He stared at Angel. "I'm ordering you to leave these premises. Otherwise, I'll be forced to have your friend—Cordelia, I believe her name is—killed, and let Cara get reacquainted with her young son."

"Angel," Gabriel croaked.

Angel looked at the artist.

"You've got to kill me," Gabriel pleaded. Fear shone in his fevered eyes. "It's the only way. If you kill me, Cara will blame Hardesty. She'll turn on him. I need you to save my son. Promise me."

"No," Angel said. "I can't. I'm sorry."

"Hey!" a child's voice rang out across the warehouse. "Don't hurt my dad!"

Gazing up, tracking the sound of the voice, Angel spotted the boy standing next to Cordelia, holding her hand. The boy had hold of the railing of the catwalk around the warehouse area and was peering over the top, standing on the tips of his tentacles.

"We got tired of waiting to be rescued," Cordelia said, "so we kind of saved ourselves."

"Jacob," Gabriel whispered.

Chapter Twenty-four

Without the slightest warning, Angel spun and threw the wooden shard toward the nearest demon standing at the top of stacked crates. The shard drove through his chest and split his heart, killing him instantly. He toppled without a word.

Angel shoved Gabriel into Wesley and Gunn, knocking them out of the way as another demon opened up with an assault rifle. A line of bullets sparked against the floor and chewed small craters in the concrete surface.

Still on the move, Angel scooped up a small bronze shield and flung it like a Frisbee, catching another demon gunner in the face and bowling him over backward. Running now, Angel barreled into a stack of crates with outstretched hands, knocking the crates over and sending them crashing into the next stack. The demon gunner atop them screamed once, but his voice was quickly lost in the carnage of toppling crates.

The stacks of crates continued falling along the left side of the clearing where Faroe Burke worked.

Only Angel's vampiric speed enabled him to reach the woman and pull her from harm's way as crates smashed into the canvas and covered the floor where she'd been standing. Carrying her in his arms, he sped toward the other side of the clearing, too fast for the demons to take proper aim at him with their assault rifles.

Angel pressed Faroe up against the wall. "Stay here," he told her. "You'll be all right."

She nodded, but her face was filled with fear.

Leaving the woman there, Angel looked at the debris spread across the warehouse. The falling crates had taken out most of Hardesty's demon guards and fallen across the Tharrolf demon as well.

The crates might have smashed the humanoid demons, but only buried the squid-like Tharrolf demon for a moment. She surged up from the debris and shook it off like a dog shedding water.

"Kill them!" Hardesty roared, pushing himself up from the wreckage covering the floor. Dust covered his suit and his features. He coughed and choked, then bared the blade hidden in his sword cane. "Kill them all but spare the woman!"

The Tharrolf demon moved with inhuman speed, aiming herself at Cordelia and the little boy.

"Angel!" Cordelia yelled, hugging Jacob to her as the little boy grabbed her legs.

Grabbing a crowbar that had spilled loose with the falling crates, Angel ran toward the demon, leaping and pulling himself up the line of crates still standing on the other side of the clearing. A demon tried to shoot him with an assault rifle. Angel threw himself up at the demon, striking him and knocking him from the pile of crates. The demon screamed, pinwheeling his arms and legs, losing the assault rifle as he fell.

Gabriel, Wesley, and Gunn battled the surviving demon guards, beating them back with the weapons they'd brought with them from Angel's car. Hardesty drew back from the onslaught that grew steadily closer to him.

The Tharrolf demon continued toward Cordelia and the little boy.

"Jacob!" Gabriel screamed. "Cara, no!"

The demon didn't even turn her head to acknowledge Gabriel's cries.

Angel took advantage of the demon's lack of interest in anything that took place behind her. He leaped twenty feet, arms outstretched for the demon. The concrete floor waited thirty feet below, filled with shards of broken wood that could mean death if he landed on them. He blocked that from his mind, concentrating on the demon grabbing the support beams that crossed the warehouse ceiling with her tentacles.

Angel slammed into the Tharrolf demon and thought for a moment that he'd torn her loose from her precarious perch. But she hung on. Her spade-shaped head swung in his direction.

"You've only come to your death, vampire," the Tharrolf demon threatened. "I cannot be killed in this world. Not as long as I can have flesh to use as mine."

Speeches, Angel thought. *There always has to be speeches.* "Then kill me if you can," he said. Wrapping his legs around the demon's tentacled body, he swung the crowbar off his shoulder like a baseball player swinging for the fences.

The crowbar smashed into the demon's head, vibrating it like a dinner bell. The huge eyes closed.

"Cordelia," Angel yelled, drawing back for another swing, "get that boy out of there."

Taking Jacob by the hand, Cordelia continued down the catwalk.

This time, the demon avoided Angel's blow, swinging her head out of the way and taking the brunt of the attack on her tentacles. She opened her huge, thin-lipped mouth and bent forward, intending to bite Angel's head off.

Moving quickly, Angel shoved the crowbar into her mouth, holding it open. She struggled and gagged, flicking a black, forked tongue out to knock the crowbar free. The touch of her tongue across the back of Angel's hand was corrosive. His flesh bubbled up into dozens of tiny blisters immediately.

Ignoring the pain, Angel hung onto the crowbar and shifted his grip. Before the demon could move, he rammed the crowbar point-first into her head.

Her skull split like a melon and black blood spilled out. She screamed in pain and her tentacles went lax, slipping from their grips on the crossbeams.

Angel stood, trying desperately to reach the crossbeam above them but missed. Falling with the demon, feeling her tentacles writhing all around him and clutching onto him out of reflex, he fought against her hold and tried to break free as they rushed toward the ground.

Angel was only dimly aware of the loud, meaty splat

they made as they slammed against the ground. Pain flooded his senses. His arms slid out from under him as he tried to get to his feet. The impact reopened the wound in his side he'd received the night before, and pain lanced through him.

The demon drew up some of her tentacles and lashed out at him. The blows sent him spinning and skidding across the debris-strewn warehouse floor. He smashed up against a stack of crates that dropped down onto him.

Gathering his flagging strength, remembering that his friends were counting on him, Angel forced himself up, standing up through the wreckage of the broken crates. A jagged board cut a painful furrow along the side of his face.

A demon with an assault rifle moved out of the shadows and fired his weapon in a continuous burst.

Angel dodged away, but not before two rounds caught him in the left shoulder and upper chest, knocking him back. Agony ripped through him but he kept moving, throwing himself from the path of other bullets. Splinters ripped from the crates the auto-fire slammed into, sudden confetti.

Turning the corner between two close-set aisles of crates, Angel leapt up ten feet and snapped his arms out, locking into position, palms pressed against the sides of the crates. He felt blood pump from his wounds, the two bullet holes as well as the puncture wound in his side, but he could tell his body was already shutting the flow down. He held his position, listening to the demon's feet slap the concrete as he pursued. Angel's arm's quivered with the strain of holding his body up, which normally wouldn't have been a problem. Black comets whirled and danced in his vision.

Come on, Angel thought, staring down. He saw the demon race through the aisle, keeping the assault rifle to his shoulder, ready to fire.

Angel dropped behind the demon, not wanting to press his luck and try landing on him. He reached for his opponent, cupping his palm under the demon's chin, and one against the back of his head. Before the demon could even try to move, Angel wrenched his neck and broke his skull free from his spine.

The dead demon dropped.

Angel plucked the assault rifle from his opponent's hands. Maybe killing the Tharrolf demon wasn't possible in this world, but Angel was certain he could introduce it to a whole new level of pain. He thumbed the rifle's magazine release, freeing the nearly depleted clip, searched the dead demon's body and found a fresh clip, and rammed it home.

He turned, ignoring the pain that filled him, trying to keep it together for just a little longer. He ran back the way the demon had come, spotting the Tharrolf demon's unmistakable spade-shaped head above the crates. With a single leap, he reached the top of crates still ringing the right side of the clearing that had existed before the left side had come tumbling down.

Cordelia and Gabriel protected Jacob, but they were being forced into the corner of the warehouse space. Gunn and Wesley stood before them with a battle-axe and a mace, adding one more layer of protection. Not far away, sidling off out of the way, Hardesty had one arm around Faroe Burke's waist and a hand over her mouth.

"Wesley," Angel called. "Gunn."

"Thought the demons had killed you," Gunn said.

"Close," Angel said. "But I'm still standing."

The Tharrolf demon snapped her head around. Her eyes blazed as she focused on Angel. Blood tracked down her body from the wounds he'd given her.

"The boy is mine," the demon roared in a voice that no longer sounded feminine. "He is flesh of my flesh, and powerful because of that. I will make him mine forever."

Angel shook his head. "Not happening."

Her tentacles whipped out as she turned to face him. "You can't kill me."

"Yeah, I can," Angel said. "Wesley, find Gabriel's painting of her. It's got to be here if Hardesty is here. He wouldn't be around her without having it to threaten her with."

Wesley and Gunn peeled away.

The Tharrolf demon immediately switched her attention back to Jacob, moving forward on her tentacles.

Angel shouldered the assault rifle and fired, blowing craters in the demon's head and upper body. When the assault rifle blew back empty, he tossed it away and stepped forward, dropping from the crates.

The gaping wounds left by the bullets bled profusely, but as Angel watched, slimy flesh poured into the holes, automatically turning into brain matter and one eye, then hardening into a skull and the flesh overlying it.

"Okay," Angel said, marshaling his focus, "it's you and me." He stepped on a double-bladed Japanese spear almost buried in the rubble before him, flipping it up into the air with his foot. He caught the spear with one hand, then swung the weapon, whipping the blade at either end in a metallic blur. "Gabriel."

"Yes."

"When they get the portrait, I need you ready to destroy it."

"I will. Be careful. She is more powerful than you believe."

Oh, I'm a believer, Angel thought, stopping the blades and preparing himself. He centered his mind, pushing away all thoughts of fear or survival. All that existed was the coming battle. He would live or die in the zero, the place of absolute nothingness for a warrior. There was no past, no future, only the present and his chosen place in it.

Uncoiling, tentacles flying in all directions, the Tharrolf demon came for him.

Angel stood in the eye of the storm as the fanged tentacles lunged at him. Whirling the double-sword in his hands, moving his body with the blades and knowing that he was spinning them fast enough to lop off his own foot or leg if he made a misstep, Angel slashed at the demon.

Tentacles peeled from the squid-like body as if the Tharrolf demon had stepped into an airplane propeller. Angel concentrated his attack on the creature's tentacles, knowing if his weapon became stuck in her body that he'd lose it and probably his life and the lives of his friends.

He ran and leaped, jumping over the tentacles that he couldn't hack off or dodge. Almost as fast has he hacked the tentacles from her body, her demonic metabolism worked to replace them, shooting out jelly-like flesh covered in blood that hardened and developed musculature in an eyeblink.

She lunged at him with her mouth, missing him by inches. Angel responded by slashing her newly replaced eye and blinding her again. She wailed in pain and fury.

Angel moved, drawing back, protecting Cordelia and Jacob, waiting for the demon to attack again.

Gunn raced across the warehouse, aiming himself straight at Hardesty. *Going to be more even this time,* Gunn promised himself. *Don't know what you're packing that makes you so strong, but unless your head is harder than a bowling ball, I'm going to win.*

Hardesty kept Faroe in front of him.

"Stay back," Hardesty warned, sliding the sword under Faroe's chin. "Stay back or I slice her pretty little throat."

"Do that," Gunn promised in a hard voice, "and you can wave buh-bye to all your world domination plans." He hefted the mace he'd taken from Angel's trunk. The weapon had a wire-wrapped handle and an iron, spherical head on it the size of a grapefruit.

Hardesty kept backing away, glancing over his shoulder at the door behind him.

Gunn figured the door let out into an alley. Since they hadn't seen the limousines inside the building or out on the street when they'd arrived, he was betting the limousines were parked in the alley.

Faroe thrust her arm up suddenly, shooting it inside Hardesty's sword arm in an attempt to lever it from her throat. At the same time, she threw her head back, breaking Hardesty's nose. She wasn't able to block Hardesty's sword completely, though. The sharp blade cut her throat.

Faroe went limp, becoming dead weight.

Hardesty released the woman, stepping back and bringing his sword cane up. He swept it toward Gunn, trying to slice him across the waist. But Gunn was closer and faster than Hardesty had anticipated.

Gunn caught the man's arm with his own, looping his left arm around Hardesty's right so that the sword passed behind him. Gunn tightened his grip, locking up the elbow, preventing Hardesty from escaping or using the weapon again. He swung the mace into Hardesty's stomach twice, knocking his breath from his lungs, then breaking ribs. He swung again, connecting with Hardesty's forehead, snapping the man's back.

The sword cane dropped from Hardesty's limp grip.

"Son of a bitch!" Gunn said, wanting to do nothing more than smash the man's face to pulp.

"Gunn," Wesley called. "Don't kill him. We may need him alive."

Trembling with the rage and helplessness that filled him, Gunn grabbed Hardesty by the jacket front and held him up. He turned to face Wesley.

Kneeling on the floor, Wesley held Faroe's head in his lap. "It's okay," Wesley said. "She's alive. The sword nicked her neck, but it didn't sever any arteries or her windpipe. She's going to need a few stitches, but she's going to be all right." He held his hand pressed to her bleeding neck.

"I saw a painting case," Faroe said in a strained voice. "Hardesty had his goons bring it in with him. It's in the office." She pointed at the office at the back of the warehouse.

"I'll be right back," Gunn promised, letting Hardesty drop unconscious at his feet.

Faroe nodded.

"I'll take care of her," Wesley promised. "Help Angel."

Gunn raced to the office. The door was locked. Drawing back, he slammed his foot into the door, shredding the lock. Inside the small room filled with filing cabinets and a computer, he found an artist's case. He broke the locks on the case, and inside it he found a painting of a creepy swampland. The artwork reminded him of Frank Frazetta's stuff, but he knew it had to be what they were looking for.

He took the painting outside to Gabriel. Recognition flooded Gabriel's tentacle-covered face.

"Do it," Gunn said.

Gabriel took the portrait and stared into it. He spoke, but the language was something other than English. Gunn thought it might have been Italian, but he wasn't sure. When he finished, Gabriel strode toward Angel and the demon.

"Cara," Gabriel called softly.

Warily, the demon stepped back from Angel. "No," she said. "I won't go. You can't make me."

"I can, Cara," Gabriel said in voice filled with scarcely controlled fear. "I will."

"No," the demon wailed. "You said you loved me, Gabriel. You told me there was no other woman like me."

"There wasn't," Gabriel said.

Yeah, and we're all thankful for that, Gunn thought, walking behind Gabriel with his mace ready.

"Don't make me go," the demon wailed.

Angel stepped back from her, keeping the double-edged sword in front of him.

A lambent green haze glowed from the painting, bathing the demon and Angel and the wreckage of the warehouse. Silver fog twisted within the light, glittering and sparkling like fairy dust.

The demon shrank, losing over half of her size. Gunn watched in wonderment, as the tentacled demon became a beautiful red-haired woman clad only in a loincloth.

The woman walked toward Gabriel, one tentative hand outstretched. "Please," she pleaded. "Please, Gabriel. You don't want to do this."

Gabriel stopped speaking, staring at the woman in bewilderment.

"Get rid of her," Gunn whispered. "Don't trust her."

"Gabriel," the woman said. "You remember how it was between us. You remember how we were together. How much you loved me."

"I did love you," Gabriel whispered. "There has never been another woman, Cara. Only you."

"See?" The woman reached out and touched Gabriel, coiling her fingers in his hair.

"Dad," Jacob called in a timid voice. "Dad, she's a scary lady."

Anger changed the woman's features. "Shut up, you little brat!" She whipped her arm toward the little boy and the fingers elongated, becoming tentacles.

Gunn grabbed the tentacles, feeling the slimy coarse hide, and stopped them.

Jacob screamed.

Whirling, Gunn delivered a back-spinning blow with the mace that wrecked the red-haired woman's features and sent her reeling back. The injured side of her face turned demonic as it started to heal, black organic pudding that turned to indigo flesh laced with deep metallic blue that in turn became flesh colored.

"Send her!" Gunn ordered, turning to Gabriel. "Send her *now!*"

Gabriel chanted again. The green light intensified as Jacob screamed. Winds roared to life in the warehouse and thunder cannonaded. Then the picture sucked the red-haired woman into it as Gabriel held it, jerking and jumping in his grip.

As the red-haired woman flew through the air, she changed back into her demon form. Her tentacles flared out, catching the sides of the portrait. Whatever power fueled the painting shrank her as she was pulled into it, reducing her size.

"I will not go!" the demon roared.

"Oh, yeah," Angel said, "you're going." He ran at the demon and used the double-bladed spear as a pole and vaulted into her feet-first. Both of them plunged into Gabriel's portrait, disappearing at once.

Angel fell through an emerald sky toward a jade-green forest below, watching the tentacled Tharrolf demon flailing as she dropped toward a small spit of land jutting out into a turquoise ocean. A pale apple-green sun hung in the sky.

In the next instant, Angel heard the *sproing!* of the demon's body striking the jungle as he plummeted into the turquoise sea. Deep water closed over him, and the spume of white air bubbles tracking his body created an impenetrable fog. Gabriel's incantation must have allowed Angel to pass through.

The water was impossibly deep. Even as far as he'd come, Angel couldn't see the bottom. He glanced up, wondering how an island could have such a shallow beach. Then he saw that the island was a patch on the ocean's surface above him.

The island's not anchored, he realized. *It floats.* He gazed around in all directions as he treaded water. There were no other islands in any directions. The one that the Tharrolf demon had lived on was adrift and alone.

Still hanging onto the spear, Angel swam toward the surface. Twenty feet from it, the pale green sun visible in the emerald sky above him, the demon dove into the water. Frothy bubbles slid around her and her tentacles spread like a jellyfish's appendages, hanging weightless around her.

As a vampire, Angel didn't need to breathe underwater, but it wasn't his chosen terrain for combat. Watching the demon glide through the water, he knew she had the advantage. If he'd been human, he wouldn't have had a chance.

She shot a tentacle at him, spearing it toward his face. Angel twisted, letting the deadly appendage go by. As he dodged, he saw small fish swimming around him in schools. The thing that caught his eye were the massive jaws they had that reminded him of piranha.

The demon coiled a tentacle around one of Angel's legs. He brought the spear down and cut through her flesh. Black blood boiled out into the sea, creating an inky cloud that spread at once.

The blood scent in the water attracted the carnivorous fish. They finned toward the wounded tentacle, attacking it at once, shredding the flesh and exposing the multi-jointed bone beneath.

He surfaced and caught hold of the island, only then realizing that it was in motion, floating across the ocean. He pulled himself up, his wounds burning from whatever was in the sea.

The demon flipped and flopped her tentacles on the ground, dislodging the predatory fish, then beating them to death with whip-like blows. The broad, spade-like head turned to face Angel, her eyes glowering and filled with hatred.

"You're going to die slow and hard for that, vampire," she threatened, "then I'm going to find your friends and kill them, too."

He fought on, slashing and parrying, because for him there was no other way. He withdrew more deeply into the jungle, using it against his opponent. Then he spotted the shimmer down on the beach, not yet fifty yards distant.

A glowing yellow rectangle formed a few inches above the sand and stone of the beach. Gabriel stood on the other side of it.

"Angelus," Gabriel cried. "This way. I can get you out. Trust me."

The demon whipped her head around, looking back toward the beach. Then she scuttled toward the glowing yellow rectangle.

Moving quickly, Angel ran through the jungle, leaped onto a boulder, and leaped again for the demon. He wrapped both hands around the spear. The blade penetrated the demon's head and Angel's weight bore her to the ground. He shoved the spear harder, nailing her to the earth.

Dodging the tentacles that flailed for him, Angel ran toward the beach. Sand slipped from underfoot, and stones provided uncertain footing. He heard her ripping through the jungle behind him.

"Hurry!" Gabriel yelled. "She's right behind you!"

Angel threw himself forward the last ten feet just as tentacles slapped against the ground where he had been. He caught Gabriel's outstretched hand and felt him pull him.

In the next instant, Gabriel let go of Angel, letting him spill onto the warehouse floor.

Angel rolled, coming to his feet, searching for a weapon, knowing the demon was going to burst through the portrait after him. Trapped by the sense of impending disaster, he stared at the portrait as one fanged tentacle started out of the canvas.

Then Gabriel unleashed a cloud of sapphire blue spray paint that misted over the portrait and froze the tentacle in place. Only a moment later, the entire surface of the portrait was painted a uniform sapphire blue. The tentacle stayed in place, as if the frame held some kind of three-dimensional art.

Dropping the spray paint can, Gabriel ran to his little boy, scooping him up in his arms, holding him close and kissing his face. Jacob giggled and complained that his father's tentacles tickled, but also said that he didn't mind it too much.

Angel sat down, morphing back into his human appearance, and with it came all the aches and pains he'd been putting off since the battle had begun.

Epilogue

"She's going to get arrested," Wesley complained. "You know that, don't you?"

Angel stood in the long morning shadow of a building in downtown Los Angeles and smiled. He was bone-tired and weary from the last day and a half, but it felt good, too. "I know that. Gunn's got the number of a bail bondsman he's done work with before."

With a bandage around her neck covering the sutured wound she'd received in the battle last night, Faroe Burke spray painted the low concrete wall that surrounded an urban park across the street. Displaying the true skill of an artist, she turned festive colors into a portrait of kids at play in a park.

Only the kids at play in the park were a lot like Jacob Dantz. They came in all shapes and sizes, some with tentacled legs like Jacob and others with the heads of animals. All of them seemed to be having a good time.

As Faroe worked, a crowd from the neighborhood

began to gather. Looking around at the crowd, Angel felt good. This was in an area Faroe and Gunn had picked, a place where most people didn't come out of doors or often let the children play. Weeds had grown up around the playground equipment in the park. Gradually, though, the kids had talked some of the parents into taking them into the park, and some of the parents were talking and working together to fix broken equipment.

Through it all, Faroe worked on, her focus totally on the wall and the world that she was building.

Cordelia sat with Jacob on a bus stop bench. She kept a blanket wrapped around his legs. The little boy kept trying to wheedle his way into the park, but Cordelia kept him firmly in hand. Maybe the neighborhood wouldn't think much of someone painting the wall, but seeing a boy running around on six tentacles was another matter.

Gabriel stood talking with Gunn, cloaked in his black garb so that he wouldn't attract undue attention.

"Did you talk to Nova Studios?" Angel asked.

"Yes," Wesley said. "Dale Foster is both impressed and appreciative of our haste in finding the blackmailer and putting an end to it."

"Is he satisfied that the blackmailer didn't going to jail? That we just scared him away?"

Wesley nodded. "Nova Studios didn't want to end up in court."

Angel smiled. "Because all the blackmail materials would end up as court evidence."

"Precisely."

"So Angel Investigations maintains its good name?" Angel asked.

"You're being facetious."

"No, actually I'm not," Angel admitted. "We do good work in this town. I don't want anyone taking that away from us."

"And if Merl lied to you and blackmails Nova Studios again?"

"I'll kill him," Angel said. "I wasn't lying." He watched in silence as Faroe finished her painting.

"It's time," Faroe said. "If you're right about all of this, it's ready."

Cordelia brought Jacob over. "He wanted to say good-bye," Cordelia said, and there was a catch in her voice.

"Good-bye, Mr. Angel," Jacob said.

"Good-bye, Jacob," Angel said. "I hope you enjoy the park."

"I will," the little boy said. "Miss Burke painted a real good one."

"Yes, she did," Angel agreed.

Unexpectedly, the little boy leaned in and gave Angel a quick hug. Frozen for just a moment, Angel patted the boy on the back. Then he released Angel and said the rest of his good-byes.

Angel was prevented by the sunlight from joining the others as they gathered around Faroe. Sometimes, though, it felt better to be removed from society; he got a better view of everything actually going on, and knew better his place in all of it.

Faroe stepped back and showed Cordelia where to place Jacob. The little boy hugged Cordelia fiercely, then scuttled forward on his six legs. The painting glowed brightly as he made contact then stepped halfway into it.

"Come on, Dad," Jacob called.

Tears streaming down his face, Gabriel shook his head. "I can't, Jacob. You'll have to go on without me."

Jacob looked at the park, then shook his head and backed out. "I want to play with the other kids, but I don't want to leave you."

"Son," Gabriel said, hunkering down to his boy, "I can't go. I—"

"Actually," Faroe said, "you can. I built it for both of you." She glanced at the other kids in the park. "That's only part of a very big world. There's a place for both of you in it."

"My God," Gabriel said, voice cracking. "My God. I brought a demon into this world, and you—you have built a paradise."

"I had someone to show me the way," Faroe said. "You didn't have that."

"You could have had anything," Gabriel said.

"I still can," Faroe said, smiling. "Haven't you seen the newspapers or television interviews? I'm a hit. Don't worry about me. And, besides, I'd rather earn it myself. I learned a long time ago that anything worth having is worth working for. This *Weid Deus*? I didn't work for that, but I can use it today to help you."

Gabriel took her hand and kissed it. "Thank you, dear lady. Thank you so much." He stood and glanced at Angel. "And thank you, Angel, for all that you have done."

"Take care, Gabriel."

"C'mon, Dad," Jacob said, pulling at his father's pants leg. People had started to gather now, staring at the little boy with six tentacles for legs. Gabriel took his son's hand and, together, they strode into the painting. The painting glimmered once more, then faded away.

For a moment, Angel saw Gabriel and Jacob walking to meet the other kids in the park, then the figures became static and it was just a painting.

The crowd around the painting started clapping enthusiastically, telling Faroe they wanted to see some more magic tricks.

Cordelia joined Wesley and Angel while Gunn escorted Faroe toward a nearby ice cream shop.

"Well," Cordelia said, nodding toward Gunn and Faroe, "there's nothing like new love."

"I don't think it's that deep, Cordelia," Angel said. "They respect each other. Maybe that's all it is."

"Maybe." Cordelia smiled. "So what are you going to do today?"

"Me?" Angel gazed at the park, watching as more kids joined the first wave that had invaded the playground. "I think I'll stay here for a little while and watch the kids. I haven't done something like that in a long time. Somehow, today, it just feels right."